# CLAIMING INNOCENCE

## by

## JoAnne Harris Michels

Based on a True Story

DORRANCE
PUBLISHING CO
EST. 1920
PITTSBURGH, PENNSYLVANIA 15238

Dorrance Publishing Co
585 Alpha Drive
Suite 103
Pittsburgh, PA 15238
Visit our website at *www.dorrancebookstore.com*

ISBN: 978-1-6442-6080-7
eISBN: 978-1-6442-6059-3

# INTRODUCTION

*I FELL IN LOVE WITH THE LITTLE BOY HE'D BEEN. I wanted to mother him, to erase his childhood—push the delete key, and replace the turbulence of his early years with a home and family who loved him. We'd go to the zoo, Disneyland, even Chuck E. Cheese. He'd have clean clothes, healthy food, and play dates with nice children, and if anyone threatened harm, I'd protect him like mothers do.*

*He came to dinner as one in a pair of Mormon missionaries. We found him remarkably gentle, helpful, and kind. After dinner, he thanked us, insisting on doing the dishes.*

*A well-conditioned athlete, he was modest about his abilities. He played basketball with my seven sons, passing the ball to anyone having a chance to score, conceding an open shot of his own. After some pleading, he demonstrated push-ups on his thumbs.*

*He prayed from the heart, speaking to God as a respectful son to his father, expressing gratitude for the opportunity to serve, and requesting blessings and protection for my family.*

*I asked if he'd begun preparing to serve a mission as a child.*

*He laughed out loud. Then he told a few childhood stories that shocked us, revealing a vast disparity between the child and the man. It was then I noticed his scarred hands, and wondered what other wounds lay concealed.*

*How could I have known he'd been an assassin, that he'd spent much of his life obsessed with revenge, and that his life was now in jeopardy? Years later he told me his story, and it begs sharing.*

# PART ONE:

# LOST

# CHAPTER 1

THEY SAY WHEN A FILIPINO CHILD IS YET IN THE WOMB, he dreams of war. When I was born, the sting of war pounded with a familiar beat in every Filipino heart, and chaos was the backdrop of our lives. Ferdinand Marcos was in power, and the corruption of his tenure saturated the soil. I walked all through it.

I recall the day that changed our family with event-by-event clarity, although only two-and-a-half years old at the time. We remember what we review, and I've run through the scenes of that day repeatedly, as though they were the sole surviving film fragments at the end of the world, watched and prized for their rarity.

Before that day I was innocent: my world-view was based on love and trust; my needs were met, and I was secure within the warm cocoon of my family. After that day, the parasite of revenge attached to me, and grew to direct and eclipse my childhood, becoming my obsession.

Papa was president of a large sugarcane company, and we surveyed the fields, my father and I, heading for home. My legs hurt. I'd been toddling alongside, taking three steps to each of his, my fingers curled around his pinkie finger as he led me along the dirt road. He hoisted me to his shoulders, and I grabbed hold of his ears to "steer" him. He laughed, "Which way now, Mark, left or right?" zigzagging in response to my ear-pulls. The aroma of pork *adobo* enticed us home.

Mama burst through the door like a quick sunrise, smiling, cradling the baby under one arm. My brothers flowed from fields with lizards and laughter, taking places at the teakwood table heaped with papayas and pineapple. Mama put Segundina in her cradle, and placed *adobo* at the head of the table near Papa. He read from The Bible, "But seek ye first the kingdom of God, and his righteousness, and all these things shall be added unto you." He said grace, and dished up a hearty portion.

During the sugarcane harvest, we stayed in our part-time home, a traditional Filipino house, securely anchored on a concrete foundation. It had a tightly thatched roof; the walls were honey-colored columns of bamboo with partitions in a checkered pattern, allowing for the free flow of air through the kitchen and living space to the bedrooms in back. Our sleeping mats were woven *pandan* leaves, dyed in colors of green, orange, red, violet, blue, and yellow, softened with coconut oil, rolled up by day, and placed close to each other at night. The windows were open-air, but screened, admitting a warm breeze that rippled over the rush of the river, carrying the wholesome fragrance of newly-turned soil, and the scent and swish of sugarcane, imparting a sense of constancy, well being, and a glow of harmony.

I was seventh of eight children: six boys, bookended by two girls. Eighteen year-old Isabel was the eldest, and had her own apartment in Manila where she worked, although when she came home on weekends, it seemed like she'd never left.

My baby sister, Segundina, was four-months old, and sucked her toes with sensual pleasure. Isabel picked her up and nuzzled in the silky, soft rounds of baby-neck, and the baby's chubby fingers tangled in her big sister's abundant, knee-length hair.

My oldest brother had left home a few years earlier, and no one knew his whereabouts. His name was Bonifacio, "beautiful face," but he was the black sheep of the family, and his name was spoken only in whispers. We wondered what he was like: he seemed mythical, from another time and place, and when Mama cried, we supposed it was for him.

I had four brothers at home, born in roughly three-year increments—José was just turning twelve; 2Tall, nine (already taller than José), Francisco, six; and Chile, four. I was two. Mama used to say that it was good to have started with Isabel, and ended with Segundina: that way the girls could smooth out the roughness of all the boys in between.

After dinner, my older three brothers hurried to race their giant marine toads. Chile grabbed my hand, "Come on, Mark!" and I toddled along after him. The toads were fat and reluctant at the starting line, their ponderous bellies sticking to the cement. But the boys prodded and poked them, shouting, "Come on," "Go Gordito," and "Jump, Baby-face!" until they finally took off. As it happened the race was solemnly declared invalid: all the toads lost by default—failing to stay the course by bounding off the sidewalk into the grass. Disappointed in their toads, the boys ran to fetch their bucket of lizards. They painted glow-in-the-dark numbers on each one and turned them loose, and Chile and I shouted and chased them as they scattered.

Numbering the lizards was Chile's idea, "When we catch them again, we'll know they belong to us, and we'll see how they're doing," he said, smiling his dopey grin. His name was Miguel, and he was four, but nicknamed "Chile" because he added spice to the family; he made ordinary things fun, and activity surrounded him.

Chile and I were constant companions. I followed him from morning to night, sat next to him at the table, and slept by him at night. We giggled as he made piggy noises and poked at Segundina's round belly, and she responded with unrestrained laughter, red-faced, pausing only to catch her breath.

Mama sat on the porch, softly singing to the steady beat of her rocking chair, Segundina in her arms. Kittens romped at our feet, and cuddled in a single fluffy white ball, purring. Our maid brought ripe mangoes, which we devoured unashamedly, ignoring the juice that ran down our faces, soaked our tees, and dribbled down our bellies. A happy hum of conversation filled the air, ebbing and flowing with the natural rhythm of the family.

Mother hens gathered their chicks, and shooed them into the coop to protect them from the hawks that would come at nightfall. Safe inside, they cooed and crooned contentment. Clouds formed a fluffy blanket tinged with melon and saffron. Softly the sun began to set.

But then came the instant that changed everything; only much later did I realize how abruptly. While in college, two decades later, I sat looking at a Dirac-curve and knew it illustrated the mere stroke of time it took to ruin our family. And left unyielding consequences.

How could I know I'd never see our house in Manila again, that within two years I'd be taken from my family, left with only names and vague memories of my siblings and parents? How could I guess we'd be scattered like lizards, without so much as names or numbers to identify us?

The sun thudded below the horizon as Chile's scream of horror tore through the air. The alarm in his four-year old voice was frightening, "Someone's after Papa!" He pointed across the garden, and all eyes squinted toward two men in the distance: one standing in shadows with an upraised machete, and Papa in his white shirt, raising his hands in protest, backing away, and turning. The machete slashed down; Papa cried out and ran, holding his shoulder. His attacker hacked through the air with the machete, as if chopping through the rain forest, chasing Papa through the field, splashing across a rice paddy, and disappearing into the woods. At first everyone stared dumbly toward the forest in a tableau of terror and disbelief.

Then came chaos. Mama wailed as she ran to help Papa; my siblings shouted and ran about in confusion; Segundina cried. Frightened by the frenzy, I pulled myself up a sloping trunk of the *santol* tree onto the grass roof of the porch, and clung to the thatch, sobbing. My nose ran, and I shivered with bewilderment.

*Chile, where are you?*

Darkness dropped like lead. After what seemed a very long time, Chile came after me. He pulled up to the roof; I slipped into his outstretched arms, and we skidded down the *santol* trunk together, dropping to the ground. Chile shifted his weight, balancing me on his hip.

"Where's Papa?" I cried.

"Papa's dead."

After that, each member of the family peeled away like petals of a spent flower. First went Isabel, who normally walked with perfect posture like a princess, but now stumbled along hanging her head, eyes red and swollen, hair tied carelessly in a knot at the back of her neck, returning to Manila because she couldn't take more time off work. Chile and I stood waving goodbye as she plodded toward the village where she'd catch a jeepney. We watched her shadow shorten as the sun rose higher, until she disappeared, dragging what was left of her shadow behind her.

No one else returned to Manila, apart from our maid whom we never saw again. Now we stayed in our part-time house, and Mama worked in the village. A young girl watched Chile and me, and a neighbor several miles away babysat Segundina, while my three oldest brothers—José, 2Tall, and Francisco—withdrew from school to work in the sugarcane factory. They labored for long hours, came home tired, and seldom felt like playing. Evenings morphed into a boring routine: making dinner, cleaning up, laundry, and bedtime.

Mama was burdened with responsibility and discord as she assumed Papa's position as president of the sugarcane company, working at the satellite office in the village, month after month, sometimes commuting to Manila, staying with Isabel in her apartment, as our house there was sold. Doom and despair surrounded her, and she was always exhausted. José joked that she should start her own church and call it, "Our Lady of Perpetual Responsibility," but she didn't even crack a smile.

Late one afternoon we went to the beach for a rare day off. Mama sat, sad and motionless, stuck in time, hardly blinking. Her parrot-green skirt was soaked with surf and crusted with sand, yet she made no effort to brush it off. We found shells and ran to show her. "Hm," she said, without looking. Soon we left her, eager to catch crabs sidestepping across the sand. The sun sank below the horizon; the moon hung small and was swallowed by clouds. A crack of lightning set us in motion, running home in the dark, except for Mama, who remained sitting, staring. The long arm of the sea withdrew its waves, leaving behind cold, compacted sand. Segundina, cold and wet, sat crying next to Mama until 2Tall returned to lead them home.

José became the man of the house. Too young for a driver's license, he nevertheless drove the pick-up truck to work every morning along with Francisco and 2Tall. Mama left before sunrise, taking the still-sleeping Segundina to the babysitter. Soon Chile and I were left without a sitter, and got used to being unsupervised. We were inseparable; I did whatever he told me. We began the day with chores, which started with feeding the chickens and gathering eggs. After we rolled up the sleeping mats, and finished our work, we were free to play.

One day José told us to prepare a chicken for dinner, and we watched our brothers slaughter it: 2Tall slid in for the tackle, securing the hen between his feet, and José and Francisco grabbed its legs, holding them steady as 2Tall lopped off the head with his machete. To our amazement, the severed head chirped while flying through the air, and when the boys let go of the headless body, it stood up, ran around the yard at least a dozen times, and finally dropped. The scene was a cartoon brought to life. Chile fell to the ground laughing, holding his sides, and mirth rolled over the rest of us. The older boys left for work still chuckling. Smearing tears of laughter across our faces, Chile and I considered the clump of feathers on the ground.

"Is it *really* dead now?" I said, scrunching up my nose.

"Well it isn't moving, so it must be," Chile grinned, as he carried it to the kitchen by the feet and plopped it in boiling water. After a few minutes, and with a bit of trouble, he overturned the steaming pot into the sink, and waited for the chicken to cool. Then grabbing it by the legs and hoisting it onto the table, he started yanking out feathers.

"Is it cooked now?" I asked.

"Mama will do that. We just have to pluck it."

"Why?"

"You can't eat feathers, you know," he said, crossing his eyes.

But Mama didn't cook it. When she returned from work she only sat outside, gazing across the fields to the forest, crying. Segundina pulled herself up to Mama's knees, holding up her arms. Mama picked her up, absently patting her back, still staring at the far-away trees with red, puffy eyes. In the middle of the night she cried again, breaking into convulsive sobs, crying first for Papa and then for Bonifacio. Toward morning I snuggled next to her, and slept with my head on her shoulder.

Chile and I were permanently assigned to pluck chickens. "See what happens when we do a good job?" Chile said.

"That's right." José said.

"We have to keep doing a lousy job on the chicken coop," Chile whispered to me.

José loaded clothes in the washing machine, "By the way, it looks like you need *more practice* cleaning the chicken coop."

Gradually, we also got to *practice* washing the breakfast dishes, watering the vegetable garden, and sweeping the porch.

Within the next two years, we practiced hanging out the laundry too. I'd get a shirt out of the basket, shake it, and hand it up to Chile, who stood on a crate to reach the clothesline. But if the crate toppled over, or the clothespins weren't on just right, the shirts fell in the dirt and need washing all over again, and José yelled at us when he got home.

~~~~~~

One day when I was four, Mama took me to the medical-mobile in the village for a booster shot, and afterwards we left in a hurry for the office. She dragged me along, unmindful of my painful arm. "Hurry up, Mark!"

I ran, trying to keep up.

"Wait in my chair while I talk to Uncle Anton," she said, going in the next room and shutting the door.

I opened her desk drawer, took out a roll of Life Savers, peeled it open, and lined the candies up by favorites, the cherry being first, the lemon last. I closed my eyes, chose arbitrarily, and happened to get the cherry one. I slowly sucked on it, savoring the flavor, trying hard not to chew so it would last a long time.

I looked up at the ceiling with white squares filled with sound-gathering holes. I picked a square and tried counting the holes, but kept losing my place.

*Are words trapped in the holes?*

Uncle Anton was talking, but I couldn't tell what he was saying until he shouted, "Don't think I can't kill you, just like I did your husband!"

I burst through the door and yelled at him, "Don't hurt my mother!" But Mama slapped my face and yanked me down the hall.

*What did I do?*

She lifted me up on the bathroom counter, grabbed a paper towel, wet it, and put it on my face where she'd hit me.

"I'm sorry," she said. Then in a little while, "Did you hear what he said?"

I nodded, sobbing.

She hugged me for a long time. Finally she whispered, "It's a game… Uncle Anton plays the bad guy, and he says really mean things. But in the game, we have to do what he says."

My head pulled back and my eyes widened.

"Mark, you have to understand. We have to be nice. He's playing a very mean man…in the game. And for awhile we have to do what he says."

I looked at her and said, "Okay, Mama."

She wiped my eyes. "You are very brave. Be polite to Uncle Anton, no matter what," she said, stroking my face. "Oh, and *promise* you'll never talk about the game. It's a secret."

"Okay, Mama," I said, crunching the cherry Life Saver between my teeth. She gave me a thin smile and lifted me down from the counter. Then she knelt, took hold of my shoulders, hurting my sore arm again, and aligned them with hers. She looked into my eyes, "This is an important promise: don't tell *anyone*."

I nodded.

She opened the bathroom door, and Uncle Anton looked at her with fierce, marble-black eyes; grabbed her arm, twisted it behind her back, and growled, "Remember..."

*He can't hurt my mother! I'll kill him!*

<center>~~~~~~</center>

Chile and I wakened to see Mama dragging herself out of bed. She dressed and trudged off to work, and we dozed off again. We were wakened by Segundina's crying, and realized Mama had forgotten her. Chile didn't know quite what to do, but finally decided he'd find a neighbor to drive her to the sitter. It was miles to the next house, but off he went.

I played with Segundina for the longest time, and gave her a piece of banana when she cried. But after a while, I felt restless, not knowing what to do.

*Should I dress her or something?*

About then Mama walked in the door, and I took a deep breath, relieved that she'd come back for Segundina. But Mama didn't even look at her. She only shuffled through the room, tired; she dropped her purse and papers on the floor, and sank into a chair. Her face was tracked with tears

"Chile went to get a ride for Segundina..." I said.

She wasn't listening, and with a tone of unspeakable sorrow she whispered, "Take her outside." Segundina, now two-and-a-half, clung to her and wouldn't go. So I went alone.

The ground steamed my feet in the morning sun. I put on flip-flops and half-heartedly chased the chickens and pigs. Then I climbed on the tire swing, but it was full of spider webs, so I jumped off, and shoved it aside. It came back and knocked me down. I wandered around the chicken coop in circles, scuffing up gravel, kicking an ant-infested turtle shell across the yard as hard as I could. I traced snail trails on the walkway, and then sat on the grass, looking at the sky. I checked the road to see if Chile was coming.

*Why is Segundina crying? Why doesn't Mama pick her up?*

I went back into the house. Segundina was standing in her playpen where she took her naps. Her face was snot-covered and red, and she sobbed in shudders. I lifted her out, wiped her face, and told her to stop crying.

Mama was lying on the floor. I stared at her. She had a cup in her hand.

*She spilled her coffee all over the place...*

I put Segundina down and knelt by Mama's side, tapping her face. She didn't wake up. I shook her softly, "Get up, Mama." Then, trembling, I shook her hard with both hands, "Please get up, Mama. Come on, you have to get up!"

She didn't. Bubbles trickled from her mouth, but she didn't move.

*Mama...?*

My movements became mechanical. I put Segundina back in her playpen, handed her a blanket, and put a well-worn pacifier in her mouth. I ran out the door, down the walk, past the fields, past the grassy pasture, and past the crossroads, heading for the village, unaware that I went in the opposite direction that Chile took, but knowing Mama used to drive this way to the village. My legs throbbed, and I slowed to a walk. Finally I reached a one-room house, and shouted through the open door, but no one answered. I ran to the next house and saw a group of women talking. I zigzagged from one to another, trying to get their attention, but apart from scolding, "Don't interrupt!" they ignored me.

*No one listens to a four-year old.*

I ran to the next house where a woman was hanging her laundry. She shooed me away like a mosquito, until I pulled at her skirt and shouted, "Mama's dead." She finally said, "Come on, I'll walk you home." We walked quickly, churning up a wake of dust.

⁓⁓⁓

An undertow of voices buzzed the house. The priest and neighbors whispered to relatives, police came and went, and we were sent outside to sit on the steps. A woman in high heels clacked down the steps between us, her shoes barely missing our hands. "Don't get stepped on," she warned.

Just before the funeral, Isabel put Mama's hanky in my hand and lifted me up to the casket. "Say goodbye to Mama," she said. I looked at Mama. She was beautiful. She seemed to be sleeping, but was completely still. I wasn't sure what I was supposed to do, so I said, "Bye, Mama," and patted her hand in the casket, but it was *cold*, and I quickly withdrew, nuzzling into the comfort of Isabel's shoulder.

We were sitting on the front row at church. Francisco, always the first to cry, was sitting by José, 2Tall, and Chile, sobbing incessantly, which provoked everyone else to tears, except Isabel, who restrained her tears so that Segundina, who was sleeping on her lap, wouldn't waken. I sat between Isabel and a woman who had her arm around me. I glanced up, but didn't know her. Her hot tears splashed on my face.

*Am I supposed to cry?*

After that we were outside, and aunts and uncles met to choose us. Isabel clung to Segundina and me, gathered the rest of the boys, and announced, "They'll come to live with me in the city!"

Uncle Anton—short, squat, just younger than Papa, and mean by nature, snarled, "You can't do that. Wherever will you put them? You can't fit them in your teensy apartment!"

"It will be crowded, " Isabel admitted.

"How will you feed them?" he demanded.

"The boys can work."

"We can work different shifts," said José, ever practical, "so someone can always be home with the little kids."

"You can't possibly support them all," said Uncle Anton, his voice harsh and gravelly.

"We'll find a way," Isabel said as the wind swirled around her waist-length hair, lifting strands in all directions. "I'll do whatever it takes to keep our family together."

A pudgy aunt with a doughy face stepped forward. Her name might have been Escolastica; I'm not sure. She said softly, "Look, Isabel, we know how you feel. But it's *impossible.* We'd all like to help—but you know we have children of our own—

none of us could take six more! If anyone can take one or two, you should be grateful."

The relatives nodded.

"I'll take two boys," Uncle Anton said, "You decide which ones," he said to Isabel.

"I can't make a decision like that!"

Instantly, the wife of Uncle Anton, Aunt Ana—skinny and drawn-out like a ferret—threw down her half-smoked cigarette, ground it into the dirt, took Chile's hand, and yanked him away from Isabel. I tried to pull him back.

Meanwhile, Uncle Anton, his eyes flaring like a scratched match, grabbed Francisco and aligned him next to Chile. "We'll make the decision for you—Chile and Francisco, you come with us," he said, prodding them toward his faded blue car. But Francisco broke away, returning to Isabel. Chile struggled, but Uncle held him fast and continued to the car. I latched onto Chile's waist, all the while kicking at Uncle Anton. No doubt trying to appear magnanimous in front of the others, Uncle Anton said, "All right, these two." He strong-armed Chile into the car, lifted me by one arm, and threw me next to him.

That was the beginning of the scattering. Chile and I didn't see our siblings again. Maybe the others went with Isabel, or maybe they were distributed among relatives like cuckoo's eggs, raised in nests not their own.

During the long journey to our aunt's house, Chile put his arm around me. "Don't worry," he said. I leaned against him, trembling, clinging to Mama's hanky. Chile stared out the window, and we sat in silence.

*I wanna go home!*

I wanted to watch frog races, chase chickens, and gather up our lizards. I wanted Isabel.

*Mama's hand was cold in the casket—it should have been warm.*

# CHAPTER 2

WE WAKENED TO THE NASTY NUDGE of Aunt Ana's foot, "Get up and pluck that chicken!" she snorted, lighting her first cigarette of the day, huffing down the hall.

I lingered long enough to scrape the "sleepers" from the corners of my eyes with my index finger, as I did every morning.

"If I save enough of these, I can figure out what they're made of," I told Chile, looking at him for approval.

Chile gave me the cross-eyes.

I put them in a jam jar, "It might take a million years..."

Chile's dimple lifted his smile.

But Aunt Ana came in and slapped us, so we went to work. We climbed up on stools and began making *champorado* for breakfast, and from then on we had one task after another—dishes, sweeping, taking out garbage...

Our three cousins, whom we'd just met, and whose names I no longer remember, were pimply teenaged boys, as mean-spirited and condescending as their parents. They berated us, treating us like the servants we'd become. "Hey, buzzard-bait, go feed the chickens!" barked the oldest, who was perhaps sixteen—lean, long, and angular like his mother. "Go get me some Marlboros!" croaked the gaunt and sulking fourteen year old, in a just-changing voice. The third, packing a paunch like his father, demanded we fetch him some food.

Chile usually complied matter-of-factly, but one day he said, "It wouldn't kill you to do it yourself!"

The cousin snarled.

"Of course, we can hope!" Chile said.

"*You* do it!" bellowed Aunt Ana to Chile, through her customary cloud of cigarette smoke.

Chile slammed the door. Fortunately for Chile, she was distracted by the telephone and let it go.

But within a few days, six-year-old Chile gave his fat, twelve-year-old cousin a punch in the paunch, and the kid went whining to his mother. Aunt Ana's wrath kindled into a roar, "Do what you're told, *by me and your cousins!* If you don't learn your place, I'll take you to live with the *cannibals*. They'll cut a hole in your head and eat that pea-brain of yours, scoop-by-scoop, while you're still alive to watch, and then chop you into little pieces, boil you in a pot over a fire, and eat you!"

We'd all heard stories of cannibals, and many Filipino children, me included, had recurring nightmares, dreaming that cannibals came to chew off fingers, toes, and noses as we slept. If it didn't scare Chile, it sure did me.

That night, I overheard Aunt Ana talking to Uncle Anton: "We can't let it happen again, not like with Bonifacio. We should teach Chile a lesson!"

I decided to warn Chile, "They're gonna feed us to the cannibals," I said. Chile smirked.

A few days later when Chile grumbled about something, Uncle Anton exploded. He turned from his mirror where he'd been brushing strands of hair over his balding head, and eyed Chile savagely: "*I'll give you* something to complain about!" he shouted, shoving him out the back door. He beat him bloody with the boar-bristle brush, and when Chile's arms went up to protect his face, he kicked him in the stomach and left him lying in the dirt.

After a few minutes, Chile braced himself against the lichen-streaked wall and shakily pulled himself up. But then he slid back down to the ground, and sat fuming. Purple bruises swelled in dots made by the bristles of the hairbrush; blood smeared his back and shoulders where repeated strikes had ripped open his skin.

I slid down by him, and we sat for a long time, not saying anything. I wanted to put my arm around him but didn't want to hurt his shoulders. So I patted his foot.

It was hard to sleep that night. Chile shifted from side to side, and mumbled, "I'm not putting up with this!"

I knew he was angry, but didn't know what to say.

"You awake?" he said.

"Uh huh."

"Papa was killed with a machete."

I bit my lip, "How do *you* know?"

"Because. His hand was cut off, and all his blood squirted out."

"Did you see him?"

"I have a photo," Chile said.

"You *do?*"

"A policeman dropped it, and I took it. It's under there," he said, shining his flashlight on a slat in the wall.

The photo looked black and white because it had been taken at night. It showed Papa sprawled on his stomach in the grass, his white shirt slashed and bloody, one arm extended with the hand missing, a pool of blood circling his wrist. The glare of the flash made a freeze-frame of horror. My stomach jumped to my throat.

I hurriedly stuck the picture back in the wall and stuffed Mama's hanky next to it. Chile pushed uncle's bulletin board over just enough to hide the slat. It was covered with green and black butterflies, stuck through with pins. Uncle took pride in his etherized, splayed, and displayed collection of delicate creatures.

We settled on our mats, and Chile switched off the flashlight. His back and shoulders had to be hurting, and he probably had broken ribs because he could barely breathe. I knew he was toughing it. I stared into the darkness, wanting Mama. A sour taste in my mouth overwhelmed me, spreading up my jaw to my ears. I thought I'd throw up, but instead, my fear came out, "He might kill you!"

"*Then* who'd do the dishes?"

I knew Chile was grinning stupidly. I said, "But I'm *really* scared!"

Chile tried to prop himself up on his elbow, but apparently thought better of it, and slightly adjusted his position. "Don't worry. He's awfully mean, that's all." Then with resolve added, "We have to keep out of his way."

I fidgeted with a hangnail, biting it with my teeth, ripping it off, causing my index finger to bleed and throb. I sucked on it, and squeezed it tight to see if it would feel better. It didn't. My stomach was knotted-up, and I was trembling.

*I can't tell Chile... But I have to.*

The words erupted: "I *promised* Mama not to tell. Uncle Anton said he'd kill her, like he did Papa. Now he'll kill *us*!"

"What are you *talking* about?"

I told him what I'd overheard at the office, and added, "maybe he'll chop us up…"

"Why would he kill *Papa*?"

"I don't know…

"Why *would* he?"

"Maybe some grown-ups know."

"Or maybe you dreamed it. You shouldn't say things like that. We could get into big trouble!"

His disbelief shattered me. I started to sob, "I would *never* lie to you."

"Go to sleep," Chile said, finished with the conversation.

I was devastated, and tears kept coming, "I promised not to tell. Now I broke my promise… and I can't even tell Mama I'm sorry…"

"Don't be a baby—you're four years old—don't be a crybaby!" Chile said.

"I'm almost *five*, and I am *not* crying!"

"How come your face is all wet?" Chile asked, wiping my cheeks with the back of his hand.

"My eyes are only *leaking*…"

"Tell you what," Chile said, easing forward on his mat. "We'll have some fun! Tomorrow, we'll play a trick on that mean old *putang ina*," he chuckled.

"It's not funny!" I pouted, scrunching my blanket against my face, rigidly turning away from Chile.

The room fell silent. I cried quietly so Chile wouldn't hear. When I finally heard his erratic breathing and occasional moaning, I knew he was asleep, and rolled over but couldn't see him. It was darker than I ever remembered.

*I'll be going to hell now. Mama said the secret was important. She won't love me anymore.*

I cried most of the night, and my face was swollen and stinging with salt. But toward morning, I thought of a way out.

*Confession. I'll do Confession.*

I was sent to the village store for cigarettes, but detoured to the church. I ran all the way.

*Do little kids go behind the curtain like grownups? I wonder if the priest stays in the booth all day, waiting for people.*

I hurried, looking back to see if scrawny Aunt Ana was following.

*Don't let her catch me; don't let her catch me.*

I saw a priest in a white robe and collar on the other side of the street. I ran across the road and tugged urgently at his sleeve.

"Padre, Padre, please help me! I have to do Confession!"

"A bit young, aren't you?" he said, amused.

"But, Padre," I said, blurting out the whole story in sobs and disconnected sentences.

"You don't need to confess," he said kindly.

"But I broke my promise…"

"It will be alright. I'm sure your mother still loves you very much." The priest looked down with a practiced smile, patting me repeatedly on the head.

"But Uncle Anton…"

"Don't worry, my son, I'll talk to him, and you must try to mind your aunt and uncle."

"Padre, I'm scared."

"There's nothing to be afraid of. Don't worry; I'll drop by tonight... Be a good boy," he said, patting me some more on the head.

I opened the door, "*Pleeease* don't tell my uncle," I said, scrambling under the table as they shook hands. But the priest did tell him. In fact, he told the whole story. Uncle Anton popped open a can of beer and laughed loudly, "That's quite a tall tale."

"Why don't you bring Mark to Mass?" the priest said, heading for the door. "And give him some extra attention at home," he added with his all-purpose smile, heartily slapping his parishioner on the back. Meanwhile, I scooted out from under the table, shoved out the window screen and jumped over the sill. The priest and Uncle Anton were drinking beer on the porch, and didn't see me.

I ran for a long time. I didn't come back until I thought Uncle Anton was asleep, then snuck in next to Chile. Used to erasing confessions from his mind, I was sure the priest had already forgotten me; maybe uncle would forget too. But he didn't. In the middle of the night, he jerked me from my mat, shook me violently, dragged me out back, and threw me on the ground. I watched with terror as he machete-chopped a willow branch, trimmed the side growths into spikes, and then made a mockery of poking his fat gut with the points, laughing, savoring their sharpness with his fingertips.

*Did he kill Papa with that machete?*

He started whipping my face and chest; I fell to the ground, rolled over and took the beating on my back. Blood-trails criss-crossed my body, and soaked the dirt. My back felt raw, as though I'd been skinned. At last, he threw the bloody switch to the side, hissing down at me through clenched teeth, "If you tell any more lies, I'll tie you in a bag and throw you in the river!"

He stomped through the back door, but his rage welled up again, and he returned to kick the wind out of me. I rolled into a sow-bug position, struggling to breathe. He left me there.

When I staggered back to my mat, I was trembling. It was hot and humid, but my teeth chattered. I couldn't let Chile think I was a baby, so I didn't waken him. My back hurt too much to sleep for a long time, and when I finally dozed, suffocating dreams came—water weighted me down, soaking through a burlap bag. I held my breath and tried to untie the knot. *A knife, where's a knife?* I kicked and thrashed about, but couldn't loosen the knot or tear open the bag. Water surrounded me: I couldn't find either the surface, or the bottom.

<hr />

I couldn't wear a shirt, or raise my arms high enough to brush my teeth for days, yet chores were still expected. Chile, angrier about *my* beating than his, did double duty, and I helped as I could. I gradually healed, with scars like Chile's. We did our best work around the house, and cringed whenever Uncle Anton, Aunt Ana, or our cousins were around, avoiding them whenever possible. Things were about to change.

We had settled on our mats for the night when a tall shadow fell across the bedroom wall. Strong hands clamped over our mouths and someone whispered:

"Shh..."

The light of a full moon beamed through the window and illuminated the face of a handsome young man with long dark hair, giving him a supernatural appearance. He was muscular in a tight, white tee shirt.

"I'm your brother," the guy said, his broad smile revealing beautiful white teeth.

"Bonifacio?" Chile grinned with delight, his dimple deepening.

Bonifacio sat down, put his arm around Chile, tilted his head to the side, and looked at us thoughtfully, "Good guess. You're Chile?" he smiled, "and you must be Mark."

I regarded him for a moment, and then burst out, "Mama's dead, and Papa too."

"I know."

Urgently, like a floodgate opening, I told him about Uncle Anton, and added, "Chile doesn't believe me."

"*I* believe you," Bonifacio said.

I gazed at his face with absolute adoration.

"Could you kill them for us?" Chile asked sarcastically.

Bonifacio's response was serious. He stood up, "I could, but I won't. They're still family."

"But they..." I began.

"I *know* how terrible they are," Bonifacio said, pushing his long hair aside, "You *have to get out of here*!"

"Can we go with you?"

"If Uncle Anton sees me, he'll *kill* me. I don't want to put you in danger."

Now I was really scared. "Couldn't we sneak out in the dark?"

"No, let me get as far away as possible! You'll be safer without me."

"Where should we go?"

"Ormoc City. Leave tomorrow night, after everyone's asleep, with as much food as you can carry. I brought you a backpack."

"Which way is it?" Chile asked.

"Go past the chicken coop, stay on the road and keep going. It's a long way; it will take at least three days. When you see lots of streets with asphalt and tall buildings, you'll be there. Find the statue of José Rizal; stay by it, and I'll find you there."

"I don't think I can remember," said Chile.

"I'll write down the name."

"I can't read much…"

"How old are you?"

"Six and three-quarters."

"And I'm four-and-a-half," I said, and getting tall!"

"Yes, you are," he said to me, ruffling up my hair, then turning back to Chile, "You can do it. Ask someone for help. They'll read it and give you directions. You *can't* stay here…"

"But…"

Footsteps creaked outside the door. "Shh…" he said, stepping back.

By the time the door cracked open, we were on our mats pretending sleep. The hall light glared like a spotlight on our faces, and we got a jolt of stale cigarette smoke.

"Told you it was nothing; they're asleep," Uncle Anton muttered to his wife, rubbing his bald spot, "Let's go back to sleep."

Bonifacio stood in the shadow behind the door, still as the statue of a saint, the blade of a long knife flashing in his hand.

# CHAPTER 3

ASSAD PUSHED THE PILLOW HARD over his grandfather's face. With both knees on the bed he shifted forward, clamping the pillow down with his elbows and forearms, pressing with his upper body weight, until the old man—*that old sack of pus*—stopped shaking.

Most of the time Assad hadn't even heard him—that bloated bag breathing in the bed next to his; that is, until the old man turned over in bed, and the broken bedspring sounded like someone stepped on a frog. Or he started snoring. Every time there'd been a sudden snort, Assad had hoped it was his last breath, and he listened... but the shallow breathing kept coming back. He felt like he was in a tomb, taking in decayed air.

Then there was his mother, always cleaning up vomit, changing her father's enormous, reeking diapers around the clock, forever putting flowers around, as if that could mask the stink.

*She's nothing but a servant—waiting on a useless old man.*

The funeral came and went, but the stench stayed. Assad stared with eyes black as tar.

*Boring.*

Adjustments were necessary: he skipped school often and went to the pool hall where he liked to hustle chumps.

Today, it was nearly empty so he amused himself practicing shots, playing arcade games, and watching TV. He saw a movie with a car-race scene, and was riveted by a red Ferrari Lusso. He had his driver's license, *but what fun was it to drive the* family *car, that broken-down bucket-of-bolts?* He imagined being behind the wheel of a red Ferrari. Suddenly he became Steve McQueen racing at Le Mans, smelling the leather and feeling the sweat in his gloves as he gripped the wheel, experiencing vibrations of pure power. The engine roared as he shifted around the bend. He accelerated to 200 mph; his body melded with the car, and the only smell was tire-burn.

To prevent the Porsche 917 from passing, he straddled the lanes, but was suddenly shocked, and keenly disappointed, to find himself back home sans Ferrari, kneeling and bowed forward on his prayer rug. He scoffed. There were his father, a weakling, and his ever-menial mother, kneeling beside him in one of their five-times-a-day prayers that in his opinion were a complete waste of time. He wanted very badly to kick them over.

*Sure, Muslims should rule Mindanao.*

He laughed out loud, drawing a scornful look from his feckless father.

*But praying won't help. At least some Muslims take action! What a coward! Stuck in his miserable life. No guts. Grandfather too—generations of stupidity. Can't picture them in a Ferrari!*

The only thing Assad liked about school was a course in Russian literature, from which came a quote something like, "Cowards have *thin* opportunities!"

*Same place, same stupid things all their lives. That's them exactly.*

"Assad," said his mother that night, wearing her usual flowery apron, "You have been missing school. How do you expect to graduate? This behavior is not acceptable, you know. I will have to report this to your father."

*As if I could ever feel threatened by my pathetic father, who knows almost nothing, although that would be news to him.*

"But, Mother," Assad soothed. "You know how I sometimes feel sick to my stomach? I was feeling really bad, and couldn't concentrate. I didn't want to be a bother, so I stopped by the pool hall for a ginger ale, to settle my stomach. Then I watched a movie until I felt better." He glanced at her tentatively.

"How are you feeling now?" she asked.

"You are the only one who understands me," he nodded. "You're the best mother in the world!" He kissed her on the cheek, winked, and left her smiling, no longer intending to speak to her husband.

When he turned eighteen, his father gave him a job in the shop. He tried weaving, making the bright red scarves Muslims wore to identify their religion. He began on a table loom, interlacing horizontal woof threads through vertical weft threads, the same exact movement thousands of times, over and over. He lulled into a dazed boredom. No wonder his father was always numb. It was hot and humid, and wiping his sweaty forehead across the weave became part of his process. He watched other workers bending over their looms with expressionless faces, their hands moving mechanically, hour after hour. The prospect of doing this all his life loomed like an assignment to hell.

Besides, he made better money playing pool, although not enough to buy a Ferrari. He scraped money from the company till and left work early for the pool hall, but played entirely without satisfaction, because bets were low, and his take was next to nothing. He began considering ways to avoid going home. The boss, drunk as usual, had forgotten to lock the door at closing time, and didn't notice Assad at a back table when he left. Assad was alone and decided to stay the night. He'd just fallen asleep on the pool table when it happened.

A man in a gray linen shirt, perhaps thirty-five and not Muslim, stumbled in, covered with blood, crying for help. He fell to the floor and reached up to Assad.

Assad locked the door, pulled down the shade, bent over the guy, and said, "Why should I help you?" eyeing the man's chest. Two bullet holes burbled blood like baby spiders hatching from their eggs, and pooled in a wide arc.

"Please," the guy begged, the blood pouring like syrup.

"You're dying, mister. God couldn't help you."

"They'll kill my family, please..."

"What's it to *me*?"

"If you could just..." the man faltered, jerking a thick, blood-soaked envelope out from under his belt, "take this to Taluksangay Mosque at noon... give to man in green shirt... pleeease..."

Assad frowned.

The man pointed toward his pant pocket, "I'll pay you..."

Assad roughly yanked a wad of bills from the guy's pocket, "Okay."

But the man only stared with dead eyes.

Assad pocketed the money and tucked the large, unopened envelope in his waistband, pulling his tee shirt over it. The bloody wetness stuck to his skin, and he was eager to see what was so valuable. He glanced at the body.

*I should go.*

He slipped into the empty street without looking back, ducked into an alleyway, keeping to the shadows, zigzagged through the streets, casually looking over his shoulder from time to time.

*Where to?*

Cutting behind someone's house, he yanked a shirt off the clothesline, tossed his bloodstained tee in the trash, pulled the clean one over his head, and ran for hours, making his way to the waterfront. The sun was rising. He ran up the steps, bypassed the doorman through the heavy door of the luxurious Lantaka Hotel, past a desk with a smiling woman surrounded by vases of yellow Vanda orchids, past a closed gift shop, into a restroom redolent with starched, white-linen towels and vases of pink plumeria. He locked the door, and counted the money, panting.

So *much money, enough to stay* here—*hum... for quite awhile. Now to open the big one.*

He made himself anticipate the moment as if he were an actor, waiting to hear, "Action!" With great ceremony, imitating the cool of Steve McQueen, he ripped off the soggy end, and probed the contents: fat stacks of bloodstained, high-denomination bills. His heart pounded. He put his trembling fingers to his mouth—tasting the bloody money—smiling.

~~~~~~~~

He made sure the door was locked, carefully rinsed the bills, dried them under the electric hand dryer, wrapped them in linen towels, and packed them under his shirt. Taking a jeepney to Anda Street, he bought a small duffle, which he stuffed with money, reserving a few bills for his pockets.

*Time to shop.*

He looked in the store mirror and adjusted the red scarf he always wore. On second thought, he took it off and tossed it in the trash. Shedding and discarding his old clothes, he bought a black button-down shirt, and black pants like Steve McQueen wore in the movie. As he left the store he clutched the duffle close to his heart.

He got a haircut, but considering himself in the mirror, was disappointed. Handsome in a symmetrical sort of way, his deep-set, raven black eyes were equally sized, and each side of his face duplicated the other. He had an even brown complexion, and straight black hair, now combed forward.

*But the cut's all wrong.*

He bought gel and tried without luck to make small curls on his forehead like Steve McQueen's. Finally he stomped out of the barbershop, his hair combed back like before, only shorter.

*Oh well, I'll be lucky in love like McQueen, the King of Cool. I'll go to Manila, away from my useless parents and their futile religion. I'll get me a beautiful girlfriend.*

He hopped a jeepney to the airport and got a locker. With hands shaking only slightly, he stuffed the duffle to the back, shut the door, and turned the key. He took a deep breath and walked with counterfeit ease to the ticket counter. "One way to Manila," he said to the girl, casting his most charming smile.

"The next flight isn't until tonight," she said.

"Oh, I'll find something to do. When do you get off?"

"No time soon," she blushed.

"Too bad," he winked, turning away.

He bought a sandwich from the vending machine, and walked out of the terminal.

*How does the guy at the mosque rate that load of money?*

He decided to find out, this time taking a taxi.

At the mosque, the noonday glare was upon him. Greenshirt was easy to spot, pacing in front of the foot-washing tap, constantly checking his watch. First the guy walked completely around the mosque, smoking a cigar. At twelve fifteen, he started chewing it. Finally he threw it to the ground, rubbed it out with his shoe, and walked briskly across the square.

Assad followed.

# CHAPTER 4

ABOUT MIDNIGHT THE NEXT NIGHT, Chile and I crammed papayas and leftover fish and rice into a paper bag. It crinkled, and we froze, listening. We stuffed it in the backpack, along with flip-flops. All was quiet. I slid Mama's hanky and the photo of Papa out of their hiding place, and tucked them in my pocket. We eased out the open window, feeling the coolness of fern fronds breaking beneath our bare feet.

We stepped out through the vegetable garden, past the musty chicken coop. The stupid rooster started crowing, and we broke into a run past the *narra* tree, onto the road, running as fast as we could, for as long as we could, then slowed to a walk. Suddenly the roar of a motorcycle revved through the air, and the flash of a headlight startled us.

"It's Uncle Anton!" whispered Chile, pushing me off the road.

We slouched across a rice paddy into a wooded area and jumped into a large hole beneath the roots of a massive fallen tree. The motorcycle came closer, churning through the rice, doing 360's, slipping and sliding, the headlight turning in frenzy like a prison searchlight. We ducked well under the shelter of roots. The motorcycle went back to the road, and we relaxed.

Chile whispered, "*Mark?*"

"What?"

"There's something moving across my legs."

I froze and felt it too—something cold *sliding* across my legs. *Snake!*

"Hold still. Don't move..."

My legs quivered, and my whole body shuddered involuntarily. My heart was beating so hard I could hear it. We stiffened against the dirt, not breathing. A six-foot cobra slithered up over the roots and across the ground—its gray scales glistening in the moonlight.

We waited, holding our breath, trying not to scratch.

Chile stifled a sneeze.

"I'll find you, and make you very, very sorry!" yelled Uncle through the dark as he turned back toward the house.

We exploded out of the hole, running separate ways through the shallow water of the rice paddy, reconnecting on the road, and then walking without talking. Chile retrieved our flip-flops from the backpack and we put them on. Suddenly he snorted and broke into a continuous chuckle. It was hard for him to stop laughing long enough to spit out: "Uncle Anton's going to be *extra* mad tomorrow!"

"He's *extra* mad already!"

"Do you know what a de-pil-a-tory is?" Without waiting for an answer, Chile blurted, "My friend at the store told me about women who take hair off their legs." He laughed until his eyes watered, wiping them with the back of his hand. "They put this cream on their legs, and it eats hair, just like magic," he snorted in anticipation of his punch line: "I filled up his tube of VO5 with hair-eating cream. When he rubs it on his head, all his hair will be gone, gone, gone."

"And he'll be bald, bald, bald!"

We laughed until our sides almost split, slapping our thighs. Holding our stomachs we fell to the ground, rolling over and over, consumed with the vision of a completely bald old Uncle Anton with his squinty little eyes looking in the mirror, tightly pursing his thin lips, his face red and swelling—a ticking time-bomb, ready to explode.

Grinning with glee, we skipped for awhile, and then settled into a steady walk. We went on for hours; our legs ached, and blisters popped up between our toes. We took off our flip-flops, sat at the side of the road, ate and rested. Leaving our thongs behind, we started out again, trudging on through the night, one tired foot after the other. Eventually we wandered into a patch of long grass by the side of the road and slept.

The sun was high when we wakened. Fascinated with dust motes in the air, we reached up, trying to catch them, barely noticing an old woman across the road, uprooting cassava from her garden. She glanced over, squinting in the sunlight, arching her hand over her brows to shield her eyes. Her entire face lifted into smile wrinkles as she realized what we were doing.

"Oy," she called, wiping her dirty hands on a thin white apron. "You're a long way from home."

"We've run away," Chile said, standing tall, "and we're never going back."

Her expression fell, and she studied us for a moment, "Are you hungry?"

We stepped over the road ruts and followed her, weaving through her garden of beets, long beans, carrots, onions, and cassava, onto a tiny porch of uneven bamboo slats in disrepair, and into her one-room house. Her graying hair was in a ponytail at the back of her neck and straggled halfway down her back. She was short for a grown-up, and wore a tattered cotton dress, red like a scarlet macaw, which went limp just below her knees. Her calves were withered, and her bare feet had gray, crusty heels, and jagged toenails caked with dirt. She turned and smiled with coffee-stained teeth, motioning us to sit on the floor.

A black and white goat stood on its hind legs, eating *nigella* from a pot on her hot plate. She shooed him away, the hanging droop of skin under her upper arm waving along with motions to hurry him out.

"Why are you running away?" she asked.

"So our uncle can't kill us," I said.

"*Kill* you?"

"He's mean, so we're going to live with our brother in Ormoc City," Chile said with gusto.

The old woman sighed and shook her head. She made rice and stir-fried vegetables. We sat on the porch to eat, and were pleased when she offered us more. Many years later, I still have a vision of that toothy yellow smile, and the upward wrinkles around her eyes.

"Do you know how to get there?" she asked.

"Our brother told us," Chile said, looking down the road.

"It's a long way," she said. "Do you have any money?"

"Money? Um, no."

"My husband left me a little," she said. "Before he died. He lived to be eighty-five years old!"

"How tall *was* he?" I asked.

"Well, taller than me, for sure!" she chuckled. "You might need some money." We followed her back into the house, and she upended her jar of change, and handed the coins to Chile, along with bananas for our bag. We thanked her, and returned to the road. She waved, along with her flap of underarm skin, said something we didn't hear, and made the sign of the cross.

〰〰〰

We were barefoot now—walking, whistling, and wishing we were there.

"Are we almost there?" I asked.

"How many times are you going to ask that?" complained Chile, pausing briefly to rub his sore feet.

"Hey, there's something gold up there," I said, running ahead. I picked up a yellow-breasted bird, its wing askew, and cradled it in my hands. Its body was stiff, its feet curled-under, and its head flopped to the side. I folded in its broken wing and smoothed the feathers, "He's dead."

"We have to make a funeral," said Chile.

"Don't put dirt on him."

"We could wrap him in Mama's hanky. We could put flowers."

"I want to *keep* her hanky."

"But she'd like it, if we wrapped him up."

We glanced at each other and nodded. I saw a clump of purple orchids and cleared a place; Chile mounded grass in the middle; we laid the little bird on it, tucked the hanky around him, and covered him with orchids. Then we sat by the grave, wondering what to do. Chile thought for a minute, and motioned for me to stand. He put his palms together, and began to recite as much of the Lord's Prayer as he could remember: "Our Father which art in heaven…" That was it. He raised one eyebrow and apologized with that dopey grin of his, and we sat in silence.

We wandered back to the road, and walked on. "Hey, where's our backpack?" I wondered after a while.

"Maybe we left it by the grave," Chile shrugged, and that was that.

The afternoon sun was hot enough to melt rocks. Humid air weighted us down, while steam shimmied from the ground, compressing us into slow motion.

"My legs are killing me," said Chile.

"Me too."

Sweat on our faces mixed with road dirt. We took off our shirts and tucked them in back of our shorts; the sun reddened us, and our shirts must have dropped to the road. Now we were bare-chested.

"When I grow up, I'm going to kill Uncle Anton," I muttered.

Chile had fallen behind. I stopped at a fork in the road, and he caught up. One was rutted dirt, and the other asphalt, with heat wavering off it.

"Let's take that one," said Chile, pointing to the paved one. But it was too hot for bare feet, so we walked along the grassy edge.

The next day, we saw a jeepney painted in psychedelic flowers of purple, red, and yellow coming toward us.

"Could we ride?" I said.

Chile looked at me with his eyes crossed.

Not much later another jeepney, painted in swirls of fuchsia and lime green, approached from behind. It passed us and pulled to a stop. There were no passengers, and the driver called, "Need a ride?"

We hesitated.

"You can ride for free," he said with a broad, toothless grin.

# CHAPTER 5

———◆·◦◦◦◦◦·◆———

THE DRIVER DROPPED CHILE AND ME OFF DOWNTOWN, and sounds of honk-and-go traffic enveloped us. Huge buildings were everywhere, taller and larger than imagined. We walked along, staring up at the tops of them. Asphalt roads stretched as far as we could see, in all directions, and were crowded with cars, jeepneys, and an enormous truck trailing billows of stinking exhaust.

"Have we been here before?" I asked.

"Of course not, stupid," Chile said, "but a long time ago we lived in Manila. It was sort of like this."

It was late afternoon, and workers poured out of shops like the exodus from an anthill. The hum of so many people talking at once made us feel disoriented. We caught a welcome whiff of fish frying across the street, but didn't know how to navigate the traffic to the other side.

We wondered what to do. So we bought Tootsie Rolls.

"I'm still hungry," I said.

"Me too," Chile groaned, "and I lost the paper Bonifacio gave me, and I can't remember where to go."

We used the last of our money to buy more candy, and then meandered around the market, standing on our tiptoes to see the food on the stands, our stomachs growling. Vendors took down outdoor tables and closed their shops. We wandered through the streets until nightfall.

"They don't have much grass here," Chile said. We sat down in a doorway and began to cry.

"But I can smell the ocean!" I said after a while.

Chile didn't say anything.

"That old woman had a nice face," I continued, "the one who fed us and gave us all her money."

"She's all alone," Chile said.

I nodded, "Maybe she has grandchildren…"

"Uh huh."

"How will we find Bonifacio?"

Chile considered the problem, "Tomorrow we'll try."

We leaned into door casings and dozed for a few hours, wakening to the low growls of a dogfight across the street. Then we saw two guys approaching through the shadows, skirting the dogs, heading through the intersection toward us.

"What are your names?" they asked us.

We told them and they left without saying a word. We went back to sleep, but soon wakened. To our great relief, Bonifacio stood over us, golden-faced under the streetlight, light reflecting off his black hair like a halo. "I've been looking for you all day. Why didn't you go to the statue?" he said.

"I lost the paper," Chile said.

"You have to be more responsible!" Bonifacio said sternly. He nodded toward a skinny kid who looked a few years older than Chile, with long tied-back hair hanging almost to his knees. The guy sprinted to an all-night market, grabbed mangoes, and ran by us, handing off the fruit. Chile and I stood there looking astonished, holding the mangoes. No one else seemed to notice, and the kid continued down the street, his hair trailing behind.

"That was Ben; he'll help you," Bonifacio laughed, absently fingering a goose egg on his forehead and a newly stitched cut along his hairline. He saw us staring. "The other guy's in the hospital," he laughed. "Come, follow me." He led the way to a near corner, and gathered cardboard. "Always sleep where you can see your enemies coming. Here's some money, but you'll have to find work tomorrow."

"Work?" Chile said.

"Ask jeepney drivers if you can wash their jeeps."

I looked up at Bonifacio with rapt attention. He was tall and good-looking, with enormous muscles, and a deep, resonant voice.

*He's like a king or something. He talks like he's giving commands.*

Just then the kid who stole mangoes returned with tee shirts. "Ben, get the kids some rice," Bonifacio said. Then turning to us, "Sorry, I can't stay."

"Can't we go to your house?" Chile asked.

"I don't have a house. We sleep on the street," he said. "It's best on cardboard."

"Can't you stay with us?" I asked. "You're our..."

"No," Bonifacio said. Then leaning down, he whispered, "Don't tell anyone I'm your brother—ever—it's important."

"Can we go with you?" Chile asked.

"Not where I'm going. Sorry." He hopped into the back of a passing jeepney and disappeared in traffic.

"He left us!" Chile said in amazement.

"Why doesn't he want to be our brother?" I asked.

Chile shrugged.

I looked up and down the street. Ben dropped off bowls of rice, and without a word went off in the same direction Bonifacio had gone, catching a jeepney way down the road. Shopkeepers had left, and we were alone on the street.

"Where did everyone go?" I said.

"Home, I guess," Chile shrugged, devouring his rice and mango.

Ragged clouds drifted across a half-moon. A dirty dog with protruding ribs scavenged the sidewalk, snarling as he passed. We began to notice smells, which infused the humid air with odors of wet cement and mud. Chile and I didn't talk, listening for uncle's motorcycle, nervously glancing up and down the street, our eyes wide. Finally we put on our new tee shirts and lay down on the cardboard. Despite our exhaustion, we couldn't sleep.

"You know," Chile said at last, "When I was little I prayed for nights to be shorter, so I'd have more time to play. Tonight, I want the night to last forever, 'cause I'm sooooo tired."

The night wind revolved in the sky, bringing in plump gray clouds, and we finally fell into a deep sleep, awaking a few hours later to the soft patter of rainfall. It was refreshing and somehow comforting. Since no one was around, we stomped a few puddles. We looked up and down the street; it was dark and empty so we twirled around with uplifted faces, our mouths open to the rain, drinking and reveling in the cool wetness.

Raindrops melted into our foreheads and cheeks. Strutting like roosters, we hopped, jumped, and crowed—overtaken by joy. We oozed mud between our toes and laughed with delight as we lifted them, making mud-suck sounds, each one louder than the last. The rain stopped. Road dirt had washed from our bodies, and we felt cool and content. At last, we settled on our wet cardboard and fell into peaceful sleep.

But toward morning, I had a nightmare that a big man on stilts was chasing me. Full of fury, he charged with the persistence of a tractor. I ran all night trying to hide, but stilt-man kept coming, towering over me like a bad guy from a cartoon. I ran through alleys, crouching in the shadows. Finally, like a super hero, I leapt to a rooftop, jumping unseen from one tin roof to another, and when I looked *down* on him, I was no longer afraid.

⁓⁓⁓⁓

Dawn came without the nudge of Aunt Ana's foot. We dozed until the sun's rays streamed through the street, warming our wet clothes. People were coming to work. Rubbing our eyes, we looked around—no uncle in sight. We began slapping puddles on the sidewalk, disrupting our images.

"No one looks at us," I said.

Chile smirked, "No one makes us work."

"And no one's mad at us."

"No one calls us names."

We watched vendors setting up for the day.

"Do they know we're runaways?" I asked.

"We're *invisible!*"

Grubby kids with dirt-caked toes emerged barefoot from the market, ranging from about four to fourteen years old. Cuts, scabs, and dirt covered their arms and legs. Most had diamond-shaped tattoos on their right hands, and cross-shaped tattoos on their right feet. A pockmarked kid with long, uncombed hair standing near a storefront stared at us, a curl of ash teetering from the end of his cigarette. Others picked their noses, smoked, and whispered as they watched us.

"They're just street kids." Chile said, as though he knew this for sure.

"Why are they looking at *us*?" I asked.

Chile glanced at them, "They don't know us, that's all."

"Oh."

"Let's eat."

Chile dug into his pocket, "The money Bonifacio gave us is gone!" He was astonished. He searched both pockets, and had me search mine. We searched our sleeping place, and looked up and down the street.

Chile frowned, "Stolen."

After a while, Ben called our names, coming toward us. He was taller than Chile, but skinny as a twig. Raising his eyebrows he said, "*Ano ba?*"

"We're hungry and our money was stolen," I said, lifting my eyebrows.

Ben regarded us, stone-faced, "Go to the back of restaurants and ask if you can wash dishes."

I must have looked puzzled, because he said with a deadpan expression, "They'll give you leftovers."

"Um, how do we brush our teeth?" I finally stammered.

Ben finally cracked a smile. "You use a guava tree stem to rub them." He handed Chile a pocketknife. "Use this to sharpen the stem. When you sleep, put the knife under your body—don't lose it!"

⁓⁓⁓⁓⁓

Chile and I hurried to a nearby restaurant, excited to eat. We salivated at the sounds of a metal lid jumping on the rim of its pan, the staccato chops of a vegetable knife, and the sizzle of fish. We went to the back, entered timidly, and asked for work. There was neither scorn nor pity in the owner's look when he saw how young we were—we blended right in. He smiled and dragged wooden crates to the sink, overturned them for us to stand on, and we climbed up. We washed plastic dishes until our hands were pruney and our backs hurt. Finally he gave us salted rice, which we consumed greedily, licking the last few grains from our bowls, hands, and between our fingers.

As we returned to the street, we decided to chase our shadows along the sidewalk, stepping along the lengths of them, trying to pin them down.

"We're street kids," I said, biting my fingernails. "We don't have a family."

Chile shrugged.

But I wasn't finished. "It's Uncle Anton's fault, and I'm going to get even."

We explored a few streets, walking for a long time until Chile said, "I'm so hungry, I could eat snails," making a grossed-out face.

We passed a cat with matted fur licking its wounds, and a stinking, mangy-wet dog with watering eyes, sniffing along the street, stopping to scratch from time to time.

We asked for work in the same restaurant and then in others, but the owners all said, "Sorry, we don't need anyone right now."

We approached jeepney drivers, one after another. But they already had boys either washing their jeeps, or hustling riders. Chile finally decided to press his dimple advantage, asking for work with a broad smile and a peppering of charisma. I stood by his side, merely trying to look pleasant. Chile was large for his age, and stood tall, looking older than his almost seven years, but it was probably his charm that finally got us jeepney jobs. I was small for a four-year old, nearly five, but I climbed up and washed the tops, then came down to clean the tires while Chile did the main part. We ended up washing quite a few.

"We have to work really hard," I said.

"*Ay*, I'm sore, tired, and *so* hungry... And we don't even have enough money for lunch."

We worked until dark and could barely buy bowls of rice. We were exhausted, and our still-gnawing stomachs aggravated our sleep.

We woke up hungry, and weren't used to it. We decided to ask for money on the street, as we'd seen others do, but no one was giving. Usually the response was "*Patawarin po*," which means literally, "Forgive me, sir," an apology for having nothing to give. But we were ashamed when a withered, old woman with arms skinny and desiccated as chicken legs, and a brown face wrinkled like the *Ilocano* cigar she smoked, looked at us in disgust, and shouted with a gravelly voice, "Get some work!"

We ran clear down the street, and finally Chile panted, "I don't *like* begging!"

"Did you see that wart under her chin? She's a witch!" I wheezed as we rounded the corner, flattening against a wall.

When we caught our breath, Chile said, "You're right about that! Let's go find work."

"Better than begging."

We made a few pesos sitting on parked cars "to guard them from theft," as we'd seen others do. If anyone seemed threatening, we were ready to yell, "Stop, thief!" although that never happened.

During the next few months, we settled into a routine of washing dishes and jeepneys. It was extremely challenging, especially for me, but we learned assertiveness: vigorously competing for jobs, determined to work quickly and efficiently. When too tired, we napped on a street corner and wakened to work again.

# CHAPTER 6

———➤·⬤⬤⬤⬤·◀———

Assad's reflections of his business start-up played like a good movie through his head, and the reruns stoked his ego. He thought of his successes in cinematic terms, and relished reliving them in his memory, like a movie watched many times, the best parts anticipated and savored. In his movie he was, of course, the writer, director, and leading man.

*So good at killing. And smart! I invented the perfect method.*

He zoomed in on his brilliance, like the day he first saw green-shirt pacing at the mosque, nervously smoking a cigar, waiting for a delivery he'd never get.

## ACT 1

*Scene one: Close up of me watching green-shirt at the mosque, merely out of curiosity. I make no move to give him the envelope. When he finally leaves, I follow him to a pay phone, and overhear him reserving a six o'clock flight to Manila.*

*Scene two: Outside, six o'clock in the evening. Davao Airport. Last flight to Manila. Green-shirt and I board the plane, me after him. He takes a window seat, orders a drink, and shakes out his newspaper. I follow unseen, and take a seat across the aisle, a few rows back. I have a drink; he has several more.*

*Scene three: Sunset. Manila Airport. We deplane and walk through the terminal to outside. I observe him against the background of a purple-orange sunset, not letting him out of my sight. We each hail taxis, and mine follows his to the ritzy neighborhood of Forbes Park. He gets out just before the security kiosk; I get out just after, and expertly vault over the six-foot stucco wall, mere moments after green-shirt did the same. I follow him.*

*Scene four: Fading outside light. Cul-de-sac. Residents turning on porch lights, some of them glance at green-shirt as he checks house numbers, and knocks on a door. A woman answers, saying, "My husband isn't home." Without a word, he pushes past her to the living room.*

*Scene five: Darkness. Backyard. I slip like a phantom through the back door to a dimly lit kitchen, then to a doorway leading to the living room. I position behind the door and watch the show.*

*Scene six: Lights up in living room. Draperies open. Three young children are sitting on the floor in front of TV. Three shots fired—BANG, BANG, BANG! No silencer. Children fall in succession as horrified mother looks on. Camera zooms on small bodies bleeding-out on pale beige carpet.*

*Scene seven: Dim light. Kitchen. Camera comes in for another close up. I'm looking on in amazement, shaking my head.*

*Scene eight: Lights up. Living Room. Next shot hits woman in the head; she's dead before she hits the ground. The next two shots are superfluous, apparently just for fun, but green-shirt doesn't smile. He walks out front door, gun in hand.*

*Scene nine: Dim light. Kitchen. Lights up, illuminating me in kitchen doorway, highlighting my face in an attitude of profound disgust. I scoff and click off the mistakes under my breath: "Seen by people in the neighborhood, draperies open, shooting possibly seen by neighbors, no silencer, waste of bullets, front door exit, holding gun. Could he possibly be more conspicuous?"*

## ACT 2

*Scene one: Broad daylight, various streets in Manila. Cameos of me following the guy, now in an orange shirt, as he meets with big-money con-*

*tacts and carries out other assassinations. Each time, he shows a uniformity of carelessness. I whisper to the camera: "Different shirts, all bright. Sloppy."*

***Scene two:*** *(my favorite): Sun low in a pink-like-fish-blood sky, fading to black. City street. I follow bright-shirt as usual, but he makes me, and doubles back. His gun jabs my temple.*

*"Why are you following me?" bright-shirt hisses through clenched teeth.*

*"I want to join your business," I say, not breaking a sweat.*

*"I work alone."*

*"So I've noticed."*

*"What do you mean?"*

*I rattle off names of some of his victims.*

*"Who are you?"*

*"Your successor."*

*"What the..."*

*Those are his last words.*

*My knife is inconspicuous.*

# CHAPTER 7

We couldn't eat unless we worked, but our need for play occasionally overtook even our hunger. It was a day too hot for Tarzan, so we headed for the ocean with abandon, running into the breaking waves—splashing, shouting, and savoring the sudsy surf. We lounged about on the sand, watching parrots, listening to the soft slap and shush of waves, as the glazed brightness of the sun rose overhead.

"When I close my eyes and look at the sun, I see red inside my eyeballs," I said.

"Me too," said Chile.

As soon as we got too hot, we splashed back into the water.

"My body stings all over!" I said, sneezing salt water and rubbing my nose.

"My feet hurt a lot."

"After a while you'll stop hurting. Papa used to say salt's the best thing in the world for sores."

I looked up at him skeptically.

Chile stood in the surf, his thick hair heavy and dripping with water, his shoulders broad and muscular, despite irregular eating. We watched kids retrieve a log from under the bushes, drag it across the beach, and push it through the incoming waves. When they got into calmer water, they mounted it, and paddled out to sea using driftwood.

"Let's do *that*!" Chile said, already scouting wood. "Maybe go to that island over there."

"But I can't swim."

"It doesn't matter, I can."

We found a log and laboriously dragged it to the water, shoved it through the waves, clumsily trying to balance our driftwood, dropping and retrieving it more than a few times. At last we were mounted, with scratched-up arms and legs, but holding our paddles. Paddling was hard work, but we were ultimately at sea. The log bobbed on the water and our brine-coated, brown skin reddened. When tired of rowing, we floated, letting the current carry us toward the island, our feet trailing water. We were relaxed and smiling, happy together.

I leaned forward comfortably on the log and was beginning to doze when I felt a sharp pain on my ankle. Snapping my leg up on the log, I saw blood streaming all over my foot.

"That was a baby shark!" Chile shouted, looking from the water to the wound. "Keep your foot on the log, and hold the blood in, so the shark won't smell it!"

"Will he come back?"

"Nah...Your blood's probably disgusting."

We resumed rowing, and finally reached the shore. The island was uninhabited, and we felt free and wild. Crabs worked across the surf, scissoring pieces of blue jellyfish and dragging bits backwards into burrows. We bypassed them and entered the forest. The soles of our feet were tough, and we stepped through the undergrowth with ease. Mottled black and brown frogs jumped out of our way. I caught one, stroked its sticky back, and thought of José, 2Tall, and Francisco and their marine toads. It jumped off my hand.

We foraged for food amid the mosquito-swatting frenzy of afternoon. Overripe *lanzones* blanketed the ground beneath multiple-trunked trees, and squished underfoot. We perched on a fallen tree trunk, and ate about ten *lanzones* apiece, then walked along the shore with slight stomachaches.

Warm surf lapped our legs, and for awhile, we watched a school of thin, silvery fish, easily visible in the shallow water. Wading further out, we tried using our tee shirts to catch them, but they swirled around and between our legs, tickling and taunting us. A flash of *déjà vu* hit me as I glanced at the shore— for a moment I saw Mama and Segundina sitting there.

The chattering of macaque monkeys diverted me, and I sloshed to shore followed by Chile, across the sand into the shade where monkeys sat, eating crabs. Babies hung suspended from their mothers' bellies, or clung to their backs. Two young monkeys tried desperately to play with each other, but their mothers scolded and yanked them back by their long, thin tails, as if their tails were harnesses. Unable to reach each other, the little monkeys screeched in frustration.

Chile and I threw rocks at monkeys in the trees, but they threw *lanzones* back with amazing force and precision, bonking our heads and shoulders.

"We're so outnumbered. Where are our brothers when we

need them?" shouted Chile.

We took refuge behind tree trunks and then a large boulder. "This will be our fort," Chile said.

We stockpiled ammunition—gathering rocks, seedpods, and rotten fruit as war began anew, accelerating into a barrage of rapid-fire throwing and shouting.

I hit one monkey solidly on the rump. He shrieked and relieved himself with a well-aimed stream of hot, stinky urine right on my head. Chile laughed hysterically, and then I laughed, and we couldn't stop until our stomachs hurt too much to laugh anymore. The monkeys chattered and watched with amusement.

A cloud of birds fluttered up from the canopy and the monkeys screeched and scattered. Then it was quiet.

"Give up?" I yelled to empty trees.

Chile shouted, "Us, one; monkeys, zero!"

But soon we understood their quick retreat: a snorting wild boar came running through the underbrush right at us. We scrambled up a tree, feeling the hog's hot breath as we pulled ourselves higher, hugging the trunk with our legs, frantically grabbing for branches, jerking our knees abruptly to our chests. The hog jumped at us, and one tusk ripped the seat of Chile's shorts as Chile puckered barely out of reach. The hog kept butting the trunk, snorting and stomping, then circling the tree, puffing steam. We clung to the trunk, climbing higher until we found a branch to sit on. We looked down at the boar. Finally we were brave enough to yell, growl, and throw seedpods on him. Ultimately, he gave up and snorted off through the bush.

We decided to sleep in the tree. The muggy air weighted us against the sturdy branches like wet leaves, and we inhaled the moisture of soggy wood.

"If Papa could see us now…" said Chile.

Clouds of chirping birds settled in the canopy and quieted. The forest was thick with the complexity of a bird's nest in varying shades of green, quickly fading to black. A few slivers of moonlight pierced through leaves far above us.

"Do you remember Papa?" Chile asked.

"Sometimes."

"Remember the pick-up truck?"

"Sort of… Could you tell me?"

"It was big. White. Once we were riding in the back," Chile began, chuckling, "Papa was joking around, with Francisco sitting on his lap, steering. 'Don't tell Mama!' he said. Suddenly Papa stepped on the gas, and we almost fell out; then we went even faster. José threw a sack of sugar out the back, and then hid under some bags. 2Tall yelled, 'José fell out!' Papa slammed on the brakes, crashing us into the cab. He jumped out of the truck, saw the sugar sack way down the road, not moving, and started to cry. Then José stood up in the truck and shouted, '*Here* I am!' Papa was so glad to see him, he wasn't even mad."

I smiled in the dark, absently picking a scab off my hand. After a moment, I asked, "Why didn't Papa teach me to swim?"

"Too young—he used to carry you on his shoulders, and you would steer him by his ears. But one time when you were two, you wandered into the sea by yourself, and a riptide pulled you under. Papa grabbed you by the heel and saved your life. You didn't even cry. He picked you up, rubbed the salt out of your eyes, and said you'd be president of the company someday because you're so tough."

"President of sugarcane?"

"Uh, huh. We were rich."

"Not like now."

"You weren't afraid of anything." Chile went on, "Papa and José used to play 'One-Two-Three' with you. Remember?"

"Um. How do you play?"

"They played catch with you, flipping you over in the air between them. You weren't scared, you just kept saying, '*Otra vez!*'"

I brushed the tickle of ants from my arms, and my mind wandered. I gazed at the stars through a break in the canopy, vaguely remembering Papa's strength, yearning to feel his arms, longing to be lifted onto his shoulders. Abruptly, I ground my teeth. Bubbles of anger simmered inside me, welling up and coming to full boil, overtaking all else. I clenched my fists until they hurt.

*I don't have parents, or a family, or a home!*

Chile hung over the next branch like a big cat, snoring. He startled at the stir of nocturnal animals. "I dreamed I couldn't sleep..." he mumbled, and resumed snoring.

The forked tree-branch was surprisingly comfortable with smooth, moist bark. I decided to think about monkeys. Finally I dozed off planning a strategy for monkey wars, and slept all night.

Chile wakened with a sweet tooth, and began singing something Mama used to sing, "*My little one came from the womb, not wanting milk, but only sugarcane...*" I was climbing down from the tree when he said, "I wish we were home and could have sugarcane anytime we want."

"What's a womb?" I asked.

"Maybe a hammock..."

We hurried to forage for food and found green papayas, but the fruit was hard and bitter. Finally we found ripe ones and eagerly bit through their soft skins, sucking out the sweet pulp.

Later, we discovered a fallen coconut. "At least we'll have coconut water," Chile said, pulling off the husk. He slammed the coconut repeatedly against a rock but couldn't break it. Finally he climbed a tree and threw it against a boulder as hard as he could. It cracked slightly. We both attacked it with the biggest rocks we could lift, hitting it over and over. Sweating and out of breath, I shrugged and looked at Chile. In frustration, Chile kicked it as hard as he could, and then hopped around for awhile, holding his foot.

"I think Papa used a wedge," he said sheepishly, as though embarrassed he didn't always remember everything Papa taught him. We found a sharp, flat rock, wiggled it into the crack, and banged it with another rock until the shell finally split. All the liquid spilled down the rocks. Chile smirked, and the monkeys chattered with delight.

Sitting on the beach, we chewed chunks of coconut, tossing pieces over our shoulders at the monkeys. Then we waded in warm bubbles that tickled our toes, skipped in the shallow surf, and ran through the sand for hours gathering shells.

"Take a look at this conch," said Chile. "It's just like Mama's. Remember?"

"Not too much."

In the late afternoon, we took a long nap under a tree. I fell asleep recalling fragments of a song Mama used to sing in Tagalog, "*Sana'y di nagmaliw ang dati kong araw...*" I struggled to remember more lines, "*Nais kong matulog sa dating duyan ko, Inay... Oh! Inay...*" That was it for words, so I let the melody play through my head, evoking the swish of her saffron skirt when she walked, the comforting smell of coconut soap on her soft arms, the sparkle of gold bracelets, her red fingernails, gold wedding band, white sandals, and red toenails. My heart ached.

*I want Mama...*

I clenched my teeth.

*Uncle Anton killed Papa, and because of that, Mama is dead. He broke up our family.*

I turned on my side, feeling a crush of leaves, oblivious to the countless insects hunting food on the forest floor beneath me. I dozed but soon wakened, itching all over.

*So that's why people sleep in hammocks.*

Chile was sitting in a tree.

"Is it night or day?" I asked, scratching.

Chile bit his lower lip, and looked up through the canopy. "Um, just about night."

Fruit bats emerged into the dusky sky, searching for fallen fruit. One bat landed fairly close to us and sucked the juice from a ripe papaya. All at once a woolly bat darted down, attacking the fruit bat, gouging its back, slashing its throat with sharp little teeth.

# CHAPTER 8

WE RETURNED TO THE MAINLAND IN HIGH SPIRITS. Unencumbered by possessions, we had only the clothes we wore, the knife in Chile's pocket, and the wrinkled photo of Papa hidden in a tree-hollow. We had nothing to keep track of, no chores, and no one to boss us around. Best of all: we had the exhilaration of going where we wanted, when we wanted, and usually how we wanted.

We found a forest hideout a day's hike from the city. It was a tiny, corrugated-tin-roofed hut with a dirt floor. Inside were a large, smelly, stain-infused mat, perhaps a dozen candle stubs, and a rusty BIC lighter that still worked. We decided to make a pond. We rolled up the mat and dragged it to the stream, heaved it across, and braced it with boulders to make a dam, diverting some of the water so the stream could continue. It took all day, but we made a great pond, and eventually fish, frogs, and pollywogs settled there, providing us with food and pets.

Our first pet didn't last long. It was a baby snake, thin as a thumb and maybe five inches long, which was the only reason I considered picking it up. I called it *Los Ojos del Gato* because it had elliptical pupils like a cat. I put it on Chile's shoulder.

"Get that thing off me!" Chile shouted, stutter-stepping backwards and falling to the ground.

So *Los Ojos del Gato* got a rapid release and wiggled its way back through the leaves to hunt tiny tree frogs at our pond, having been our pet for all of thirty seconds. We were both fine with toads, so we caught fat and warty Asian Horned Toads and raced them like our brothers had done a few years earlier, making a racetrack with lit candles along the floor of the hut. Chile's toad was so fat he could hardly budge off the ground, so usually mine won. I got to drip hot wax from the candle onto Chile's arm, because Chile had the loser toad. Those were the rules.

Our toads were black with brown side bands, and nearly invisible at night, so we tethered them in the doorway to guard us from mosquitoes, and named our hideout, The Palace of the Toads. It was ours—we discovered it, named it, and carved our names inside.

~~~~~~

When we returned to the city, we skipped to the market, and noticed two boys about our ages. The youngest had a freckled face, sunken chest, and was skinny as a starved dog. Leaning against the wall, he wound heavy-gauge sewing thread around a loose front tooth, while a tiny monkey sat on his head, picking through his mop of hair.

"What're you doing?" I asked, lifting my eyebrows in greeting.

"Juan's going to pull out my tooth," he said, coughing. "I've wiggled it for two days, and it's ready."

"What's your name?" I asked.

"Perito."

"That's a funny name."

"Just like a puppy," Juan interrupted, "except he doesn't *whine* like one," he said, yanking out the front tooth. Perito looked up with soulful puppy eyes, lifted his tee shirt and wiped his bloody mouth, hiccupping.

"Put this in your mouth and move it into the hole with your tongue," Juan told him, shaking salt into Perito's hand.

"How old are you?" I asked.

"Six or seven."

"I'm five, maybe." I said. "What's your last name?"

"I just have a front name," Perito said, his mouth puckering as he maneuvered the salt with his tongue, his freckles shifting as he shuddered.

Chile and I laughed.

"I'm Chile; he's Mark," said Chile, pointing to himself, then to me.

"I'm Juan," said the older boy. His broad smile radiated warmth as he put his arm around Perito, and handed a burro banana to the monkey. We all walked toward the covered market like we'd always been friends.

The market had a corridor, covered by corrugated tin, and a dirt walkway. Small stalls lined each side, selling everything from clothes to knick-knacks, as well as food. The clamor of shoppers and sweet aroma of fish, rice, vegetables, and freshly cut fruit filled the air.

As we entered the market, I asked, "What's his name?" taking hold of the monkey's tiny hand.

"Mano."

"Can I hold him?"

"Sure..." said Perito, grinning.

Perito lifted Mano off his head and put him on the ground. I held out my arms. Mano curled his fingers around my hand, jumped onto my chest, and with practiced speed, his hands darted into my pockets, searching—nothing there. He grabbed the neckband of my tee shirt, searched inside with the same rapidity, and then gave me a quick nipple-twist. Laughter erupted and rippled through a half-dozen kids. Juan convulsed to the ground, his bushy black hair rolling in the dirt, his arms holding his stomach. Chile, out of breath with laughter, sat down by Juan and rocked back and forth, slapping Juan on the back. Meanwhile, Perito slanted his arm to the ground, and Mano scampered back on top of his head and looked around, exultant with the show he'd put on.

As the amusement subsided, Mano jumped down and began gathering snails from outside the marketplace.

"Want to play squishy?" Juan asked Chile.

"Sure," Chile answered in his "I'm so cool" tone of voice.

The snails tested the air, and then quickly withdrew into their shells as we piled them into pyramids of six. Mano handed a snail to Perito, who expertly tossed it under a bicycle tire, and we heard the crunch of shell. Juan skidded one under the wheels of a passing jeepney. Everyone got six tries, and crush and ooze smeared the street. A few snails didn't get run over, but it was only a matter of time. Perito got lucky with the only perfect score and grinned broadly, showing the vacancy left by his tooth. Juan strutted over and put his arm around him, "We'll call you 'Perito Perfecto' from now on." But because we were boys, his name soon was shortened to "PP".

As the sun went down, the city quieted, and we gathered cardboard and staked out places to sleep in the covered market. Although the alleyway was open, the shops inside were closed with iron grates. Shopkeepers were gone; only the homeless were left behind, most of us children. Chile and I watched kids we didn't know: two boys finished a game of chess and shared memories of a friend who'd been killed in a gang war; one kid stitched his torn shorts, then handed the needle and thread to someone else; a kid in the corner torched a pile of cockroaches with his BIC lighter; another told about setting fire to a hornet's nest, and his triumphant escape, his friends listening eagerly; a kid with a badly torn shirt and a scarred face scratched his mosquito bites; another methodically pulled legs off a grasshopper, while still another jumped up abruptly and ran outside.

"Diarrhea," said Juan, knowingly.

Juan was built like Chile, and resembled him—big for his age, about nine years old, a year older than Chile. But the ravages of living on the street were apparent on Juan. He had a thick red scar above one eye; his complexion was yellowed, as though he'd had malaria, and he had tattoos on his right hand and foot. A bit thinner than Chile, he had the care-worn look of one with too much responsibility. Yet when he smiled, he brightened the space around him, and conveyed genuine affection. He lit a cigarette. Chile asked to try one, and Juan was

71

quick to share. Smoke filled the air, blending with a smoky, pungent smell coming from down the corridor.

"What's that?" I asked Juan.

"Oh, the weed? Sorry, I don't have any."

We slept on cardboard, but some kids spread out on their stomachs or curled up like sow bugs directly on the ground, unbothered by dirt against their faces. One kid lay splayed as if dropped from a tree, his limbs at all angles, looking almost boneless. Sleeping in a variety of positions, they looked like strewn about pick-up-sticks. PP slept at Juan's feet like a puppy, sucking on a tattered blanket with Mano curled beside him, his tiny monkey-face burrowed in PP's armpit. Just then, a mischievous kid yanked away PP's blanket. Mano scolded. Chile jumped up, punched the kid, grabbed the blanket, and tucked it back in PP's hand. Everyone resumed positions. Juan flashed Chile an upward nod of gratitude; they smiled, and the bond between them took root.

---

The enticing aroma of sizzling fish greeted Chile and me following a hard day's work, and we were hungry.

"Let's get fish," I said.

"With rice, eggplant, sweet potatoes, green beans, and..." Chile began.

Variations of this conversation had persisted all day, as we become more famished. Now we were exhausted, but we'd cleaned seven jeepneys and had finally earned enough for dinner. We rushed toward the vendors, stomachs growling, licking our lips.

Suddenly we noticed two big kids coming toward us.

"Give us your money, coward!" one demanded, staring at Chile. A few adults stepped around us and hurried on. The kid took a deep draw on his cigarette, leaned forward, and blew smoke in Chile's face, along with a spray of spit.

"No!" Chile said.

With a contemptuous smile and toss of his head, the other kid, puny as a stick, flicked away his cigarette and sucker-punched Chile in the stomach, sending him to the ground, then socking me in the chest, knocking the wind out of me. Chile struggled to his feet, but the first kid returned him to the dirt with a roundhouse kick to the side of the face. Skinny Kid ground Chile's face in the dirt with his foot, grabbed our money, and sauntered off. Chile stumbled to his feet, rubbed his eyes, and stood there seething.

Later at the covered market, we met up with Ben and told him what happened.

"Do you know who they were?" I asked.

"Just predators. They're lazy, so they steal from shops, restaurants, and street kids. Stay away from them," he said, and then with a tone of sympathy, "Sometimes they surprise you."

"Are there lots of them?"

"No. No one respects them. They're dirt."

"Do *you* usually see them coming?"

"I'm a *Tibay*—they don't mess with me. Before I joined though, I watched for those *putang inas* all the time. Sometimes it helps to fight hard. Once when they ambushed me, I fought like a mad dog, and they gave up pretty easily. Usually they won't put out too much effort for just a few pesos."

"What's a *Tibay*?" Chile asked.

"You don't *know*?" Ben said, round-eyed.

"Not yet."

"Only the most powerful gang in the city!"

We looked at him in amazement.

Ben laughed and changed the subject. "Some of us are going to the cinema to see 'Rocky.' Come with us."

~~~~~~~~~

"Mark, we have to learn how to fight, and we have to get strong," Chile said after the movie. "We have to work out, do push-ups—maybe even five or six sets."

By the next afternoon, we were terribly sore; we could barely walk, and every part of our bodies ached. We hobbled down to the park to watch the daily kickboxing competitions. The sharp sting of sweat filled the air. We were enthralled: fighters were strong and powerful—the action fast, tense, and mesmerizing. Adrenalin spread from the contestants to the crowd.

We decided to go every day, vowing to learn defensive moves, and how to *really* fight. Privately, I resolved to become tough enough to face Uncle Anton, and confident enough to exact punishment. I planned to show up at his house, tell him who I was, and what I knew.

*Then I'll kill him.*

Whenever possible, Chile and I sparred, imitated moves, and practiced roundhouse kicks to banana trees until the bones in our feet hurt, competing to see who could kick a series of trees the fastest. Over the next few months, we developed a few street-fighting skills, and even entered a few daily fights.

Occasionally, Bonifacio dropped by and gave us advice. "Put the stare on them; don't look away. No fear!"

"Sometimes we get beat," I said.

"Everyone loses sometimes," said Bonifacio, putting his hand on my shoulder. "You need a master to train you. I'll get someone." Then he put his arms around Chile and me, drawing us close, "Remember, don't ever tell anyone you're related to me. Not anyone. In fact," he said, shaking his head and pursing his lips as if sorry he didn't think of it sooner, "you two pretend you're just friends—not brothers."

"Why?"

"There are those who'll kill your whole family if they have a problem with you. We can't put each other's lives in danger by admitting we're related. That's the way it works."

From across the park, a group of kids nodded respect to Bonifacio. Two boys approached and stood as though awaiting orders. He spoke to them in a huddle, and they sprinted away. Another nodded as if indicating a completed assignment, and glowed with his approving smile. We didn't see him around much, and when we did, he was often going elsewhere. We supposed he had other responsibilities, but never guessed what they were. So we were shocked when Ben said, "Bonifacio's the leader of the *Tibays*, all three divisions. We're under his command."

Chile and I were a mix of thunderstruck, proud, and humbled.

"You respect him, don't you?" Chile said.

"I'd give my life for him!"

Chile asked, "Are the tattoos part of the *Tibays*?"

"You guessed it. They show our rank: diamonds on our hands, crosses on our feet, and triangles on our arms."

"What's yours?"

"I'm a *Papa,* the highest rank," Ben said, pointing to the triangle on his right delt.

"What about your other ones..." I said, "the ones on your hands and feet?"

"What about this one?" interrupted Chile, pointing to the diamond on Ben's right hand, just between and above his thumb and index finger.

"It's the first one you get. It shows you're a *Laya,* a beginner."

"What do *Layas* do?" I asked.

"They're spies," Ben smiled. "And they make the best beggars, because they're so young and cute," he laughed, glancing at me. "Usually, they're younger than six."

"But the *Papas* are the best ones?" I asked.

Ben laughed, "The *Papas* have the power."

"What about the tattoo on your foot?" asked Chile.

"That's the second rank. *Batas* serve under *Papas*—they don't make decisions, but they fight, run errands, and do what they're told. Usually, they have jobs to help support the gang."

"So, they get the cross?" Chile asked.

"Yes, the *Batas* get the cross," Ben nodded, pointing to the tattoo just above his big and second toes. He paused to lite a cigarette.

"What do *Papas* do?" Chile and I asked, almost in unison.

"We advise Bonifacio."

Chile and I tried to take it all in.

"So this triangle on your arm shows that you're a *Papa?*" I asked.

Ben nodded, "It's also our job to fight, control the money, and teach and protect the *Batas* and *Layas*—we're their leaders."

"Do you have any more tats?" asked Chile.

"I will," Ben said, puffing out a ring of smoke. "The 'mark of the assassin' goes on the back of the neck. After you've killed at least ten people…"

⁓⁓⁓

"I don't want to join," I said to Chile when we were alone. "I want to be on my own."

"We probably wouldn't live to be fifteen," said Chile. "I heard six kids died in the last gang war."

My stomach cringed.

I didn't want to die. The vengeance parasite that had attached to me after my father was murdered had grown into an obsession. I *couldn't die* before I reclaimed the family honor. My mind was set.

Paradoxically, though, the appeal of the *Tibays* increased: the gang was like a great big family; I admired the camaraderie, organization, and loyalty. I also loved and respected Bonifacio.

"Man, he's strong," Chile said, "I want to be…"

Our conversation ended when Ben joined us. "You two should join the gang," he said, lighting his cigarette.

Chile said, "We prefer independence."

"Is that why you're learning martial arts?" asked Ben.

"I want to earn big money fighting," Chile said.

"I want to be tough," I said.

"Difficult when you work."

"We work during the day, and train later," said Chile.

"We're awfully tired," I admitted.

Ben nodded unsympathetically, and changed the subject. "I looked for you last night. Where do you sleep? I don't usually see you."

"Wherever we can—in the pool hall under the table, the park, or the covered market," said Chile.

"Or the street," I said.

"And when it rains?"

"Sometimes warehouses. We make friends with the security guards, and give them cigarettes."

"Do you get cold?"

"We pull rice sacks around us."

Ben laughed. "Movie theaters are better. The owners kick everyone out before locking up, but I know where there's one with a hole in the wall. I cover it with particleboard during the day. At night after everyone leaves, I crawl in and sleep on cushy seats. I'll show you sometime."

"Does anyone else know?"

"Three of us now," he smiled, putting his arms around us.

"Do you sneak into the movies?" Chile asked.

"No, it's so cheap to get in. Besides, I wouldn't risk losing a good place to sleep."

"What's your favorite movie?" Ben asked me.

"'Rocky.'"

"Chile?"

"I'd have to say 'Thriller,' on TV. What about you, Ben?"

"I like cartoons."

"Except for the subtitles," Chile said, in a Donald Duck voice.

We spoke Spanish, having been born in a Spanish colony, but now our language had become mixed with Tagalog, and a sprinkling of Cebuano, Visayan, and Letenio. Often movies were in English, with subtitles in Tagalog or Spanish, but most street kids didn't read very well, if at all, and we were no exception. We watched the 'Rocky' series repeatedly to stoke our workouts, and learned a little English in the process.

We watched TV at the pool hall or went to the cinema with Juan and PP, and sometimes Ben. When cartoons were on, it was always jammed with street kids. Word of mouth communicated the playbill; we never kept track of days, weeks, or months for that matter—time was irrelevant, and we only knew two seasons: hot and humid, or hot and humid with rain.

# CHAPTER 9

SHE WORE DESIGNER JEANS and Via Spiga heels. She bumped her Prada bag across his lap without apology as she slid past him to the window seat. But it was the delicate fragrance of her perfume that provoked a glance. He quickly took out the flight magazine and pretended to read. She was stunning. He forced himself not to look, but as her arm brushed his, he quivered; his awareness was acute, and suddenly he couldn't think of anything but her. He purposely looked away, and yet he sensed she'd turned toward the window. He fidgeted with his Rolex, as he often did when nervous, then jumped up and headed for the restroom.

"What's the matter with me?" he asked the mirror.

The flight wasn't full and he resolved to find another seat, yet he walked right past several empty places, and sat next to her again. She had dozed off, and he took the opportunity to look. He was amazed to see how small she was, petite in fact.

Her jet-black hair was pulled into a twist above the back of her neck, exposing a softly curved nape that excited him. Her eyebrows arched gently, and her almond eyes were fringed with dark, full lashes that fluttered slightly in her sleep, giving her the appearance of innocence. Her mouth was soft and begged kissing.

"What are you staring at?" she said abruptly.

"Um, your necklace," he said. "It's unusual... Um, a, does it have some kind of special meaning?"

"It's an abstract design," she answered with annoyance. She brought her chair to the upright position and crossed her elegant legs.

He studied the necklace intently. "I wonder how someone comes up with something like that?" he said. "It's, um... strange," and then fumbling for conversation, "probably made by a strange person."

She didn't reply.

"A crazy person with thick glasses and frizzy white hair in a secret underground lab..." he continued, rolling his eyes.

"Could be," she laughed. "I designed it."

"Nope, you don't fit the picture."

She unclasped the necklace and handed it to him. "See, it's quite intricate," she explained, tracing her manicured finger over a variety of overlapping circles in contrasting gold and silver.

"It is that."

She smiled, replacing the necklace around her neck. "Could you help me with this?" she asked, motioning for him to fasten it.

He held it awkwardly, his fingertips brushing her soft neck. "This must have a secret combination," he said, apparently unable to fasten it.

"This is a timed test," she said.

"I think I flunked; maybe you'd better do it."

He handed her the necklace, their hands touched for a moment, and a surge of electricity sparked between them.

"What do you do?" she asked, ignoring the unspoken connection.

"Ah, I'm a teacher," he said quickly, "…a professor."

"What do you profess?"

"Ah, I teach warfare."

"Sounds boring."

"Anything but…"

She licked her lower lip, "Where do you teach?"

"All over the country—private lessons."

"So you're a tutor?"

At that point, the flight attendant interrupted, asking what they'd like to drink.

"Champagne?" she asked.

"Make it Krug Rosé," he added.

As they sipped their drinks she said, "My name's Dameana."

"Assad," he said, offering his hand.

# CHAPTER 10

STREET KIDS WORE THE SAME CLOTHES FOR MONTHS, rarely getting new shirts or shorts, almost never doing laundry. We bought blocks of Palmolive soap, chopped them into chunks, and bathed in the sea, wearing our clothes so they got cleaned-up too. Sometimes we were lucky enough to have shampoo to play with—slathering our long hair into shampoo-horns, and molding bubbles into beards. We bathed and romped in the ocean for hours, while salt water healed our wounds.

One day, Ben, Juan, PP, Chile, and I hiked about eleven miles from Ormoc City to Lake Danao, which was called Lake Imelda in those days, and shaped like a giant guitar. PP, Chile, and Juan swam, while Ben and I waded the perimeter, gathering skimming rocks—flat, disc-shaped ones—and had a skimming contest. We stockpiled a mound of good rocks, and tossed them until our arms were sore. One rock in particular had all the features of a winner—flat, smooth-as-silk, and just the right size, so we kept it as a trophy of our excellence. We called it "the best skimmer of all time," and I kept it in my pocket.

Before we knew it, the sun went down.

Chile stood up, "I'm starving!"

"We don't have any money," said Juan.

Night came upon us suddenly. It was pitch dark, but Ben guided us back by the stars. We found a field of sugarcane where we cut joints of cane and peeled back the purple casing, sucking and chewing the good part. As we walked along, pacified by sugar, Chile cheered us with a happy thought: tomorrow might be Sunday.

In the morning, we headed for the nearest church, hoping it was indeed Sunday, and that Mass was about over. Things were looking good—we saw lots of street kids waiting outside.

"It's a holiday too!" Ben said as people poured out the door. A man handed us more than enough money for food; a group of women distributed small bags of shampoo, combs, candy, and toothpaste.

"No work today," Chile grinned, delighted that religious holidays brought out the generosity in people.

<hr />

After months of working with our master, Chile and I entered daily fight competitions at the park more often, and made much better money than we could by working. I was still small, and looked *younger* than my seven years, which worked to my advantage, because no one expected me to fight as well as I did.

On the other hand, Chile was now almost ten, but he looked *older*, and competitors were wary. He was a tough, fearless fighter who packed a punch and a powerful kick. One day, he entered the more prestigious weekly fights, held at the gym where bets ran higher, and won a hundred dollars.

He took great pleasure in spending it. Juan had given him a beat-up radio, and he played it whenever he had either an outlet or batteries—tuned to a station of American rock. He learned to Moonwalk, imitating Michael Jackson, always drawing a crowd. But currently his biggest magnet was money: kids came to drink beer, sniff gas or glue, smoke marijuana, and occasionally to snort crack. Chile paid.

He still wanted to fight, and entered another weekly, no doubt wanting the encore of another large purse. His contender moved his head around like a rooster ready to fight, and entered the ring with quick kicks. Chile gave it all he had, but his timing was off; he was hammered, and actually got knocked out in the third round. Bonifacio doused him with water, and led him out of the gym.

"You just can't *do* this. Drugs and fighting don't mix!"

"Gave 'em up just this morning," Chile said, unshaken, and grinning sideways. The three of us went to the park and sat down together.

Chile leaned against a tree, nodded, and then turned on his radio, cranked up the volume, and the rhythm and lyrics of "That's the Way I Like It" drowned out all else.

Later that day, I found him in an alley with new friends, smoking marijuana. "Why are you hanging with these parasites?" I demanded.

Chile shrugged, "You can join us."

"I want to *train* with you."

"You should have some fun! You can't work *all* the time."

"You're wasting your time!"

"It's what I feel like doing right now."

"And what am I supposed to do without you?"

"How should I know?" he said, slipping me a wad of money.

I left, but I took the money.

⦚

Now I lived, worked, and trained by myself. I fought in the dailies, and my reputation for winning grew. Unlike Chile who'd become overly casual, I was exceptionally serious. I worked my advantage of being small, encouraging opponents to underestimate my strength, ability, and quick reflexes, holding back full force until necessary. I entered the weeklies.

As I made my way to the ring for my second fight, a hush filled the air, but it wasn't for me. Someone was parting a path through the spectators. He wore a tight black tee with dark shorts, had slick-backed hair, and a flank of bodyguards. He moved with confidence. Whispers coursed through the crowd, "Assad's here, bet on the same guy he does."

*Who's Assad?*

At the last minute, bets were placed on me. I won the fight and earned a good purse. I looked around for Assad, but he'd gone, to my disappointment. Yet the person I really wanted was Chile; it was a hollow victory without him.

Finally when all his money was spent, he returned, wanting to get back in shape. It took a while, but we were happy together again. One day I said, "Don't you ever think about getting even with Uncle Anton and Aunt Ana?

"Are you kidding?" he jeered, conversation over.

*He'll change his mind.*

He lit a cigarette, smoked it to a nub, paced back and forth with a quickened stride, and said, "Fighting in the weeklies is better, and we can beat them, you know," he said in his Donald Duck voice.

So we restricted ourselves to the weeklies where betting was bigger, and liked fighting in the ring rather than the dirt of the park. It was a good time for us: we won quite often, and I appreciated Chile more than I used to.

We were thrilled when Bonifacio came to watch us. A deferential hush spread through the crowd as he approached. We were stoked when he said in front of everyone, "You're both good. I'm proud of you!"

We smiled at the spectators.

"Join the *Tibays*," he said.

"Why would we give up our independence?" Chile asked.

"You'll be safer, because we protect each other. You won't have to work; we'll support you while you train."

"But gang members work…"

"Not always. Ben and Juan don't. The old guys, the *Abuelitos*, work to pay for protection, but everyone else has assignments based on ability and circumstance. Both you and Mark are potentially great fighters, and you should train full time. Chile looked up.

Bonifacio smiled broadly, revealing straight white teeth, "I just won a monthly fight. *That* should be your big goal—to fight in the monthlies."

We nodded. Although we'd never seen him fight, we'd heard kids brag about him.

He continued, "By far, the best money's in the monthlies. You have to train exceptionally hard, and while you're training and getting experience, you should join the gang."

Chile looked at him cross-eyed.

"You'd get better food," Bonifacio said.

Chile looked puzzled.

"It's true."

Chile's interest stirred.

"Of course, parties…"

Chile became attentive.

"You'd make lots of friends—we have hundreds of members."

Chile's interest spiked. "Okay, okay," he said, "I'm in."

"What about you, Mark? Ben and Juan want you to join, and now Chile…"

I hesitated, grinding my teeth.

*Chile gave in; I can't believe it. We do everything together. He must hate Aunt Ana and Uncle Anton. He doesn't get it.*

"Think about it, Mark, and tell me when you're ready," Bonifacio said, and putting his arm around us both, he turned to Chile, "No favors, you've got to be initiated."

"Oh goody."

I headed for the beach with everyone else for Chile's initiation. It was warm and quiet apart from the slam of the surf. The sand was clean and stretched for miles up and down the coast. The sun was down, but the moon was full, ringed with a pale haze, and the strand was illuminated with melon-colored lights.

Eight *Tibays,* Chile's age or younger, were assigned to fight him. Bonifacio and I took places on the sidelines with fifty or so gang members, including a few adult *Abuelitos.* The appointed fighters gathered around—all eight of them. I tried to size up Chile's opponents. There were no kids bigger than him, but two looked about the same. The other six were probably assigned much like second-string players, to give them experience. Chile signaled ready, and the gang members circled like wolves—putting on the stare, egging him on:

"Think you're tough?"

"Let's see what you've got!"

They closed in with the rhythm of a wolf pack, poking from one side, then the other. The first punch hit Chile solidly on the jaw. Then came a quick kick to the chest he didn't see coming. He moved forward like a bulldozer, knocking one guy to the ground, and breaking the nose of another with a lucky punch. There was a fairly even exchange of kicks, but then a roundhouse kick opened a cut above his eye that bled profusely. He took a beating to his face, and both eyes became puffed slits. He managed a few more punches, although he could barely see. He swung a blind left hook and missed, and connected with a roundhouse kick that downed a kid. Then a hard right hook sent him down. He got back up, but was pummeled from all sides. A crisp left jab knocked him to the sand, and he rolled painfully to his side.

I shouted, "Stay down! Stay down!" but Chile struggled to his feet, refusing to give up.

A swell of respect rose from the sidelines. Everyone chanted his name: "Chil-ee! Chil-ee! Chil-ee!"

Bonifacio stepped in and stopped the fight, and the gang had a new member. Ben and I brought ice-filled rubber gloves, bandages, and beer, and the gang's artist gave Chile the diamond-shaped tattoo on his hand between his thumb and index finger. He was a bonafide *Tibay*. Caught up in the enthusiasm, I was proud in a way. "Hotel California" was playing on Chile's boom box, and I joined in celebrating his exceptional initiation. Later he switched to reggae, and the gang drank San Miguel Beer to a Rastafari beat far into the night. But when all was quiet, in the hours just before dawn, I sank into despair.

*Chile betrayed me. He just cut his life expectancy; he won't live long enough for revenge. And how can Bonifacio still consider Aunt Ana and Uncle Anton family after what they did? I will be the one.*

I decided not to share my continuing revenge plan with either of them, and wondered what they'd think of my goal. I couldn't be dissuaded. Vengeance had taken hold.

~~~~~~~~

Chile spent a lot of time with the gang, while I worked and trained solo.

Occasionally he joined me in the evenings, and once brought his gun.

"You could get one. Why don't you join?" he asked. "Ben…"

"I'm okay."

"You wouldn't have to work so *hard*."

"I don't want to."

"You're seven. It's time for you to be a man…" Chile said, tossing down his cigarette.

I tried to ignore him.

"You're being stubborn."

"I have my *own* life!" I said, turning my back on him and walking away.

*And I'll make Papa proud.*

I'd grown tall enough to make washing jeepneys easier, and I knew which restaurants had food to spare. Tumi, a good friend I'd made when Chile had abandoned me for his druggie friends, worked as a cook in an upscale restaurant. Fifteen, and weighing well over two hundred pounds, he was affectionately called "Soft Serve" by his boss, and soon by everyone else, because of the rolls of fat that began at his neck, descending in concentric circles to the pool of his corpulent belly. He had a gentle nature, uncommon generosity, and was whip-smart. He got a kick out of teaching me to read and write, and to play chess. His gang assignment was stitching wounds, but he also baked cassava cakes for them, and was a great cook. I did kitchen jobs and errands for him, which was steady work. The pay wasn't much, but I loved being around him.

I made much more money winning the weeklies. There were times, of course, I got too beaten up to do much of anything. But I thrived on fighting, and tried hard to please my master. I don't recall his name anymore, but he was extremely patient.

Chile continually tried to persuade me to join the *Tibays*. He sent a kid with black front teeth to provoke me into joining. For awhile, the kid showed up every day, rubbing his chronic pinkeye with filthy knuckles, shouting abuse with his combustible breath, and forever pestering: prodding, poking and punching. Finally I got annoyed enough to knock him down. The kid was so shocked that he swallowed his gum, walked away, and never came back.

# CHAPTER 11

As I dipped my rag into the bucket and soaped the back of the last jeepney, I thought only of dinner, and finally had enough money. I glanced up at a sky as white as a movie screen and watched a couple leisurely walking along the street. Profiled against the horizon, they leaned toward each other, talking ever so privately—*probably going home to family dinner.*

I looked toward the restaurant and noticed an old man with cotton-fluff hair, long ear lobes, wattles of skin at his neck, arms shriveled like dried trumpet mushrooms, and a face of up-turned smile wrinkles—*probably someone's grandfather.*

The man glanced at his pocket watch, walking slowly, creakily, with the forward-leaning posture of an old person, leading with his cane toward the cinema. He bought a ticket. I collected my payment for washing jeepneys, and forgetting my hunger, paid admission, and followed him as though hypnotized, sitting next to him. But he got up and moved to the other side. I slumped in my seat, overcome by rejection and sadness. When the movie ended, the lights came on, and I gazed wistfully toward the grandfather-man. At precisely that moment, the man lifted his eyebrows in greeting, and looked across at me with a smile of infinite kindness—radiant and enduring.

*He didn't reject me!*

Warmth surged through my body. I burst out of the theater glowing, entirely forgetting my hunger. As I walked along the street, the murmur of the city faded and I tried to recall the words of Mama's song: "*Sa aking pagtulog na labis ang himbing; Ang bantay ko'y tala, ang tanod ko'y bituin...*" I could feel her soft hands, see her beautiful red fingernails, and sense a soft surround of coconut soap in the air. I smiled thinking about the warm scent of cordovan polish Papa used on his best shoes, and how shiny they were. Scattered memories of my parents were like pinpoints of light behind a movie screen, where the rest of life took place. I was transported to a barely remembered time of belonging.

I snapped to reality when five kids moved in on me, blocking my way. They pushed and taunted me from all sides, grabbing my hard-earned money. As they sauntered away, my anger erupted, and I followed them, shouting, "Give it back!"

"Come and get it," a rat-colored kid said with a savage stare.

"I don't wanna fight. Just give me my money."

"Coward!" they shouted. They took turns shoving and slapping me. A tall, thin guy with a missing front tooth made a show of cracking his ball-bearing knuckles, pushed me down, and spat in my face.

I reacted. I rolled over in the dirt, eased my fingers around a fist-sized rock, jumped up and smacked the guy across the head. Blood gushed all over the place. The next guy, not having seen the rock, stepped back, incredulous. I threw him off balance with a kick to the shoulder and my best three-punch combination, the last one a power punch. Two attackers restrained my arms, but I wiggled away.

A crowd formed.

I concentrated on the biggest guys, fusing frustration and fury into the fight. "Want my money? You'll have to kill me!" I screamed, hands fisted, eyes shooting sparks.

I was downed, but rolled over and got to my feet, grabbed the biggest kid, and landed a punch. The kid bounced back, but I gave it all I had—rapid-punching his face and ribs.

The other big kid, of the steel knuckles and bloody face, returned to the fight, but I dodged, kept focused, and landed a kick that snapped his forearm like balsa wood.

*I can do this! I can win!*

A jab to the jaw and a series of stomach-punches made the last kid pull back and bend over like a sprinter, breathing like an old bicycle pump. I was exhausted, but I grabbed a two-by-four and whacked him across the legs as hard as I could, sending him howling to the ground.

My face was swollen and bleeding.

The smallest kid, who'd never expected to fight, looked at me, and I put the stare on him. He recoiled, clenched his eyes, and skittered away like a frightened beetle.

I glanced around. I was standing alone, having gone through the whole pecking order.

"Give it back," I said.

The leader scowled up at me and thrust out a wad of bills. I counted out what belonged to me and put it in my pocket. I wiped the blood off my forehead with the rest, and threw it in his face.

Under a bruised sky of blue and purple, I ventured down the street a week later, limping and battered, but not bested. Word had spread. Kids, including *Papas*, crowded around for a chance to hang with me. Bonifacio came with congratulations and everyone nodded respect to us both, "You know, one of those kids was twice your age!"

"But half the man," Ben said, putting his arm around my neck with affection as we walked down the street together.

"I can't believe it! You were great! Everyone's talking about you!" Chile exclaimed, dancing in circles around Ben and me as Boston's "Don't Look Back" boomed from the radio.

"Hey, Chile, this is my friend Tumi," I said.

Chile appraised Tumi's bulk, "More like 'Three-Me,'" he said with affection.

"Everyone calls me Soft-Serve," laughed Tumi, bringing food.

We ate, played poker, and Soft-Serve taught us more chess moves. When I really thought about it, I wasn't hurt all that bad.

I decided the strategy of going for the biggest guys first had been a good one, and found a new master, whose name I've also forgotten, to teach me more. My confidence soared when even

Chile started betting on me. No longer insignificant, I now protected a few kids who asked for my help, and I did my best for them, usually without violence. They confided in me and sought my advice. I loved the big-brother role. I began to notice how well the *Papas* trained gang members—always looking after their needs and treating them with respect. This had tremendous appeal for me: I wanted to be a *leader*.

The next time I saw Bonifacio, I said, "I want to be a *Papa*."

"You want to join?"

"I want to do what the *Papas* do."

"First you become a *Laya,* and when you're ready, you get promoted to the *Batas,* and then you *earn the right* to join the *Papas.*"

"Couldn't I just be a *Papa*?"

"That's not the way it works."

I was deflated. But then I remembered the exception to working up the ladder. "What about the *Abuelitos*…those old guys who just hang out? They didn't start as *Layas*, did they?"

"No… they only pay for protection; they don't have any responsibilities—or power."

I pursed my lips. "I don't know about joining. I like independence."

"Look, Mark, why don't you hang with us for awhile, and think about it? Except for sick kids like PP, most kids do." He paused and changed the subject, "Why don't you come to Davao for the monthlies? I'm fighting."

# CHAPTER 12

DAVAO SPRAWLS OVER MORE AREA than any city in the world, yet everywhere we went, Bonifacio was known. As we walked down Anda Street, a path cleared: people whispered, raised their eyebrows, and gave him the upward nod of respect. Kids on the street deferred to him, and some shouted, "Good luck tonight!" Bonifacio was radiant. His whole entourage reflected his glory, honored just to walk in his shadow.

We took a bus through boulevards bulging with traffic, then to streets with a steady flow of cars, finally to a winding road at the base of Mt. Apo, where cars eased around the horseshoe curves of the mountain single-file. As we chugged up the incline, a warty pig trampled through a patch of green orchids into the bushes; carnivorous pitcher plants, no doubt full of flies, dotted the edge of the road, and a monkey-eating Philippine eagle with a ten-foot wingspan took flight, soaring through clouds that whipped the sky. The paved road became gravel, then dirt, narrowing even more, snaking up the hill. Moisture from decades of rain swelled from the forest floor to meet us, through thick and tangled vegetation. Buzzards circled.

"It's a dead end," I said.

"It's not a dead end if it takes you where you need to go," said Master David, who was Bonifacio's master.

We had arrived. Eight guys pulled a vine-covered net away from the entrance to an enormous secret cave, known only to the illegal kickboxing crowd, and of course to cops who took kickbacks. Everyone ducked through a dark, damp passage into a vast cave. Bleachers for hundreds of people were filled to capacity, and a hum of excitement echoed through the interior. Bonifacio usually liked to be first to enter a room, at the forefront when the gang went somewhere *en masse*, but now two armed bodyguards and Master David preceded him, pressing through the crowd to a partitioned dressing area, followed by two more bodyguards. The rest of us pushed through spectators to ringside.

Preliminary fights were in progress. Three major kick boxers fought successive opponents, all fighting at least three times. With little matching by size or ability, some fights didn't last long. Occasionally fighters returned to the ring after losing, in a desperate gamble for the purse. There were no referees, but both fighters and spectators were fair-minded and courteous.

Then came the main event. Bonifacio entered the ring shaking hands and talking to his opponents as if they were old friends, and some of them were. But when the fight began he was all business. He dispensed with his first two opponents quickly, mostly using conventional, but forceful, well-timed and positioned roundhouse kicks.

His third fight was much more interesting. A hush fell over the audience as the challenger entered the ring with a self-assured stride, towering over Bonifacio: buff, muscles oiled to shine, a weight advantage of perhaps fifty pounds, and like Bonifacio, bearing all three of the usual *Tibay* tats, as well as "the mark of the assassin" on the back of his neck. They shook hands, exchanged pleasantries, and assumed starting positions. Bonifacio rotated slightly to the left, so the guy prepared for a kick from the right, but then Bonifacio quickly rotated to the right, and the guy readjusted; then in a flash, Bonifacio shifted back and followed through with the intended roundhouse from the left. He followed with a quick combination—a powerless front kick to the solar plexus, a tap on the left shoulder which made his opponent think he was too close to kick again, then a hook kick to the guy's jaw with the point of his right heel. His opponent was stunned.

Chile elbowed me, "That's why he's the best!"

I thought the fight was over when Bonifacio turned his back, appearing to walk away. But with fluid motion came the third surprise. Bonifacio looked over his right shoulder as he stepped forward with his left leg, quickly aligning his legs with his opponent's, stepped, pivoted on the balls of his feet, glanced over his right shoulder again, and landed a hard spinning back kick to the guy's lower abdomen.

His opponent tried to muster a roundhouse kick, but the attempt was lame, and Bonifacio delivered two snapping round kicks, and repositioned for a switch-step round kick to the back of the neck that ended the fight.

The audience stomped the ground in respect, chanting: "Bonifacio! Bonifacio! Bonifacio!" which reverberated through the cave.

Bonifacio reached down and helped his opponent up, putting his arm around him. "You okay?" he asked, checking for broken bones.

"Great match," the guy said, gently thumping Bonifacio's stomach.

Exuberance rocked the house. Fans held up their arms and cheered. Chile, Ben, and I scrambled into the ring, and dove out across the mass of upraised hands, bodysurfing the wave.

Despite the general excitement, there was a pocket of hush surrounding someone, which had mesmerized a kid near us. We turned our attention to a well-dressed man, surrounded by bodyguards, and two guys following him with crates of beer. He had slicked-back hair and black eyes, fierce as a falcon's, surveying the crowd. Some backed away to let him through.

Never shy of strangers, Chile asked the kid, "Who *is* that?"

"A powerful man," the guy said, "by the name of Assad."

"So, should I introduce myself, or what?" asked Chile, in his Donald Duck voice.

"Only if you want to be an assassin," he said, "Rumor is; he trains them."

I'd heard Assad's name at the weeklies, when he'd bet on me. My curiosity peaked. Chile hoisted me onto his shoulders, and I scanned the audience to get a better look. Assad had on an expensive white linen suit with a black shirt and tie, and his bodyguards wore tight black tee shirts. He searched the crowd with a raptor's intensity and elbowed his way toward the champ, ostensibly to pay homage with cases of San Miguel Beer. But Bonifacio's fans clogged his path, and Assad turned and made a brusque exit with his entourage. I was spellbound.

Fighters and spectators alike continued to applaud Bonifacio, wriggling through the crowd for a chance to touch him. Those who managed to get close patted his back, put their hands on his chest, and their arms around him, praising him all the way to the dressing area. He pulsed the glow of success.

Sponsors and spectators were well mannered and orderly as they bought food and celebrated. Friends clustered around congratulating him, bringing tributes of *balut* (fertilized duck eggs), and banana leaves with roasted chicken, fish, or fruit with coconut fillings.

When Chile, Ben, and I were finally alone with him in the dressing room, it was time for payment. Master David limped in with a fat wad of money. Having the flat nose of a prizefighter, he was constantly pushing his glasses up, sometimes holding them in place while he focused on something in particular. He put his arm around Bonifacio, counted out a hundred thousand dollars, gave Bonifacio his cut of ten thousand, put aside most of the remainder for paying off government officials, and took his cut. Being a man of few words, he smiled, gave the upward nod of respect, and left.

"Do you always make that much money?" I asked, drop-jawed.

"Only when I win."

"The most I ever made was one hundred dollars," Chile said, "and it took me two weeks to walk again!"

Bonifacio laughed, "When I first came to Ormoc City, I fought in the dailies, and spent more time recovering than fighting. I trained hard, but without a master. I moved up to the weeklies, almost two hundred fights, and still got trounced quite often. Then I had a stroke of good luck. After Master David injured his leg in the ring and was unable to fight, he agreed to train me. Six months later, I'd made huge progress, and was hot for a monthly. Although I was in great shape, I was arrogant, and got beaten to a pulp. Afterwards Master David gave me the advice that made the difference: 'the monkey knows many tricks, and the crocodile but one. But it's a *good* one.' He said I knew many useful moves, trained well, and had some experience. I was already a monkey, now I had to be the crocodile with a trick, and it would be—*strategy*!"

"Is that why you put the first two guys down so fast tonight?" Chile asked.

"Exactly—to conserve energy," Bonifacio beamed. "I knew if I beat the first two quickly, I'd be warmed-up and still fresh. I didn't know who'd be next, and planned for the worst. As it turned out, the guy's a friend. He's a great fighter. He's beaten me twice, and quite possibly would have beaten me tonight. So I had to surprise him, catch him off guard."

Bonifacio paused to open a soda, and I wondered briefly if martial arts had enticed him to leave home all those years ago.

Then he astonished us by saying, "Why don't you start training for the monthlies? You both fight well, but you have to train differently."

"Could you sponsor us?"

"Master David could. You'd have to do everything he says." Chile nodded.

"Okay," I said.

"I'll ask him," Bonifacio said, and then turning to Ben, "You're awfully quiet over there. Are you interested in training?"

"Oh no, not me. I've got you guys to protect me. And..."

Before Ben could continue, Bonifacio turned back to me, as though he'd forgotten something, "...and this week, while

we're in Davao, learn how to swim," he said, "to build en-
durance."

I was too excited to sleep that night.

~~~~~~~

The next day, Chile, Ben, and I walked onto the bridge on the
Bangkerohan River in Davao, and looked down at the murky
water, rushing and gurgling far below.

"We'll jump from here, all together," Chile said.

I backed up. It was a long way down.

"Couldn't we..." I began.

Before I knew it Chile and Ben flanked me, and on a fast
count of three, grabbed my arms, took a few steps, and jumped.
We screamed all the way down, me the loudest. A shiver pierced
me as I hit water. The brown river gulped me to the bottom and
I couldn't see the surface through the muddy water. But in a few
moments, I bobbed up like a cork and was carried along with
the current, gasping for air, swallowing mouthfuls of gritty
water, dog paddling down the river.

Chile was already laid back on the shore, spreading his cigarettes out to dry. "Hey, you swim great!" he said, laughing.

"Not bad at all," said Ben, hauling my soggy body up on
the bank, "How do you like swimming?"

We met up with Bonifacio, found a place to stay for the
night, and bought dinner. Ben asked if we could take a few extra
days to return to Ormoc City, so we could explore some of the
small islands—and practice swimming.

# CHAPTER 13

*WHY DOESN'T SHE RETURN MY CALLS?*

Assad paced the floor of his Forbes Park estate. He stared at the phone yet again and finally dialed her number. No answer.

He remembered her face when he'd given her the earrings—drop diamonds with a total of four carats. They'd gone to the magnificent Chinese Cemetery in Manila and toured the air-conditioned houses of the dead with the crystal chandeliers, running hot and cold water, and even kitchens. Dameana had walked like a queen among her mother's ancestors, placing her tribute of food and flowers in their eternal home. It had been an elegant setting, a classy prelude for giving her the earrings.

They'd had a first-rate dinner at the Shangri-La Hotel: *Camaron rebosado* (heavily battered fried shrimp), *paella*, okra, eggplant and tomatoes, a coconut vodka, and *leche* flan. The candlelight had cast a warm glow over a centerpiece of white orchids; music had played softly from the piano bar, and the moment had been right. He'd handed her the black velvet box. She'd opened it slowly, and had glowed from someplace deep inside, punching him out with her smile. Without a word, she'd put on the earrings. Beautiful jewelry was meant to pay her homage—her slightest movements had made the diamonds sparkle around her face like a sudden sunrise.

*So what's wrong? Why doesn't she call?*

He didn't want to marry; yet he wanted her all to himself. Sometimes when other men looked at her, rage had boiled inside him.

*Maybe I could adjust to the idea of a wedding ring in the far distant future... Shudder. But the earrings should hold her for now, flashing around her like fireworks!*

She had an unlimited capacity for adventure that energized him. Sometimes when he called she'd been deep sea diving, or hiking, or spelunking. He never knew quite what she'd say or do: her unpredictability sharpened his desire, and her rough edge excited him.

He hated not being able to reach her. He'd call again from the airport in Davao. Unfortunately he spent much of his time away from Manila where most assassinations took place, because it was always better to recruit and train operatives elsewhere.

He boarded his flight, found a window seat, and thought about Dameana. Finally he shook out and refolded his newspaper to the sports section. He made note of a Mixed Martial Arts match he wanted to see. He had special regard for fighters; it was while watching illegal kickboxing in Ormoc City that he'd gotten the idea that made his fortune:

*Who would be less conspicuous than kids? Street kids are invisible—the ugly problem everyone ignores. They'll be my as-*

*sassins. No one will notice a street kid walking toward him. I'll train street kids in Ormoc City and Davao, fly them to Manila for the job, and whisk them out again.*

In three years, his business had grown into an empire of assassinations and corresponding drug traffic.

# CHAPTER 14

As the months passed, I was consistently tired, and found it difficult to train after working all day. Master David was patient and kind. He put his arm around me, pushed up his glasses, and regarded me with penetrating interest, "You've got talent, Mark, but if you want to excel, you can't waste time and energy working."

"But, Master, I have to work."

"Now that you've seen Bonifacio fight, you know what kind of money you can make. Join the *Tibays*; they'll support you while you train. If you want to be a *great* fighter, you have to *completely* dedicate your energy to training."

"I try my best."

"Look, you have to work *smarter*, not harder…"

With that, I caved. It seemed that becoming an exceptional fighter required me to join the gang.

*I'll use it to prepare for revenge.*

My resolution finally made, I found Bonifacio and said I was ready.

"Good decision..." he said, putting his hand on my shoulder.

"About time!" said Chile, cross-eyed, flashing his best dopey grin.

We went to the beach at night for the initiation. The sky was black as charcoal. A bonfire raged a hundred yards down the coast, and the only breeze carried smoke from the fire. A crowd gathered, lots of kids and a few adults, smoking, and drinking beer. Both joy and fear circulated, filling the air with palpable energy. Eight gang members were assigned to oppose me, and waited for my signal.

Standing still as stone, I planned my strategy, and put the stare on each one—two were only slightly bigger. I stretched my legs, shook out my arms, and cracked my neck to each side. Then I took a deep breath, and nodded. They began moving in, but I made a preemptive strike, kicking the biggest kid in the face, breaking his nose. He stumbled to the sideline, splattering blood, as I snapped a front kick to the other big kid's sternum and followed with a spinning back kick, which dropped him.

A third kid threw an uppercut to my jaw that felt like a whack with a hammer. Someone followed with a hook to my mid-section, and I countered with a snapping sidekick that didn't connect. A right-jab, left-cross hook combination caught me by surprise and knocked me down. Still on the ground, I got a few painful kicks in the ribs and kidneys before grabbing a handful of sand and throwing it in several kid's eyes. Another kid belly-flopped across me, but I kneed him hard in the groin and staggered to my feet. While being pummeled from all sides, I got in a few strong roundhouse kicks, and maybe one six-punch combination. But someone kept punching my face. My eyes were swollen to slits, and my pulse throbbed through my teeth. Exhausted, I punched two more guys, and then the details became blurry. I took the worst beating of my life—cuts around both eyes dribbled blood; my nose was broken and bled profusely, and I was a mass of pain. My legs quivered, my knees buckled, and down I went.

When I woke up, guys with bloody faces and black eyes knelt around me, congratulating me and saying what a great fighter I was. Two of them apologized for hurting me so badly, but when *I* fought so hard, *they* did too. My rib cage racked with pain and I shallow-laughed at their good-natured apology. One kid, still holding his groin, nodded respect, however grudging.

"That's the longest initiation fight I've ever seen," Ben said.

"Good opening! Great strategy!" said Chile.

"Going to the hospital is against gang rules ..." began Soft-Serve, gently cradling my head.

Bonifacio stepped in, "Ben, bring the ice."

Soft-Serve's belly made an ample cushion for my head. I glanced into his rounded face, and he winked at me, then put on the face he usually reserved for poker, and began stitching my forehead with sewing thread. Determined not to flinch, I clenched my jaw. My bruises, cuts, and abrasions throbbed like neon signs. I didn't know what hurt the most, but I thought my cracked ribs might be number one. I hardly noticed the gang's tattoo artist etching the diamond on my right hand.

"Welcome to the *Tibays!*" Ben said, his eyes sparkling with delight as he rotated rubber-glove ice packs.

The adrenalin rush sustained me through a few jokes that hurt when I laughed. A few guys wound a wide elastic bandage around my ribs. I couldn't eat. I vaguely remember downing a few pills with Mello Yellow, but it was becoming less possible to see through the slits of my eyes, and I finally yielded to sleep.

The morning sun pierced through the acacia tree like the glint on a knife blade, waking me. I found myself nestled under bushes in the park. I could barely move. My bloody shirt was stuck to me; new scabs pulled off as I rolled over. My tattooed right hand throbbed. I dozed off and on, dreaming about other tats I'd earn: next would be the cross on my foot, then the triangle on my arm—all with embellishments.

*I'm a* Tibay—*and I belong! I have respect. And I'll be tough enough to live as long as I have to!*

*I'll be a Papa soon... But what I* need *is the tat on the back of my neck: "the mark of the assassin."*

# CHAPTER 15

WELL ENOUGH TO ACCEPT MY FIRST GANG ASSIGNMENT, I was excited to prove myself. My first task was to spy on other gangs, but I got into immediate trouble. As I approached the area of a rival gang in the late afternoon, I alerted to a buzz of excitement. Lowering my eyes and moving in closer, trying to be inconspicuous, I heard disturbing fragments of conversation:

"We can't get near Bonifacio."

"Our best assassin couldn't even…"

"Impossible!"

"With both our gangs, we can ambush him."

"Tomorrow."

"At night!"

Too inexperienced to maintain cover, I broke into a run. Instantly, kids were dispatched to hunt me down. I ran my fastest, but they gained on me, and I darted through the gate of an old cemetery.

"He's not here, maybe that side!"

"Over there!"

Sweat poured down my back: *They're going to kill me.*

There was only one way out—the way I came in, and they had it covered. My adrenaline became pinpricks of terror. I saw a bone-white crypt in a neglected part of the cemetery, the lid slightly ajar. Inside was a rotted wooden coffin, topped by a few displaced planks that were weathered and broken. I pushed them aside and scrambled into the coffin. The bones inside were dry and brittle, and there was a faintly bad odor. I heard kids getting closer. I frantically wedged in with the fetid skeleton, pulling the rotting planks over me, my heart pounding like a captive bird.

I held still for a long time, barely breathing. The sun went down, and the disc of the moon cast an osteoporotic light across the cemetery. I listened to the continuing search, to wild dogs: squalid scavengers padding around, sniffing. Then at last, all was quiet. I felt claustrophobic—as though the coffin was closing in on me—compressing me into the smallest, darkest, and most disgusting of places.

*They'll be guarding the gate.*

Knowing I would surely die if I got out, I resolved to settle in. I shuddered and began speculating about ways to die.

*Getting shot wouldn't be too bad—if I died right away— beats drowning. Poison? Not like Mama. Probably won't get it with a machete like Papa. These guys will use knives...*

Scared spit-less, I was terribly thirsty, but the odor had taken away my hunger. My bladder was full, but I held it. Then I reconsidered.

*A bit of urine won't bother the bones under me.*

I tried to think of something pleasant, so I imagined being at the Palace of the Toads with Chile, sitting with our feet in the pond, watching an occasional sailfin lizard run across the surface of the water. I decided to pray, thanking God for my narrow escape, and for every good thing I could think of. Finally I slept, for hours. Toward morning, I dreamt about the grandfather-man at the cinema and felt the warmth of his smile. He put his warm arms around me, and embraced me as a grandson. But I wakened with a start, finding myself in the arms of a skeleton.

I stayed in the coffin until I felt safe—which wasn't until about noon. It was knife-bright. Squinting, I eased over the edge and tentatively made my way around the crypts and tombstones. I glanced at mourners huddled around a newly dug grave, lighting incense to ensure that neighboring corpses would welcome their loved one. They didn't look up. I took a deep breath, inhaling the pleasant fragrance of incense, seeing its soft gray curls blend with sunrays.

Sprinting all the way back, I told Bonifacio everything, breathless, yet lifting my chest with pride. He put his arm around my shoulders, and I still remember the glow of his smile when he said, "Well done, Mark; you've saved lives today!"

⁓⁓⁓⁓⁓

The sky became gunmetal gray, darkening into night. An allied gang joined us and we prepared to fight. Sentries posted throughout the city watched, waited, and smoked. In the middle of the night, when the streets would normally be empty, two of them spotted dozens of enemies approaching, some on bikes or skateboards, but most running quietly, armed with *panas* (sharpened four-inch nails, propelled by slingshots), knives, and guns. Bonifacio appraised the situation and directed us into position; we would ambush the ambushers! Excitement and loyalty carbonated my veins.

A kid from an enemy gang, his uncombed hair jutting out at rakish angles, rode his bike full tilt toward Chile and me; we were revved for combat behind a garbage bin. I grabbed a fluorescent light tube from the trash. The biker got near, doing a wheelie onto the sidewalk, and when his front wheel touched ground, I smashed the tube across his head, and Chile stabbed his side. The guy was down and dead.

Adrenalin boiled through the street. Knife fights and *pana* shooting broke out everywhere, accompanied by shouting, dogs barking, and the sharp crack of gunshots.

Ben shouted, "Look out for the twins in the alley!"

I was kickboxing with another kid when one twin emerged from darkness with a two-by-four, and hit me on the head. Lacking space, he didn't have enough force to do much damage, and I pivoted and punched him in the stomach. The other twin moved in with his *pana* aiming at my chest. Ben dove to shove me out of the way, but the nail caught my left knee. I fell in agony, curling into a fetal position, my leg burning like a hot poker. Ben reloaded his gun and shot both the kid and his twin, tucked his gun in his shorts, and pushed me under a parked jeepney.

Sirens ripped through the streets. Cops swarmed all over the place, shooting every kid who had a gun, and some who didn't. Gun smoke filled the air. Ben ran down an alley, keeping his .45 hidden. Gangs scattered, leaving the street blood-soaked, resounding with the cries of the wounded—and littered with the dead.

Sometime later, I heard Chile calling me, but I couldn't make my response heard over the shriek of the sirens. When he got close, I gathered my strength, reached out from under the jeepney, and grabbed his leg. He tripped and fell on his face, gashing his forehead. Blood streamed down his face, but he pulled me out, scooped me into his arms, and carried me through an alleyway to the beach, awkwardly wiping his bloody face on his shoulder along the way. Ben caught up with us and helped carry me. No one else was around, except PP, who materialized through the gun smoke. Chile and Ben gently laid me on compacted sand, under the streetlight of the strand. Chile blanched at the sight of the arrow, but said, "Don't worry, I'll pull it out."

"We need something for him to bite down on," said Ben.

Chile glanced around, "A piece of wood…"

PP's freckles paled, and in his panic he grabbed a flat rock. "Bite down on this."

"All right, hold him," Chile said to Ben and PP, and pulled the *pana* with all his strength. It didn't budge. I bit on the rock and felt like my teeth shattered. PP started to cry, then Ben, then me.

"Stop the bleeding; use your shirt!" Chile shouted to Ben.

Ben shoved the shirt so forcefully against my knee that I screamed in agony.

"I'm going to pull again!" Chile put his foot on my hip for leverage and yanked.

I screamed again. Nothing.

"It's stuck in the bone. I have to dig it out with a knife!"

I felt dizzy, nauseous, and clammy. I turned my head away, heard the knife scrapping my bone, and someone screaming. I felt a rotation as Chile finally yanked the *pana* out, and realized I'd been the one screaming. When I saw the hunk of flesh on the arrow, I fell into an unconscious stupor.

# CHAPTER 16

AGONIZING PAIN PIERCED MY LEG. Chile and Ben bumped along, carrying me, weaving through the whine of multiple sirens, as ambulances backed into the hospital emergency entrance. PP shouted for people to move out of the way; Chile and Ben maneuvered me inside, past workers in scrubs rushing to receive stretchers laden with the wounded, dying, and dead. Two doctors triaged victims and pointed to various areas; no one took time to pull curtains between gurneys. Many, including me, were sent to a line at the admittance desk.

"We couldn't find Bonifacio," Chile said, with swampy eyes. "So we brought you here."

"We thought you'd die," Ben said, unashamedly shedding tears.

"Name?" said a thin woman behind thick-rimmed glasses and her desk.

"His name's Mark," said Chile.

"Can't he talk for himself?" she asked, concave behind her desk, not looking up.

"I'll talk for him," Chile said.

"Last name?"

"He doesn't have one."

"Street kid. Put him over there," she said, pointing with the chin of her prognathic frown.

Chile and Ben carried me to the chair indicated, and stayed with his arm around me until a merciful nurse came with ice and morphine.

"Ooo," she said, glancing at my knee. As she injected my arm, she said, "You'll feel much better in about twenty minutes." Then she continued in a tone meant to be soothing, "When the big hand gets to here, Honey."

But the pain was almost more than I could bear, and I held onto Ben and Chile's hands in desperation, squeezing hard. We all watched the slow ticking of the clock—tick... tick... tick... tick. PP, pale as paste, paced the floor faster than the clock, dropping tears. The big hand seemed stuck.

*So this is dying. I must be dying; no one could live through pain this bad.*

The sounds of the hospital hovered in a hum, indistinct as though coming from under water. At last, the pain retreated into a hot, low buzz. I unlocked my teeth, stretched out my hands, and relaxed my leg muscles, surrendering to the morphine. A doctor in green scrubs took an x-ray, and irrigated the wound, which had picked up some sand. "Take a deep breath—this will hurt a little," he said, swabbing it with Betadine. I gritted my teeth and white knuckled the sides of the gurney. Mercifully the doctor finally flushed out the stinging Betadine with sterile water. He patted the wound with gauze, injected local anesthetic all around the site, and took multiple stitches. A young nurse with a pleasant smile propped my leg on a pillow, holding it ever so gently while the doctor wrapped it, then inserted an IV needle into my arm, attached a bag of saline solution with glucose, and injected the line with antibiotics, and more morphine. She was kind; the morphine even kinder.

"The wound is serious," the doctor said, discarding his mask. "Unfortunately, the chance of infection's high because of the humidity here."

Pulling off his gloves, he said to me, "You'll have to stay awhile."

Approaching Chile, Ben, and PP he said, "You kids can go now." They looked up to thank him, but his eyes had moved onto the next patient.

An over-worked orderly rolled me down the hall, keeping his eyes on the gurney as we passed others moving in both directions. There were no vacancies, so I was given a cot in a storage room. Without windows, it was hot and stuffy, and I was terribly thirsty—my throat was closing up. I rang the bell they gave me, but no one came.

I'd never been on a cot before. It was strange and uncomfortable, so I eased to the edge, my toes feeling for the far-away floor, and slid slowly and painfully down to the cooler linoleum and slept there, waking in the night to find water placed beside me on the floor. When the morning nurse came in, she scolded me with her tiny tadpole mouth, pouting disapproval, and helped me back on the cot. She left, and I returned to the floor.

During the next week my knee throbbed constantly, and I impatiently waited for shots of morphine, or codeine pills. I dozed often, waking to pain and unbelievable boredom. I tried channeling my thoughts to pleasant things—great fight moves, rock skimming, and The Palace of the Toads. But the thought that Bonifacio might be dead kept intruding.

Finally Soft-Serve came waddling into the room I'd been transferred to. He wore a clean button-down shirt tucked into long pants, his belt making a gully around his belly. He heaved his bulk onto the end of my bed, overflowing the edge.

"*Hola!*"

"Is Bonifacio okay?" I asked.

"Invincible."

"What does that mean?"

"No one can touch him!"

I exhaled. "Chile and Ben?"

"Chile, Ben, and PP are all outside. They wouldn't let them in. Could be their clothes..."

I grinned. "Did we win?"

"We were prepared, thanks to you. We took out three of their leaders."

"Is it over?"

"They're disabled. It'll take a long time for them to regroup."

"What about us?"

"Lots of injuries, and we lost quite a few. Cops killed a lot." He clicked off names of kids I didn't know well, and then abruptly changed the subject, "So, how's the food in here?"

"Um..."

"I know you. You're so tough, you could digest tacks."

"Doesn't mean I like them."

He grinned and opened his backpack. He'd smuggled in fish, rice, and mangoes, and we ate without talking, licking our fingers. Then he taught me to write a few more words, after which we played poker on my chest and told jokes, laughing louder and louder.

An over-caffeinated nurse rushed in like an angry chicken, hands on her hips, clucking something about bothering other people. She stood at the doorway tapping her toes until we were quiet, and then strutted off.

Soft-Serve, dimpled in many places, imitated her—flapping his arms like a chicken, jutting his head forward and back, forward and back, "*Bluck*, bluck, bluck.... *bluck*, bluck, bluck, bluck," strutting around in circles. It was something to see, his fat jiggling and all, and we laughed until our faces were red, and our sides hurt. Then Soft Serve crowed like a rooster, because she actually looked more like a rooster than a hen.

The head nurse came in wearing a uniform starched to a state of rigor mortis. She glared at Soft-Serve with laser eyes, "You have to leave, *now*!"

He did, but of course came right back. Carefully settling his girth on the edge of my bed, he set up a chess game on my chest. I restrained my laughter, mostly to keep the pieces in place. We became more serious as we got into the game, concentrating and sipping Mirindas. He won the first game, I won the second, and the third was a stalemate.

He took his time putting away the pieces, dawdling. He lit a cigarette, and immediately stubbed it out, realizing he couldn't smoke in the hospital. Then, looking away from me he said, "One of your good friends was killed."

"Who?"

He paused, bowed his head, sucked in a quick breath, and said, "Juan."

"*Naku!*"

Nurses came rushing to the door, "What's the matter? Are you alright?"

"He's okay," Soft-Serve said gently, putting his hand on my shoulder.

"Are you sure?" they asked me.

"*Es nada.*"

Exasperated, they left, neglecting to kick Soft Serve out again.

Not wanting to press his luck, Soft-Serve continued in a subdued voice, "Chile was shooting it out with a cop, when another cop aimed at him from the side. Juan pushed Chile out of the way, and was between them when the bullet hit."

"Oh, Juan..." I choked.

Soft-Serve teared up.

"Did he die right away?"

"He just said, 'Take care of PP,' then he was gone..."

Soft Serve lit another cigarette, remembered he couldn't smoke, and stubbed it out. He continued, "Right after that Chile went to help you."

"How's PP?"

"We didn't even tell him until the next day. He usually hangs with Chile now."

⁓⁓⁓

That night, lying there on the floor, I thought about life in the *Tibays*. With a visceral shudder, I imagined getting it with a gun, and felt keenly aware of my mortality.

A crushing sense of gloom overcame me as I remembered that first night when Chile had said those simple, little words, "Papa's dead." DEAD. But the words weren't simple or little; they were huge and heavy, like a rock that pulls a sack of baby kittens to the bottom of the river and holds them helpless. Alone in the dark, I descended into convulsive weeping, remembering Juan, remembering my family, crying until my eyes felt sandpapered.

I considered my stolen life and security. I reviewed my list of happy things: Mama's swishy skirt, her red-polished fingernails, her singing... Papa's shoes, and strong shoulders. A porch with a rocking chair. Sugar cane. I clung to every precious moment I had stored in an effort not to lose my family altogether.

There were memories just under the surface that I remembered only once in a while, and deeper ones that were vague. Some had faded altogether, leaving an elusive residue. I tried to recall Mama's face, but what came to mind was the coldness of her hand in the coffin. I couldn't imagine Papa's face, but I had the photo showing his slashed shoulder, and his wrist bleeding on the ground where his hand should have been.

When I ran out of good memories, my thoughts flipped, and became anger—red hot like molten, hardening into lava—the rock-hard resolve of revenge.

*In return for taking my family, and the hell they've sent me to, I'll make them pay.*

Three weeks later while waiting for the doctor, I hopped back and forth across my room, either practicing the alphabet, or counting to a hundred. I looked out the window, drumming my fingers on the sill. Finally someone came in.

"I'm okay now. Please can I go?" I asked.

"There's the problem of your bill," the doctor said. "Unfortunately, we ran out of charity money long ago, but you can work off what you owe."

I hobbled around using a crutch, doing odd jobs, and saw other kids working too. It was difficult. The work wasn't hard, and I enjoyed helping patients: giving them water, toothbrushes, or something to read. But after a week, there was an incident. A stern doctor saw me giving water to an old man and scolded me severely, "That patient can't have water! You are *not* a nurse! Stick to mopping and cleaning!" I was humiliated, and wanted to run out the door, but security guards always manned the exits. I looked out the window at a sky hung like a wet blanket, and cried.

*Five stories above freedom.*

The next day, a nurse gave me an envelope. I ripped it open, and read the words: "We're coming."

That night, Ben and Soft-Serve came in separately, as though visiting, dressed up like rich men's sons with button-down shirts, long pants, and leather sandals, carrying a couple of heavy backpacks. After visiting hours, they hid in the storeroom, cramped and craving smokes. Sometime after midnight, they slipped back into my room, and tapped my shoulder. Just then a couple of nurses came down the hall. "I saw two kids pass the station with backpacks," one said, opening my door, as Soft Serve and Ben positioned behind it.

*The thick and the thin.*

The hall light glared across my bed, and I rubbed my eyes. "Did anyone come in here?"

"What?"

"Have you seen anyone?" a nurse asked, not expecting an answer.

As they turned to leave, she tripped on the strap of a backpack that looped near the door. Ben yanked it out of sight before she righted herself and looked at the floor. She swore under her breath, and hurried to the next room as the self-closing door clicked shut. Soft Serve and Ben stayed in place for a few moments, taking shallow breaths.

Then they sprang into action, knotting two long ropes together with a square knot, and tying one end to the heavy cabinet in the corner, while I slipped out of the hospital gown and into a tee shirt and shorts. Ben knotted the other rope end around my waist, and Soft-Serve eased me over the sill.

I clung to the rope, overtaken by panic, not moving.

"You have to do it!" Ben whispered. "Slide down slowly, and kick against the wall with your feet as you go down."

Well, that didn't work, but I learned fast: I could only rappel with my good leg, awkwardly slipping down, painfully skinning my hands, bruising my foot and knocking my good knee, while they held tight, gradually measuring out rope all the way down.

When they met me outside Soft Serve explained how they'd gotten out. "A 'code blue' message blasted over the intercom, and we heard the hallway fill with people. We thought they had us. I cracked the door and saw a rush of nurses pushing a cart down the hall. It wasn't about us! We blended into the crowd, took the elevator to the lobby, and walked out the door. No one even noticed. Nothin' to it—easy."

"Me too, easy," I said, sweating profusely, barely able to walk without crutches.

We headed for a party at the beach—Soft Serve and Ben strutting, and me doing my best to move. The party was a welcome event: I was excited to see my friends; four weeks had passed, and the war was behind us. We felt the strong bonds of brotherhood, and put aside the wretchedness of war, injury, and death. Glue, gasoline, and marijuana circulated.

"I've looked forward to this all day," Chile said, dazedly inhaling his joint, absently rubbing a few track marks on his arm. He tuned his radio to Guns 'N Roses singing, "Sweet Child O' Mine," and put his arm around PP's freckled shoulders. PP was clutching his even more ragged blanket, and being groomed by Mano. I grinned at PP, and edged in next to them on the ground. Mano jumped from PP to me, and started checking my hair for lice.

"Juan saved Chile's life!" PP said.

"He was a hero," I said, regarding PP with affection.

A *Papa* with a ropey scar on his face joined us, putting his arm around me, "So are you. What if they'd caught us by surprise? You saved Bonifacio's life, and probably the gang!"

"Thanks," I blushed.

*His scar's as thick as a worm. How amazing. New skin grows right up over the wound.*

The kid saw me staring, "Pretty cool, huh?" he said, slapping me on the back. "Let's see the knee."

A cluster of friends circled to see my leg, and to show off their wounds. "You never saw *my* wound," Soft-Serve inserted, lifting his shirt above the gunshot crater in his side that formed a second navel. "It hardly even hurt. Took the bullet out myself," he laughed, his belly jiggling all over.

Bonifacio and Ben interrupted with *barilis*, long green beans, eggplant fried with scrambled eggs, plantains, beer, Mello Yello, and enough rice to replace all the sand on the beach. I forgot the rope burn on my hands, the still-throbbing pain in my knee, all my other aches and pains, and the depression of the hospital. I delighted to see Chile and PP wrestle and fall laughing into the sand, both drinking beer. I played with Mano while most everyone took to the ocean. Bonifacio brought me more scrambled eggs and eggplant, and as we sat eating together he put his arm around me and said, "When you lose someone in the gang, you don't have to lose them alone. We're a family." Then he whispered, "Mama used to make eggplant like this."

I smiled, eager to hear more, but a group of swimmers called him to the water. Soft Serve came to sit with me, and I asked him how to spell "revenge." We practiced writing in the sand.

Later, we all played a card game called Mexican Speed. That night, I advanced to the *Batas* and got the tat of the cross on my foot, together with many embellishments, while Queen sang, "We Are the Champions" from Chile's radio.

# CHAPTER 17

"WHAT'S A PROMOTION?" asked a five-year old named Jhimmy as he tagged along behind me, occasionally running to keep up. His clothes were exceptionally dirty; cigarette burns dotted his arms, and his long hair was impossibly tangled. He was a new member of the gang, but hadn't been required to initiate yet because of his age.

"It's a contest," I answered. "This time we're going to play 'chicken.' The winner will be last off the railroad tracks when the train comes."

"Oh," said Jhimmy, catching up. I put my arm around his shoulders, and limped along beside him.

"The winner gets extra stuff on his tat, like the designs on my diamond," I said, showing him my hand, "or the ones on my foot decorating the cross. He might even get a higher ranking in the gang. My next rank will be *Papa*, and I'll get a triangle tattoo on my delt, here."

Soft Serve, Ben, Chile, and two other kids lit cigarettes, and got out their drugs of choice. Everyone began drinking and drugging, sitting on and between the tracks. Chile passed me a beer, but it was relatively new to me, and I didn't like it; nor did Jhimmy, so we walked off arm-in-arm, sat on old crates, and practiced our smoking.

"You have a family?" Jhimmy asked, brushing his matted hair out of his eyes.

"Nope," I said, glancing back at the tracks.

"I have a mother, but she's forgotten all about me," he said, hunching forward, elbows on his knees.

"What about your father?"

"Stepfather," Jhimmy sneered.

"Guess you don't go home much."

"Not for anything."

"Did he beat you?"

"He used to tie me up in a burlap sack, throw the rope over a branch, and hoist me in the air. Then he'd light a fire underneath and say he was gonna roast me."

"*Putang ina!* Did your mother know?"

"She was afraid of him. She never said *anything*. Usually he burned me with cigarettes, but one time he threw me out a second story window when I wet the bed. I got a broken arm."

We sat talking for several hours, shallow-sucking our cigarettes and coughing. Suddenly aware of a low roaring vibrations under our feet, Jhimmy shouted, "Earthquake!"

"No, no, it's the train!"

Jhimmy looked toward the tracks, "I can't hear anyone..."

We strained to hear laughter or talking, but heard only the rumble of the train, and started jogging toward the tracks.

When we couldn't see our friends, we broke into a run. Then we saw them—lying on the tracks—none of them moving.

"They're stoned!" Jhimmy exclaimed in horror.

"Let's pull them off the tracks!" I shouted, running to Chile.

We dragged Chile off by his arms. Then we got Ben. But Soft-Serve wasn't budging. I frantically pulled on his feet; Jhimmy slapped his face, pulled his hair and yelled, desperately trying to get him off the tracks as the train sped closer.

We didn't make it. We fell backwards as the train rolled over Soft-Serve and two other kids, and continued on its course. I looked over at Jhimmy who was gaping at the tracks, staring vacantly. Soft-Serve's severed head rolled across the tracks. Jhimmy collapsed like a rag doll. I glanced after the train. The ground was covered with blood, flesh, and crushed bones, dragged along the tracks. The remains of Soft-Serve's feet were in my shaking hands.

After the train incident Jhimmy couldn't speak for months, and when he did, it was babble. Gang members were kind— they brought food and looked after him, even washing, cutting, and combing his hair. They always made an effort to include him in activities. But he withdrew into a shell, like a turtle in hibernation, unable to comprehend what was going on. Nuns finally took him to a mental hospital, and we never saw him again. Months later, we heard he'd committed suicide—he was only five.

My friends thought I might end up like Jhimmy because I stuttered for a long time. I was also depressed, shuddering unpredictably. I withdrew into a stupor when anyone talked about it, but talk about it they did—most gang members saw death often, but not like this. Chile and Ben frequently thanked me for saving their lives. But I was preoccupied with the ones I didn't save—the two smaller kids—how they'd looked before, sleeping there on the tracks.

*I could've saved* both *of them, gotten them before trying for Soft-Serve. Which I* knew *was impossible. Where was my strategy?*

I became haunted by a variety of nightmares. In one recurring dream, I was strapped to a gurney in a hospital room and heard a train charging down the hall. Trying desperately to shake my profoundly heavy sleep, I struggled toward consciousness and managed to open my eyes, yet I was paralyzed. I looked around and saw Soft Serve and some little kids standing in the hall, oblivious to danger. I shouted a warning, but no sound came out of my mouth. There was only the chug-chugging of the train...

*Don't let it catch them; don't let it catch them.*

# CHAPTER 18

—◆✶✶✶◆—

Assad couldn't wait to see her. When they were apart, he thought about her with a constancy that astonished him, and when he slept, he dreamed of her. He felt captivated, unable to focus on work without her invading image. His rhythm was off, and he was consumed with frustration.

He hadn't considered marriage, but he'd bought a house in Forbes Park with her in mind. It had four bedrooms, seven bathrooms, a maid's room, and a driver's room. It was on two floors, and had an extra large kitchen with commercial-grade appliances, an entertainment area, and a three-car garage. But the attic had been the dealmaker: a room with windows on all sides, like a control tower, where he could look down on everyone in Forbes Park.

Around the clock decorators and gardeners worked on improvements. The master bedroom had a huge Belgian-lace canopied bed, placed on a riser as the focal point of the room, spread with saffron silk overlaid with lace, and piled high with Chinese-embroidered silk pillows. Several antique wardrobes, an elaborate Louis XVI chest-on-chest, and a cluster of red velvet Century sofas dwarfed a black-lacquered grand piano, which stood inconspicuously in the corner, the fallboard closed over the keys.

The living room was larger still. A custom-built, floor-to-ceiling display case with specialized lighting held rare Chinese vases he'd been accumulating. Three seating areas were arranged to showcase Chinese art, a Renoir, and a Picasso. White marble floors framed richly colored Persian rugs, and white marble statues echoed the elegance of the floors. Chairs and sofas were upholstered in jewel tones of gold, blue, and burgundy. The room was an aesthetic masterpiece.

He participated by phone in auctions held around the world, buying all the enrichments he could think of, including European stained-glass windows, beveled and leaded windows, and wood paneling from an old English estate to wainscot the rooms and hallways. He bought six-inch crown moldings, carved ceiling medallions, and a brass railing from the salvage sale of Le Figaro in Paris. His curving staircase was custom-made with oak, patterned after one in Atlanta, Georgia. He bought Venetian chandeliers and Murano glassware to add sparkle to the dining room and bathrooms.

*I'm gonna take her breath away.*

He had no spending limit as long as Marcos was in power. There were plenty of contracts yet to fulfill, drug trafficking was booming, and of course, no taxes. He opened a Swiss bank account in case he needed to leave the country, or wanted to build vacation houses elsewhere. Eventually he'd travel, taking his time deciding where to buy property.

*South of France?*

He didn't spend as much time in Manila as he wanted. His inventory of boys came mostly from Ormoc City or Davao. He observed them fight in daily and weekly matches, looking for tenacity and motivation more than martial art skills. He watched gang members, and knew the significance of each tat. He liked the *Tibays*, and looked for kids with triangles on their right delts, preferably with embellishments—*Papas* who had excelled. He recruited the best, and trained them separately without knowledge of each other, to the degree that he could. It was a huge time commitment, but he was good at what he did: in fact, unique.

He trained, fed, and paid the boys well. In exchange, he demanded absolute loyalty. They must accept and complete all assignments. No information about him or his operatives could be spoken to anyone. Failure to make the kill resulted in death for them and their families.

He was fiercely jealous of Bonifacio. Assad had power, and if he wasn't respected, he was certainly feared. In his business, boys were the ones at risk—he stayed well in the background, and rarely felt endangered.

On the other hand, Bonifacio had power *and respect*: Assad knew gang members would willingly sacrifice their lives for Bonifacio, but he had no illusions about anyone doing that for him. His single consolation was that Bonifacio probably wouldn't live long; after all, he fought *right next* to the boys—on the front line.

Standing on the fringes of the crowd, Assad watched the weeklies. He saw Bonifacio, his arm around Ben, leaning toward him as though sharing a confidence. For Assad, that eclipsed the action in the ring, commanding full attention. Ben paused for a moment, then replied to Bonifacio, who nodded, and they laughed at what had to be a private joke. Assad ground his teeth, and spit.

# CHAPTER 19

———✦∿∿∿∿✦———

OVERTAKEN BY A SURGE OF RESTLESSNESS, I wanted to hack apart the rainforest, chopping and slashing, faster and faster, until I could escape the clickety-clack, clickety-clack, unrelenting ghost of a train that chased me, chugging and chewing at my heels all night long.

*Where can I hide from the clacking in my head?*

Tormented by nightmares when I slept, and exhausted by day, I often drifted out of reality, disconnecting from the world around me. Nothing mattered; I had tumbled into a different dimension. Mindlessly, I rewound tape around my left knee. Conversation surrounded me, but I was on the outside, not even looking in, but shelled in a stupor.

As though from underwater, I heard Bonifacio's voice, "Mark, I want you and Chile to go boar-hunting."

*Is he still talking? Yes, but to Chile… about me.*

"Make sure Mark's in on the kill—that'll get him back in

the game. Take PP; maybe he can cheer him up. Ben should go—he's a first-rate hunter... let Ben pick a few others."

Ben had something else to do, but was persuaded to come anyway, bringing along Leo and Mickey-Mole. Leo, a pock-marked kid with an affinity for flora and fauna, picked a stack of elephant-ear leaves. Mickey-Mole, the oldest at perhaps twenty-five, was an *Abuelito*, and came for the fun of the hunt, plopping a half-dozen rusty shovels down near the water, as his out-of-breath girlfriend stumbled like a rhino across the sand toward us, dropping a bulky backpack. "Here's food for you," she panted, "coffee, condensed milk, rice, cigarettes, candy, and even chicken."

"Will you take care of Mano? He's afraid of water," PP asked.

Mickey-Mole smiled, along with the mole on his mouth. As Mano jumped into his girlfriend's arms, Mickey-Mole patted Mano's furry back, and dismissed his girl with a nod of thanks.

But I saw this as though watching a movie, where I couldn't relate to, or interact with the characters. I made no objection as Chile hoisted me onto his shoulders, and the next thing I remember was sitting on the sand surrounded by a blur of activity: Chile wrapped a machete in cloth, tucking it in his backpack, along with knives, fishhooks, and *panas*; PP threaded a vine-rope through holes punched in the tops of empty coffee cans, and draped them over his neck; Mickey-Mole strapped on the backpack of food, and carried the shovels. We mounted two logs, three kids to a log, and using shovels as paddles, set off to an island reputed to have plentiful boar. I vaguely noticed the splash and spray of ocean water stinging sores on my body, the sucking in of hot air, the relentless sun scorching my back, and the wind-dried, salty-crust streaking over me. But only my body was there.

Slipping into the water like eels, Mickey-Mole, Leo, and Chile took turns cooling off in the sea, floating on their backs. Ben and PP swam along side, both too skinny to float well. But PP got goose bumps; he started coughing, and his lips began to turn blue, the only color on his face being his freckles. Chile laughed good-naturedly, "Come on up, Squid-lips," he said, pulling PP by his stringy arms onto the log, shivering and still coughing. Ben struggled back on the other log, weighted by his wet, super-long hair, which clung to his back, and shone with the iridescence of beetle wings.

Mickey-Mole remounted. "Hey, Ben," he said, "Ever had a haircut?" He began compulsively raking his fingers through his own newly cut hair, over and over, his fingers continuing their course through mid-air, as if he still had long hair.

Ben gathered his water-soaked mat of hair, wrung it like a mop, and tied it back. "Doubt it."

"My girlfriend cut mine; she can do yours if you want," Mickey-Mole said, turning his attention to the food she'd brought.

I was detached as everyone ate: they pulled apart pieces of chicken, devouring them, licking lips and fingers, chucking the well-cleaned bones out over the water. Chile handed me a leg, but almost immediately a sea bird swooped down and snatched it. Chile tilted his head, dimpled with amusement, and offered me another piece, but I waved it away.

We reached the first island and spent a few sunny hours on the beach. While the others jumped across patches of seaweed, popping pods with their feet, running up and down the shore, I slumped, nearly sleeping, on the sand, and didn't see them gathering. The cold water they dumped on my head shocked me into momentary awareness, but I soon shook it off.

Then Leo, who had on a once-blue tee shirt he'd worn for two years straight, caught a sea snake and was fascinated by it, unlike most Filipinos, who are afraid of snakes. He waded out of the shallows and showed it around. The snake was about five feet long, banded in grayish-white and black. Ben nervously supported the front end while Leo confirmed the snake's paddle-tail.

"Of course, he's *venomous*," said Leo casually.

Ben dropped the head, jumping backwards.

"But," he continued, ignoring Ben, "a sea snake is so mellow, he'll hardly ever bite," shifting his hands along the length of the snake, holding up its head. "Look at the yellow design on his mouth," he smiled. "He's so *beautiful!*"

He shouted for me to look, and I nodded dismissively. Then he let the snake down into the water and it swam gracefully away, provoking a collective sigh from Mickey-Mole, Chile, PP, and most certainly Ben, who had faded to a shade of pale.

Sour-gray cloud curds hung dribbling, then pouring, as we pushed off toward the next island. Not even the pounding rain disrupted my apathy. Someone held a huge leaf over my head, but I didn't even notice until PP and Mickey-Mole reached under to offer me a drink from coffee-cans of collected rainwater. When the clouds moved on and the wind came up, Leo and Mickey-Mole tried to use the elephant-ear leaves as sails, but couldn't catch the wind.

By late afternoon, land was spotted and we maneuvered to the beach. Tired, sunburned, and sore, we sat on the sand and ate candy. After a while, Ben and Mickey-Mole made a hiding place for our supplies behind rocks and driftwood; Chile and PP foraged for food and found sweet potatoes growing near an abandoned hut, while I tried unsuccessfully to nap under the elephant-ear leaves.

Fishing attempts failed, so Ben decided to catch a bird. He threaded his fishhook through a shrimp for bait, placed it on a leaf near the water, patted the line under the sand for about five feet, tied the end to a large piece of driftwood, and waited. Not long after, a sea bird swooped down, swallowed the bait, and was already tethered.

Ben roasted the bird over an open fire. Our elephant-ear leaves now became plates, torn to size, loaded with sweet potatoes and rice, and a smidgen of gull. After dinner, we drank coffee with condensed milk and lit cigarettes, taking deep drags, puffing out long, gray columns of smoke.

As usual, I had trouble sleeping, thinking of nothing in particular, staring at the stars for hours. I watched a full moon slide up over the horizon, making a pathway across the surface of the sea. I fell into a restless sleep at dawn, but was soon wakened.

"Look for pig tunnels in the undergrowth," Ben ordered, as he began hacking a trail with his machete. We single-filed into the foliage, PP just behind me, bringing up the rear, stepping over a procession of leaf-cutting ants carrying leaf-triangles back to their mound. Ben plucked a scorpion from the watery leaf of a bromeliad, showed it around, and dropped it back on the leaf. Then he thumped a tree trunk with the handle of his knife, and hundreds of moths took to the air.

We climbed a small waterfall slimy with moss, grabbing branches and roots, pulling ourselves up, while a cool spray of water fell over our bodies. The marinade of misery I'd been soaking in began to wash off, and I discovered a cold sore on my lower lip, which I couldn't help licking and biting.

Sun beat down on the canopy; wet wood and leaves misted underfoot. The sweet fruity aroma of the forest enveloped us as we threaded through tangles of looping vines.

Just as I was beginning to pay attention, Ben held up his hand and our procession came to an abrupt stop. Leo, who'd been looking at the ground, bumped into me, and there was a ripple effect through the line. Everyone fell, and Ben, being first in line, was last to go down. As we scrambled to stand he pointed through the undergrowth. We froze and listened. A slight slithering sound came from leaves in front of us.

"Sss...ss...sna...ake!" Chile said, hopping sideways. We slowly and carefully made our way around the back end of an eight-foot reticulated python, and watched it scale a tree in front of us.

Glimmers of sunlight penetrated the undergrowth, barely lighting our way. Now and then I heard something small scurry through the bushes, against a background crackling with insect static. Ben picked up the dark-green scat of a boar, squished it in his hand, and whispered, "It's fresh." He perused the area and pointed to a possible pig-track. Bending low to the ground, we entered a tunnel in the vegetation—well trodden, moist and gray.

Maybe it was the camaraderie, or the thrill of the hunt, but whatever the reason, the exhilaration was contagious, and I began to meld into the team. Ben moved forward on the balls of his feet, turned and signaled silence with his index finger to his lips, motioning us to follow. He made eye contact with each of us, and signaled us to stop. With fingers and toes gripping like a gecko's, he climbed a tree. Soon he pointed across the heavy vegetation, and quickly slid down. "There's a fat sow on a trail crossing this one, but there's no room for us to position an attack. We'll have to do the 'bait-and-fall.'"

"And here comes the bait now!" Mickey-Mole whispered, shoving PP forward.

PP's knees locked.

We grabbed our shovels and dug a hole in the middle of the trail about four feet deep, four-feet wide, and four-feet long. Then we cut and laid leafy branches across the top, perpendicular to the trail.

PP practiced long jumping, air running over the pit a few times, and then went down the trail to get the boar's attention. Soon he came bounding along the path, screaming, the hog's hot breath steaming his scrawny bare legs. He undoubtedly made his personal best run, skittering over the branches. The pig, right on his heels, fell through into the hole. I laughed for the first time in weeks.

Ben raised his eyebrows in my direction, and we simultaneously jumped on the pig's back. Ben reached down and stabbed her belly, and as she turned, I raked my knife across her throat. It was quick and perfectly synchronized.

I felt her sticky, hot blood burbling over my hands, and it felt good—*satisfying—the hot, metallic-stinking gush*. I smiled. *Like killing Aunt Ana—a quick slash across her neck. And for Uncle Anton—spilling his disgusting beer belly.*

My heart was pounding.

The pig lay still.

Everyone whooped with excitement. We shoved ropes under her belly, behind her front legs, and in front of her hind legs.

Ben and I stood on top of her, smiled, and shared a moment of mutual triumph.

We climbed out and were patted on our backs and chests, and given knuckle-rubs in our hair, along with PP. Then we all pulled together to hoist her out of the hole. She was heavy, bloated, and gray with white stripes banding her snout; bristles of straight, wire-like hair poked through her tough hide.

Ben extended the cut across her belly, and we carved out the intestines and vital organs, and strung her up to bleed. A coppery odor steamed the air.

PP stood with his mouth open, mesmerized. "There's so much blood. Look at the guts!" He poked them with a branch, tentatively at first, then with a frenzy of stirring.

"Did you see how Mark stabbed her, and kept the knife going?" said Chile.

"Like he'd done it a million times!" Leo said.

I stood there smiling. *I'm good at this.*

We sat smoking for a few minutes, and then braided tree vines into more rope in the dim light of the forest. When we finished and Ben tried to get up, he found that some of his hair was caught in the rope braid.

I sawed off a chunk of his hair with my knife, "Your first haircut!"

"Real professional," Chile joked, giving the cross-eyes, "except for the bloody knife."

"A little blood doesn't bother me," Ben said, standing, looking at us, and then at the boar. "We need a pole-pack: Bring me the biggest leaves you can find, and two long, sturdy branches."

Chile, PP, and I brought body-sized leaves and Ben showed us how to shred them into strips nearly to the edges. "Like this," he demonstrated, placing one shredded leaf across the other so the strips were perpendicular. The he began weaving the strips together. Chile and I finished it, forming a large mat. Mickey-Mole and Leo lowered the carcass onto the mat; Ben and Chile tied the fringes up over the sow, making a sow-sack. Mickey-Mole and Leo brought the branches and attached each end of the sow-sack to them with vine-ropes, shoring up the middle weight with more rope.

"Flies on her guts," said PP, still coughing from the exertion of his run. Wiping his nose with his arm, he said in a hoarse voice, "Let's throw 'em over the cliff." PP and I lifted the guts with sticks and flung them across the ravine. A few made it to the scree on the other side, catching on protruding branches, dangling and dripping down the cliff.

Hoisting the pole-pack up over our shoulders, we hiked back to our hut, stumbling until we got used to the weight, dipping through the foliage of pig tunnels, occasionally stopping for a breather. Finally arriving back at the beach, we buried the boar in sand, and rested.

After a while Ben and PP went to swim naked in the pool at the base of the waterfall. Holding their breath, they swam up under the falls, and stood shivering with their backs tight against the rocky face of the ridge, screaming at the top of their lungs through the rush of water pounding down in front of them.

Chile put his arm around me, and we set off to explore the ravine, with Leo and Mickey-Mole following, this time taking a steeper trail to the north, looking down on the winding river below. Not finding a place to cross, we hacked down a tree with the machete, positioning the last few chops so the tree bridged the narrowest part of the ravine when it fell. We took turns shimmying across to the green shadows on the other side, and walked south close to the rock face, wondering if the sow guts were still hanging there, but by the time we arrived the cliff was picked clean.

We hiked for a long time. The ravine had now widened considerably and we began looking for a way to cross back over. We finally came upon a dilapidated suspension bridge made of frayed rope and splintery planks.

"I'll go first," Chile shouted. Smearing dirt across his face with his sweaty shirt, he stepped tentatively onto the sagging bridge, grabbing frayed bits of guardrail. He tensed as a hot breeze flowed through the canyon, swaying the bridge slightly. The roar of rapids below drowned out all other sound. He glanced down through missing planks to water crashing over boulders. Then looking toward the guano-coated rock face of the other side, he wiped his palms on his shorts and stepped out. The planks wobbled, and several dislodged, falling slowly, gliding back and forth until they hit water and were slurped under. I watched with alarm as he continued, my heart pounding out of my chest.

He took a quick look over his shoulder at me, and continued with resolution, his knuckles clamped on the rope guardrail. With each successive step he gained confidence, and at last reached the other side. He stepped off the bridge onto solid ground. Nonchalantly swatting a few mosquitoes, he motioned to me, "Next?"

Finally on the other side, Chile and I sat by a cascade of small waterfalls that flowed into a tributary stream. We put our faces in the water, drank, and dunked our heads to cool off. When Chile raked back his wet hair with his fingers, I had a flash of *déjà vu*, "Remember how Uncle Anton kept pushing his side hair up over his bald spot all day?"

Chile slapped his thigh and chortled. "I'd give anything to see him going crazy when all his hair came off!"

"Would you ever go back?"

"Last place on earth I'd go. Don't want to set foot on their street."

"Don't you want revenge?"

"They live in a hell of their own making... I wouldn't want to deprive them of that." After pausing for a moment, he shook his head, "But I hated to miss Uncle Anton having a bald-guy fit."

When we headed back toward the beach, we opted to hike back to the tree we'd originally crossed, rather than crossing the suspension bridge again, "so we wouldn't get lost," we all decided. Once we shimmied across the felled tree, reticulated light confirmed our way through the forest, as did the aroma of roasting pork. Soon we saw the red-yellow burn of wood, and heard the sizzle of fat dripping into the fire. Ben and PP were squatting on either side, turning a rotisserie of juicy pork shoulder.

We devoured chunks of pork, rice, and roasted sweet potatoes from leaf-plates, relishing the feast. I poured hot coffee into cans, and passed it around with condensed milk and sugar. We rubbed warm pig fat onto our thorn-scratched legs, and shoulders sore from carrying the pig-pole through the forest. We recounted our adventures for awhile, and then thoroughly exhausted, sat in silence, sipping coffee and smoking.

The fire crackled. Every cell in my body stoked; I felt rejuvenated, supremely alive, savoring the satisfaction of the kill. I dozed, taking pleasure in how the pig's blood warmed my hands. The smolder of greener wood, slow to burn as the fire fizzled, mingled with the aroma of roasted pork, and I was content. I offered a silent prayer of gratitude for happy days like today, and watched a thread of smoke work its way into the night.

When I finally fell into a deep sleep, though, I dreamed of the train again. Uncle Anton was driving, and snarled down at me; the train was about to run over my friends. I wakened with a start. Now wide-awake, I was haunted by the events of the "promotion," and thought about Soft-Serve.

*I tried so hard...at least I could have saved the other two... I wish I could turn back time. If I could do it all over...*

Jhimmy's face was clear in my mind—*sad, so young, cigarette burns on his arms—a good kid, given the chance.* I was overwhelmed with tenderness, and felt exceptionally close to him, having shared that life-altering experience.

My thoughts wandered. *I could have done better all right, but the drugs were also to blame.* I decided the price of their drug use was too high, and I made a promise to God which I have kept: *to stay away from alcohol and drugs for the rest of my life.*

# CHAPTER 20

THE *TIBAYS* INFUSED US WITH VIGOR UPON OUR RETURN: they were holding a feast. First the girls who stayed with the gang ate, then boys from youngest to oldest, as was the custom. Everyone sat engrossed with our story of the hunt. Told from many points of view, each time it gathered elaboration, almost achieving legendary status the first night.

Ben called me aside, and whispered, "I want to take a pork shank to my family. Will you come with me?"

"Didn't know you had a family."

"Only Bonifacio knows. Don't tell *anyone*."

"I had no idea."

"I try to help them when I can. Come on, I want you to meet them."

We wove through a labyrinth of narrow streets, doublebacking a few times, Ben frequently looking over his shoulder. We crossed a large plot of dirt, finally coming to a dilapidated two-story house, with chipped white paint and a tin roof. Ben's five-year old sister, Peachy, slid down the slippery-slide and ran to meet us crying, "Mama, Mama, Ben's here, and we have meat!" She was a hummingbird sort of child, delicate and flitting. As Ben and I dipped under a line of laundry, she hugged his legs. He handed her a piece of taffy, and she bobbed up and down with glee, her ponytail bouncing after her to the front door.

As we entered the house, Apple, who was two and wore a faded pink sun suit, toddled over, holding up her pudgy arms to Ben. He scooped her up against his skinny chest, laughing at the tickle of her hair tied in lop-sided bunches on the sides of her head. Bing-Bong was a chubby six-month old with gobs of black hair extending several inches down his back. He wore a tee shirt, cloth diaper and plastic pants, and had thighs with multiple rolls of baby fat. He was learning to crawl, but preferred scooting. Now he pulled himself along the floor with his forearm.

Ben's mother came to greet us, wiped her hands on her apron, hugged us both, along with the pork shank, and hurried to pre-heat the oven.

Ben grabbed a sofa-cushion from the only piece of furniture in the small living room, and headed upstairs carrying Apple, followed by Peachy, both girls squealing with anticipation. Ben sat with Apple on his lap; Peachy positioned behind him, and all three rode the cushion down the stairs.

I sat down next to Bing-Bong and did my daily knee-rehab exercises. Then I extended both legs in front of me, painfully forcing the back of my injured knee against the linoleum, like the hospital therapist had shown me, counting slowly to sixty.

I bent it slightly and took a deep breath, re-taping it despite "help" from Bing-Bong, who mostly wanted to teethe on the tape, and was drooling all over the place. We watched and laughed as Ben and the girls tumbled over each other at the bottom of the stairs.

"Come on!" shouted Ben.

I grabbed Bing-Bong along with the remaining cushion and bounced down the stairs in turns with Ben, the baby shrieking with delight, fully distracted from his teething pain. After a few hours of play and a pork dinner, we prepared to leave, but Peachy and Apple clung to us, crying.

"We'll come back," Ben said, pulling both girls to him.

"Oh, Benjie, I wish you'd come more often..." said his mother with a broad smile, "I hope your father's home next time. Thanks for the pork." She turned to me, apologizing for the baby-drool, just as Bing-Bong planted an open-mouthed goober-kiss on my nose. I laughed as she gently disentangled Bing-Bong's arms from around my neck. "Come back anytime, Mark—you're *always* welcome."

〰〰〰

As we returned to the party, I said, "Ben, it's so good you can help them."

"Soon I'll bring home more money than my father," he said.

Our conversation was cut short as we reentered the party, which had morphed into a game of "running-rumble" on a narrow street, adjacent to the park. The challenge was to run through three increasingly difficult sections: in the first section, defenders tried to stop us with body slams; in the second, we got body slams plus boxing. But the third part was "the suicide course," no holds barred—body slams, boxing, kickboxing, and tackling.

When Ben, Chile, and I hobbled off to the cinema to sleep, we were sharing quotes from the movie, "Rocky," "Ya gotta be willing to take the hits…" We were bruised, battered and could barely move, and found cushy seats to sleep in. My knee throbbed, and I held it against a cool metal armrest.

Soon I heard Chile and Ben's even breathing, and knew they were asleep, but my mind kept going. I smiled thinking of Ben's sisters and brother. I felt almost like one of his family, and reveled in the newly stored memory. But my stomach recoiled as my thoughts switched from Ben's family to those of my own.

*I wonder where Segundina is and if she's okay. I hope Isabel isn't a prostitute... And my brothers?*

I reviewed their names—José, 2Tall, Francisco—savoring the sound of them, as if by clinging to their names, I could have them back.

*Maybe they're street kids too, and had to join gangs. At least Ben gets to see his family.*

After a while, my sadness and loneliness churned into the rage I often cultivated when alone—nourishing it, gorging on it. While Chile and Ben slept peacefully, I thrived on hatred, and let it consume me. I longed to feel the knife-plunge and the reward of blood-gush on my hands, just like with the sow.

*Would it be different killing humans?*

My fury took the form of a knife, and was my obsession. I imagined stabbing Ana and Anton over and over, cutting her throat, jamming the knife deep in his gut, raking it to his neck in a single motion. My jaw shifted, and my teeth ground with rage; my arm muscles became rigid; my hand clenched as if holding the knife. I felt the steam and smelled the stink of their blood.

# CHAPTER 21

DISINTERESTED IN FIGHTING HIMSELF, Ben often came to cheer my fights. But I hadn't seen him recently, and I missed him. I ached to visit his family again, and to play with the kids.

*He's probably with them now.*

I was wondering about him after just winning a difficult fight, when I noticed Assad talking to another fighter and nodding my way. It was hard to tell whom he recruited; I hoped he'd just picked me. He walked toward me; I felt flattered, and met him halfway.

"Want to talk?" Assad asked, resting his hand on my shoulder.

"Yes," I said nervously glancing up.

"Come down to the gray house behind the pool hall tomorrow morning."

Light quivered across the rooftops as I walked past the familiar blue-stucco pool hall the next day, knowing my life was about to change. I took a deep breath.

*Now I'll learn exactly how to kill them.*

The door was halfway opened. I pushed it all the way open, entered, and closed it behind me. Was Assad already there? The shades were drawn; the inside was somber and dark, smelling of spidery dampness. My eyes slowly adjusted. A whiff of cologne overpowered mold as Assad entered from the back room.

"Do you know why you're here?" he asked.

"Yes," I said, dry mouthed.

"How old are you?"

"Seven, I think."

"Are you an orphan?" he asked, squinting into a hard stare.

"Yes."

"What do you think you'll learn from me?"

"To be an assassin," I answered, clearing my throat, forcing myself to look into his eyes, which were pot-holed deep in his face, his pupils like punctured pools of black ink leaking into the irises, so that his eyes were completely black.

"Why would you want to do that?"

"To kill people."

"Uh huh. You'll mostly be killing cops, like the ones who shoot gang members."

"When do I start?" I said, nearly wetting my pants.

"Now. You'll train first in stabbing, and then knife throwing. Eventually you'll get a gun."

I nodded, trying to still my shaking knees.

"This is your main weapon," Assad said, unsheathing a ten-inch knife. "Tuck it in the back of your shorts. Now this is what you do: walk toward the victim but don't look at him; pull the knife out quick and jab him, hard as you can—in the gut, here," he continued, touching his lower abdomen with the point of the knife. "Keep the sharp side up, like this. Use both hands to jerk it upward with all your strength," he said, drawing the knife up, "then pull it out, run until you're sure he can't come after you, and tuck the knife back in your shorts. You must be fast so he can't grab you."

I took in every word. "Push the knife clear up to his neck?"

"That won't happen because of this bone here," he said thumping my sternum. "The rib cage protects the heart and lungs pretty well. That's why you do *exactly* as I showed you."

"What if it only wounds him?"

"You *must kill* him. You'll learn how to do it correctly. It's important he bleeds to death quickly."

He paused for effect, keeping his eyes on mine. "If *he* doesn't die, *you* do."

"Oh," I said, rubbing my palms on my shorts.

"You won't know your target."

"What if he sees the knife?" I stammered.

"He'll have no idea you're a threat. You're young and too small to be noticed. You have great reflexes and a lot of grit— the best possible combination of attributes. To him, you're a street kid he's used to ignoring. He won't even know you're there. You'll catch him completely by surprise."

"What if I get caught?"

"You won't."

"Okay. Then what do I do?"

"We'll be waiting in the car where we dropped you off."

I nodded.

"And, Mark, you don't tell *anyone* about this."

"I'll *die* before I tell anyone."

"Or shortly thereafter," he said.

"Oh."

That night I was a mix of excitement and terror. I decided to think about my tattoos. The one on my arm showing my promotion to the *Papas* was promised because of the lives I saved during the train incident, but overdue. The tat on the back of my neck—the "mark of the assassin," given for killing ten people—might take a while, and of course assassinations done for Assad couldn't be part of the count—those must be well under the radar.

*Of course, the tat isn't all that important. What I* need *is the practice.*

# CHAPTER 22

DAMEANA MET ASSAD AT THE MANILA AIRPORT with a radiant smile, and they drove to the restaurant, ecstatic to see each other. But the evening ultimately went sour. While having dinner, Assad noticed a man repeatedly looking at her, and when a bottle of Dom Perignon was delivered with the guy's compliments, Assad shouted at him, "Who do you think you are?"

The man raised his glass to Dameana and mouthed, "You're gorgeous!"

"She's with me! How dare you!" Assad said.

The man ignored him, continuing to stare at Dameana.

Assad fixed his stare on him, and then looked at Dameana, who said, "This is embarrassing," shifting uncomfortably in her chair.

"Do you know him?"

"No!" she insisted, pushing her chair back from the table.

When Assad saw the man *still* watching her, he jumped up,

rushed over to the man's table, pulled him from his chair by his lapels, and punched him repeatedly. The assault was so quick, and the blows came so fast and hard, the guy passed out and fell to the floor. Assad kicked him.

His anger unabated, Assad glared at Dameana, who was in a state of horror. He grabbed her arm and jerked her roughly to her feet, out the door, across the street, and shoved her into the car.

"You were flirting with him!"

"No, I..."

"You encourage men to look at you!" He raised his fist to hit her.

She slid to the floor, her arms shielding her face.

Maybe it was the way she looked so helpless that made Assad soften, "I want you all to myself," he said.

She was crying.

He reached out to her.

She cringed.

He drove her home, still cowering on the floor, without a word. He parked, yanked her out of the car abruptly, walked her to the door, and said merely, "I'll call you."

During the successive weeks they made up, and Assad was especially attentive, sending flowers daily with notes of apology, and taking her out whenever he was in town. He assumed all had been forgiven and forgotten, and apart from a brief hour of self-loathing after the incident, he went about his routine, business as usual. He reassured himself he had control of his temper, and had for several years—except where she was concerned—a fact that he found annoying but certainly not paralyzing.

But for Dameana, that night had been an eye-opener. She was now tuned to his frequent jealousies, possessiveness, and how often he was gone. Not only that, after more than a year of being together, he'd never mentioned marriage.

*I'm just an ornament to him.*

He spent time in Ormoc City, with only brief phone calls to her, and then had done exhaustive recruiting in Mindanao for several weeks without calling. He was taken aback when he finally called and she wasn't home.

*But I'll see her soon.*

The beginnings of a trip to Taal Volcano formed in his mind—they'd ride horses to the top and spend tranquil evenings watching breathtaking sunsets, then ride to a beach resort where they'd swim and lay on the sand. He made out an itinerary and mailed it in a beautiful silk gift box, but she didn't call, and he wondered if she'd gotten it.

*A week. Should have gotten it by now.*

When he finally called, the maid said she'd gone to White Sands.

"Who with?" Assad interrogated.

"Oh, I don't know. Oh, her aunt... Yes, her aunt."

"How long will she be gone?"

"Only six weeks, I think."

*Why would she go without telling me?*

He was furious she hadn't told him. He'd have to wait weeks to see her, and he longed to hear her voice. She should be available when he called or wanted to see her!

*I'll have to talk to her about this.*

Still, now he'd have time to train a new batch of recruits before returning to Manila, and then he could spend more time with her. He was, after all, raking in the money, and that would impress her.

*The new Ferrari, and then the* house!

He waited the six weeks for her return, and then two weeks more, not wanting to seem too eager. But when he called, she wasn't home, so he left a message. Then he left more messages, but she never returned his calls, and no one gave any explanation. Anxious and then frantic, he flew to Manila and rushed to her house. No one was home. The soap factory owned by her family would be closed by now, and he didn't know where to look. He made a frenetic attempt to find her in places they'd been together, to no avail. She was nowhere to be found.

<hr/>

It took two months to find her. He'd called and gone by her house many times—either no one was home, or they'd said she was out. Even his private investigator had no luck. Then, when wandering down a street where they'd once bought fruit together, Assad thought he saw her from afar. He pushed through the crowd, running toward her. Her hair was different, and the dress unfamiliar, but as he called her name, she turned.

He rushed to her, "Dameana!"

She gasped, and her hands covered her mouth in shock.

He noticed her rounded belly. "You're pregnant!" he said, jerking away with revulsion.

She didn't reply.

"But…" and then looking up to her face, he saw the ring. "And you're… married?" he said.

She nodded.

"How long?"

She swallowed. "Five months," she managed to whisper.

"How could you do this to me?" he said, clenching his fists.

"Assad…" she trembled.

"That's right, say my name! Say it like you *used* to!"

"I'm sorry…"

"Who *is* he?"

"You don't know him," she stammered.

He raised his fist.

She winced, more terrified than she'd ever been, crouching low to the ground.

People in the street gathered to watch the excitement, and a few shopkeepers positioned as though to protect the pregnant woman.

But Assad abruptly turned away. He started walking, determined not to look back, and broke into a run. He kept going all night without destination, walking, turning it over in his mind. He shook his head.

*That didn't just happen. Only a bad dream. The time I gave her the earrings, could we go back to then? Things would be different. I'd run to her, and she'd welcome me with open arms and that bewitching smile. Married, and pregnant? I'll kill the guy! How could she?*

He returned to the house he planned for her in Forbes Park, ran to the bedroom, took his knife and stabbed the bed repeatedly, slashing it to shreds. He smashed the vanity mirror that would have been hers. Rushing to the living room, he attacked his display of Chinese vases with a vengeance. He triple-stepped to the attic and drew his knife across the portrait he'd commissioned of her, hacking it to pieces. His appetite for destruction temporarily satiated, he ran through the house over a crunch of glass, and bolted through the front door, slamming it shut. With curious neighbors looking on, he jumped into his Ferrari and screeched down the hill, heading for the airport.

⌁⌁⌁⌁⌁

"Ben," he said the next day, "I've got another job for you," and they flew back to Manila. It was Ben's first time flying, and he could barely contain his excitement.

*Manila! Probably a politician—can't wait to see mother's face when I give her all that money! By the time Mark comes to visit, she'll have a new sofa, and a TV that works. If he could see me now... Wonder what he'd think?*

During the next few days Assad completed the stakeout and chose the time and place, while Ben cleaned up the mess at the Forbes Park house. As with his first two jobs, Ben wouldn't know anything about the victim. Assad would point him out; they'd drive past, then Ben would get out of the car and walk toward him, not making eye contact, and do an abdominal stab. It was time. No one was around. It was a few minutes after sunset, the park was poorly lit, and it was just dark enough.

*Ideal.*

Ben focused on the job at hand and walked toward the target, thinking only of the stab.

*Soon the crooked politician will be gutted like a fish, and I'll have a sock full of money.*

Ben walked casually down the path toward his prey, deliberately not looking. As he neared, his right hand settled on the knife handle in his waistband. His peripheral vision barely made out the form of a person approaching. He looked at the ground until he got close, and then glanced at the victim, assessing where to plunge the knife. Perhaps it was the scent of her perfume, or the flash of *déjà vu* Ben had glancing at her belly that caused him to hesitate.

*It's a woman, and she's pregnant!*

Dumbfounded, he dropped his knife.

He picked it up and tucked it in his waistband before the woman saw it. Then in a voice as soft as a hymn, she said, "Would you like some money for food?"

He turned and ran. The path was unsteady beneath his feet.

# CHAPTER 23

ONE EVENING, BONIFACIO AND TWO OF HIS BODYGUARDS entered the gym, soaked with rain. I was stretching and taping my knee as I prepared for a fight.

"He can't fight tonight," Bonifacio informed Master David, giving him an upward nod of respect, and pulling me aside, "We need your help."

"Whatever you need…"

"It's about Ben."

"Is he okay?"

"There's a problem—I just found out."

"What's the matter?" I said.

"It's about his family. Do you know where they live?"

"Yes, are they okay?"

"Assad gave Ben an assignment that he refused."

*So that's why he's been gone!*

"That isn't acceptable to Assad," Bonifacio went on, "so Ben was given an ultimatum—he has to kill his family."

"He won't do that!" I said.

"My guess is that Assad threatened him with something worse…"

"What could be *worse*?" I cried.

Bullet taps of rain pounded the roof. We looked at each other, and broke out through the rain, along with Bonifacio's bodyguards. Ben's house was dark, and we didn't know what to expect. But even before we got there we heard crying. We hesitated on the porch, and everyone but me drew guns. Then, without knocking, I kicked the door open and turned on the light. Ben was alone, slouching in a ladder-backed chair, facing the door, head in his hands, sobbing. We glanced around the room; Bonifacio checked out the kitchen, one of his bodyguards walking ahead. The other finished sweeping the downstairs with his gun, and went to look upstairs, but soon returned to the landing, lowered his gun to his side, and shook his head.

Bonifacio put his hand briefly on Ben's shoulder, squeezed, tilted his head to the side and said softly, "Ben, what happened?"

Ben cried uncontrollably for a few minutes.

I brought a chair from the kitchen and sat down facing him.

"I…" sobbed Ben, his face red and swollen.

"What?" I said, leaning forward.

"I… killed them."

"*Who?*" I said, incredulous.

He wiped his arm across his runny nose, and choked with chest-heaving spasms.

After a brief silence, I wrinkled my forehead, "Your family?" I paused for a long time, trying to imagine the possibility, and then said slowly, "Bing-Bong?"

"Dead," Ben coughed through his sobs, rocking back and forth.

We both cried for awhile, and no one else spoke.

"How could you *do* that?"

He didn't answer.

Bonifacio knelt down beside Ben, pursing his lips. "You know *Tibay* rules." He paused, and murmured, not unkindly, "The penalty for hurting your family is death."

"Didn't you think the gang would find out?" I said at last.

"I didn't think about it," Ben stammered. "Assad gave me no choice... He said he'd torture the children in front of my parents before he killed them all—except Peachy..."

"And so you..."

"He was going to sell her to pimps!" Ben sobbed. "I wanted to warn them, to help them get away, but Assad had guards everywhere. I couldn't do *anything* to save them."

"What kind of a man *is* he?" I cried. "Oh Ben... *Ben...*"

Then Ben turned abruptly to Bonifacio. "I *know* the rules. Go ahead."

"Mark," Bonifacio said, fixing a silencer to his .45 and handing it to me.

I didn't respond. The gun hung limp at my side.

"Do it *now!*" Bonifacio said.

I glared at Bonifacio.

Everyone looked at me.

*Why don't you do it yourself, Bonifacio? Why do I have to do it?*

But I said to Ben, "You know what I have to do."

"Yes."

I looked at him, hesitating, and cried.

"Don't worry," Ben said, suddenly straightening up in his chair, his eyes meeting mine, "If you don't do it, I will."

I held the gun out with both hands, shaking.

"It's okay, Mark. I'm ready," he said softly.

The bullet shot through the room, hitting Ben in the forehead, knocking him backward to the floor. A pool of blood spread from the back of his head through the tangles of his long black hair. A profound silence settled on the house.

Bonifacio took the gun and patted me on the shoulder, "Stay here," he said gently, heading for the stairs. The soft sandpaper sound of his sandals on the steps broke the stillness, and he signaled the others to follow. A minute later, he clomped heavily down the stairs, compressing his lips, shaking his head, "They're all dead..." Then with trembling lips he said, "The family is sacred!"

For a moment we were quiet, and then Bonifacio said to me, "Stay awhile if you want." He leaned down and put his arm around me, and said, "As long as you want. Ben used a silencer, so probably no one heard. Don't worry; the neighbors won't get involved. They'll keep their doors shut and mind their own business." He regarded me carefully, "You okay?"

I nodded slightly, hanging my head.

"Eventually the police will get an anonymous call," Bonifacio said to his bodyguards, "This never happened." They walked out the door, leaving me alone with Ben.

I sat in a virtual coma, staring without seeing, and then slumped my head to my knees. After a while I stood up and looked at Ben's face, still wet with tears. I brushed the hair from his face, stroked the sides of his hair back, caressed his shoulder, and held his hand. His skinny arms were askew and punctured with recent needle marks. The blood pool expanded across the floor; blood splatter and bits of flesh covered the wall behind, and was sprayed across the side of a new sofa. I put my hands in my pockets, paralyzed. Finally my fingers closed around a flat, disc-shaped rock, the one Ben and I had found when "skimming" on the lake—*the best skimming rock ever.* I placed it gently on his chest and rested my hand on it for a moment. Then I turned and walked into the rain, leaving the door open.

A shadow moved under the slippery-slide, and down the hill. I stood and listened, but could only hear wind moaning through the rain. I headed uphill, and wasn't followed.

*But I don't really care.*

It was strange out. The rain stopped, and the moon was gray against a darker gray sky, casting an eerie pall over the earth. Stars had withdrawn, and flowers were closed for the night. I walked aimlessly. The hoot of an owl pierced the air, and I found myself on the beach. It was high tide and the waves crashed against the shore, consuming the land. I knew some of the smaller islands Ben and I had explored together were completely under water tonight, as though they'd never existed.

I slept fitfully, dreaming of a house with familiar rooms, and heard the rush of a river, and the whisper of wind over it. Scents of coconut soap and cordovan shoe polish embraced me. My father and mother were there, and my brothers and sisters, and they were all talking softly, sitting around a table. I couldn't hear what they were saying. Then I smelled a distant sugarcane field burning.

# CHAPTER 24

In the early morning hours, shadows as thick as tar unbraided. Sunlight struck the city and penetrated my hiding place. I stirred from my dry spot beneath the bushes to the smell of mud, and knuckled open my eyes.

I was late for my daily routine, but automatically headed for the gym. Master David, always well groomed, unfolded from his lotus position, and stood tall, his straight black hair tied at the back of his neck. His voice was mellow, "Let's get started."

I bowed slightly, automatically did my knee exercises, and we stretched together. He revved up his motorcycle and drove slowly down the street, as I jogged along side. I ran without rhythm. Soon my eyes swelled with moisture, and I barely noticed a three-legged dog trying to keep up.

"Stop," Master David said, pulling to the side and dismounting. I hung my head. He pushed his glasses into place and said, "Your mind is the athlete; your body the means of expression. Relax your mind, and run freely."

"Yes, Master," I said, and we restarted.

I focused on relaxing and my movements became more fluid—I looked toward the next tree, and the next street, and the next hill. The morning air was damp but not hot; there was a warm breeze, and I imagined myself as a deer effortlessly running across the horizon. I got my second wind after two miles, and ran the last four without thinking, a buzz of blood pounding my temples. The three-legged dog had dropped out long ago, slinking off into the weeds.

After training, I bought *adobo*, but couldn't eat, and returned to my hiding place in the park. With heavy eyelids I slept soundly for a few hours, but when I wakened, the reality of the night before intruded with brutal clarity. I struggled to my feet, and headed for the street. The sun was a spotlight overhead that shone only on me; I felt raw and exposed, more crippled than the three-legged dog, as though I had fallen behind and could never catch up.

*Ben stole mangoes for us that first day.*

Images of him haunted me as I wandered through the city; everywhere I went I'd been with him. I expected to see him coming around the corner any minute, and once or twice, extra-long hair caught my eye. Memories swirled around, underlining every moment—swimming, the hospital, chess, *panas*, watching Bonifacio fight, boar hunting, and most painful of all—Ben's mother, Peachy, Apple, and Bing Bong. Every time I remembered the children, my tears came in torrents, and I tasted the sting.

*This is too hard.*

I felt incredibly close to him because of all we shared.

*And his death? Yeah, you could say we shared that. How could we have shared anything more intimately?*

By afternoon, my eyes were sore and red-rimmed with crying and fatigue, but my wanderings took me to the gym. I made a feeble attempt to spar with a new kid, but saw Ben's face before me, and got walloped.

"Maybe I should bet on the other guy," said PP, while Mano scolded from the top of PP's head. "Hey, you look terrible..." PP said.

Ignoring him, I ran outside to the black car pulling up in front. Assad's eyes were as hard and black as the car. He didn't look at me. "Get in," he said. "Ever held a gun?"

I hesitated, hating his guts, and sweating with fear.

Not expecting an answer, Assad continued, "After you get some experience with a knife, I'll teach you how to shoot."

---

I immersed myself for weeks—focusing on training, pushing thoughts of Ben and my revulsion for Assad out of my mind. The goal was avenging my family, and I always had that in mind when I trained. Many times Assad had me practice walking unnoticed by his assistants, catching them unawares, making fake stabs, turning, and running. Every time I stabbed the raffia mannequin, I was enacting fantasies I'd rehearsed in my head for so long.

*This is exactly how I'll kill them.*

Then I got my first assignment. I never knew who the target was, perhaps a cop or politician; it didn't matter, and I didn't care.

I only cared about getting on with my goal. A scout had followed the intended victim for weeks and knew his routine. Assad and his driver took me to the selected spot and pointed him out. It was dark. I got out of the car well ahead of my target. With my knife tucked in my waistband in back, under my shirt, I casually walked toward the man, trying to minimize my limp, preparing mentally for the task ahead, full of hatred and revving with rage. Then, as trained, I focused on the job. I didn't look at the man, but slipped out the knife when he got close, plunged it in with all my strength, well below the ribs, cutting edge upward, and raked it up with both hands. I yanked it out, turned and ran, slowing only when safe. I jumped into the black car; the door slammed shut as we sped off, my heartbeat accelerating along with the car.

We drove to a house on the other side of town. "You did great," Assad said, knuckling my arm. "Don't think about it, or talk about it. It's just a job. *Only* think about what's ahead."

*So I can be just like you? You creep.*

I showered, standing under the water for a long time. The water turned cold.

*Now I'm an assassin.*

I underwent a transformation—cut my hair short, threw away my old clothes, bought Bermuda shorts, a button-down shirt, and my first pair of leather sandals. I could have passed for a real kid.

I stuck to a rigorous schedule, following the training schedule set up by Master David, wondering if he'd guess I was an assassin, and what he'd think. Chile would be surprised, but of course I wouldn't tell him, or anybody for that matter. As for Bonifacio, if he didn't already know, he'd find out, and I wondered how he'd react. I couldn't let myself think about it, so I kept busy—running, kickboxing, stick fighting, and occasionally target shooting with a gun. I trained for a few more weeks and went back to the gang.

When I returned to the old neighborhood, I sold my blister-making sandals, and reveled in the feeling of earth under my bare feet. I bought a used tee shirt and shorts, soon looking like a street kid again, apart from the wad of money in my pocket, which I promptly and proudly gave to the gang's treasurer.

Before long I had more assignments from Assad—cops, I think—all done with my knife. There were two who may have been politicians; I wasn't sure. Each time I approached with steely focus, did what I had to, and then forgot about it. I don't remember being especially nervous. The whole thing was more methodical than exciting; there was no thrill in the kill. It was just a job like washing dishes, something I never thought about. But then I got an assignment that had a different outcome.

The moon was a boar's tusk against a black background. The air seemed to coarsen, and I was imperceptibly on edge. I circled to the pathway where the victim would come. I looked at the ground and kept walking, glancing ahead from time to time, and finally saw my target approaching. But the guy turned abruptly and hurried to a parked car with its hood up.

*This isn't the plan...*

I moved in slowly, keeping to the shadows, and as I got closer, and saw the man lean under the hood.

*Adapt or die.*

I decided on a "kiss of the dragon" stab to the back of the neck. If I got it right, the man would be paralyzed, and I'd follow with a major organ stab. I walked past the car, then quietly doubled back, casually stepping into the street, moving silently behind the man, knife drawn. But in a flash, the man pivoted, grabbed my arm, twisted it behind my back, and took the knife. He slammed down the hood and roughly shoved me in the back seat, diving in after me. "Keep down," he shouted, ducking and pulling me down as gunfire shattered the back window. The driver, who'd been hiding in the front seat, pulled up under the steering wheel while accelerating. The back door slammed shut as the car sped off.

The black car drove after us, Assad shooting. A side window shattered as our driver swerved into an alley. I felt handcuffs clink on my wrists, held firmly behind my back, and noticed the uniform. The man was a cop. I lunged unsuccessfully for the door. The cop pulled me back on the seat, and said, "I'll take you to Bonifacio."

Our driver was first-rate, and after a half-dozen harrowing turns, lost Assad. With lights off, we pulled up behind a small house and parked in a shed. Bonifacio came out to meet us, and put his arm around me. The cop unlocked the cuffs, and Bonifacio sent me inside.

A few minutes later, I heard Bonifacio say, "Thanks, I won't forget it," as he and the cop walked to the shed.

"Anything I can do. Try Davao, and soon," the cop said.

"Watch your back," Bonifacio called after him. He came through the door, closed it, barked orders to a few gang members, and motioned me to a chair.

"Sit down," he said softly. "There are things you need to know." He opened the fridge, pulled out a beer and a Mirinda, and handed me the soda.

I popped the top and took a gulp.

Bonifacio looked at me, pulled the flip-tab on his beer, and drank. He didn't say anything.

"What just happened? How'd that cop know who I was? And to bring me here?" I asked.

"He has informants, like I do; he was expecting someone to come after him, and he was also looking for you."

"I don't get it."

"I asked him for help when I learned Assad was out to kill you."

My eyes widened, "Why would Assad kill me?"

"He found out you killed Ben, and he's furious."

"How did he find out?"

"He has tentacles everywhere."

"But..."

"Because you killed Ben, there's a contract out on you, and I'm so sorry. I had no idea you were linked to Assad then."

I glanced at Bonifacio with a look of panic on my face, because up until now I thought he knew pretty much everything. "But you..."

"I wouldn't put your life in danger! I was in Davao preparing to fight, then fighting and recovering. I didn't know anything about Ben *or* you recruiting with Assad until I came back. Then I learned Ben was in trouble."

I blinked a few times, twisted in my chair, and set my jaw, "I'm valuable to Assad; he's invested time in me. I've always completed my assignments and done everything he asked!"

"You missed killing the cop tonight."

I nodded.

"But Assad planned on killing you even before that."

"Then why didn't he just kill me, after Ben?"

"He probably didn't find out until recently. Then he figured he'd use you for one more job, this one being riskier than most."

"He set me up to fail."

"I doubt it. I'm sure he hoped you'd make the stab. Either way, he'll come after you—the contract is irrevocable."

"What does *that* mean?"

"It can't be cancelled."

"I don't believe this!" I said shaking my head.

"Accept it—he controls his operatives through fear, and makes examples of those who disappoint him. He has no conscience."

"He'll hunt me for the rest of my life?"

"You've got it," he said, taking a long swallow of beer.

I tried to take it all in.

"Why did Assad make Ben kill his family?"

"Ben must have crossed him. Whenever that happens, Assad gets the *whole family*, one way or another."

I choked on my Mirinda, "Do you think Assad knows Chile's my brother?"

"I doubt it. But if he *has* made the connection, he'll hit him for sure. Just to be safe, Chile should go to Davao too. Go to Butuan, and then separate—you shouldn't stay together."

"What about you?"

"He doesn't know about me; he wouldn't mess with me if he did."

I tossed my empty bottle into the trash, shifted positions,

and finally stammered, "About Ben's sisters, and the baby. I... couldn't go upstairs."

"Better not think about it."

"They were my friends... I *have* to know...were they...?"

Bonifacio hung his head and said tenderly, "Two little girls were lying on mats with rag dolls, and the mother was next to them with a baby in her arms. They were probably all shot in their sleep. The gun was on the stairs; there was a silencer. The father was at the top of the stairs. He was shot twice: through the head—and through the heart."

I hated to cry in front of Bonifacio, but I did, a lot.

He sighed deeply, and lit a cigarette. After a while, he held my shoulders and looked into my eyes, "Think of it this way— you helped him." He handed me a wet cloth, and looked at me with compassion. "You *know* he didn't want to live after that. You did what only a truly good friend would do."

"I didn't want to."

"You were tough enough to pull the trigger. It was necessary."

"I miss him."

"Me too. You gave him some of the best times of his life. It was Assad, *not you*, who took that away. Assad is the one responsible."

Then concentrating on the ash of his cigarette as if it were the most important thing in the world, he said, "That was probably the hardest thing you'll ever do. It was the only option. Part of leadership is doing the best thing you can. I don't know what Ben did to provoke Assad, but for sure it was serious. Forcing Ben to kill his family was extreme, even for Assad. You can also be sure that Assad wouldn't let Ben die easy after whatever it was; you had the guts to spare him a horrible death. We didn't ask for life on the streets, but we have it. You *must* be tough." He paused. "You have a great deal of love in you, and the ability to lead." He looked directly at me, "One day you'll lead the *Tibays*."

"What?"

"You are my heir."

Incredulous, I could only think to ask, "What about Chile?"

"You're more focused than he is."

"But he's bigger, and a better fighter!"

"Not necessarily, you will be better. Chile doesn't like responsibility."

"And Assad?"

"It's more complicated now. Hopefully I'll live for awhile, and who knows what will happen to Assad during that time? For now, you have to survive the immediate danger, and now you know what Assad is capable of."

He stood and gave my shoulder a reassuring squeeze.

"What about the cop tonight?"

"He's a good friend, one of the few honest cops. He refused a bribe from Assad."

I took in a slow breath and sat up straight, "What should I do now?"

"Assad stays mostly in the north, and doesn't like Mindanao, so that's where you should hide. Davao is large enough to get lost in."

"Okay."

Bonifacio gathered a change of clothes for me, and put food and a roll of money in a backpack. Reluctant to go, I stalled, rubbing my hands together, "Why did you leave home?"

"I wondered when you'd ask. I left to save our family. I was working with Uncle Anton, and discovered he was stealing money from the company. He put a knife to my throat and said he'd kill the whole family if I told Papa."

"But…"

"He did it to support his cocaine habit."

"No one knew."

"No."

"So you just left without saying goodbye?"

Bonifacio hung his head, "I was afraid of what Anton would do, so I left in a hurry. I wanted to come home and tell Mama I loved her," he choked, "but I couldn't."

"Why didn't you come later?"

"I don't know what lies Anton told about me, but from then on I was an outcast—no one respected me. I thought it best to stay away."

"Mama cried for you," I said.

With that Bonifacio broke into tears, and we both cried.

After a while, he went to the sink and splashed cold water on his face. Finally he said, "When I heard you and Chile were with Uncle Anton, I had to come."

I wiped my face on my shirt, "Why did he kill Papa?"

"Papa probably found out about him stealing money, and was going to do something about it," Bonifacio said, crushing his beer can in his hand.

I ground my teeth.

"Mark, you can't look back—only forward. You have to worry about Assad now. He's a powerful enemy."

"Can't you get him? With the gang's help…"

"He's connected to top officials in government, and extremely well protected. If I made a move against him, the gang would be wiped out in a day."

I made no effort to get up from my chair.

"You need to go; we don't have much time. Assad will do his best to track you down. Don't underestimate him. He knows you're a *Tibay*—he'll be asking around, soon," he said with some urgency. "Here, take this hat."

I put the hat on, and pulled it down over my forehead.

"I'll help all I can. Don't worry—I'll put out word that you've gone north. Is there a safe place Chile could meet you?"

"Um... Tell him to meet me at the Palace of the Toads."

Bonifacio grinned, and hugged me.

I slid into my flip-flops, slipped out the back door, moving slowly through the shadows until I felt safe enough to run, and then kept going, running through streets, then the pitch-dark forest, guided only by the sound of the river, reaching our hide-out in the middle of the night, exhausted.

I settled on the dirt floor, but couldn't sleep, worried about Chile. Lyrics from "Hotel California" tormented me, "You can check out anytime, but you can never leave..."

Hours later, Chile burst through the doorway, and slumped down. "You okay?" he panted.

"We're safe now," I said. "We can sleep."

A fly buzzed erratically around our heads. We tried to ignore it, but it swirled and zoomed with insistence. Chile groped for the stub of a candle, and lit it. We swatted at the fly unsuccessfully, but I finally caught it, grabbing its wings. The buzzing stopped. I looked at its hairy legs, twitching and probing, and then studied its eyes.

"Someone told me there are millions of little eyes in each eye," I said.

"It probably sees everything," said Chile.

"It doesn't blink."

"It doesn't have eyelids."

"If it can't close its eyes, how can it sleep?"

# CHAPTER 25

---

RAIN SLASHED IN SLANTS, by the bucketful, and both passengers and crew bailed water from the boat as we tossed through the choppy waves of the Bohol Sea, and past the southern-most tip of Leyte. The storm slowed and abated as we reached the Mindanao Sea. Chilled, soggy, and exhausted, we went below deck, wrapped in blankets, and slept until docking in Nasipit.

In Nasipit we blended with people around us, apart from our wet clothes, but as soon as the fog dissipated, the afternoon sun warmed and dried them—potato-colored tee shirts, shorts, and farmer's hats pulled down over our hair—we looked like everybody else. We decided on new names, Rodel for him and Bayani for me, which were the first of many aliases. We wanted more time together, so we decided not to split up until we reached Davao. We took a jeepney to Butuan and were the only passengers, so we stretched out on the benches and slept.

We spent a few days roaming Butuan, getting short haircuts and exploring, ending up near a tributary of the Agusan River. It was pleasantly warm, and we felt free and secure. We headed toward the water and heard families of long-tailed monkeys chattering from the edge of the swamp.

"I wonder what Mano's doing now," I said.

Chile shrugged. "PP has malaria."

"Is he in the hospital?" I asked, picking a scab.

"Mickey-Mole's grandma is taking care of him; I gave her some money," said Chile. "I think he'll be okay. I told him about Assad, and that we had to go. He cried, and said not to worry, he'd find us someday."

Chile stuffed his gun and the money Bonifacio gave me in a rocky crevice, and we sloshed through the marsh without further conversation, shedding shirts, hats, and flip-flops, hanging them in the reeds. At river's edge, we tossed rocks over the river and jumped horizontally to catch them before they hit water. We swam further out, and the current pulled us downriver, so when we returned to the shore, we were a few miles from where we'd begun.

We took our time walking back and retrieving our clothes. Chile pulled a joint stub out of his tee-with-a-pocket, and lit it. The ragged photo of Papa spilled from my tee pocket, and I replaced it. Beginning to get hungry, we rushed through the reeds to the rocks where we'd hidden Chile's gun and our money. They were gone.

"*Sumpain!*" Chile shouted, smashing a boulder against the crevice, over and over, "No gun. No money to buy one with! I *need* a gun!" He paced back and forth, and after a while, kicked up some sand, "*Sumpain! Sumpain! Sumpain!*" We sat on a flat white rock, and picked at green moss that had pushed its way into the cracks. Chile lit another joint and sucked it in. "Well, let's go back to Butuan."

Hunger overtook us in the city, and we decided to steal some food. We edged into the back of a restaurant, moving behind a cook too busy to notice, grabbed two orders of rice and vegetables intended for paying customers, and in one motion slid into the alley, instinctively turning in different directions. Suddenly I felt a firm grip on my shoulder. I squirmed, dropping my food. My captor was strong and tightened his hold. "I'm sorry. I only want to talk to you," the man said quickly. "Could I buy you something to eat?" he asked, looking at the spilt food, loosening his grip.

I glanced up suspiciously. The man had short black hair, a face textured like sandpaper, but kindly, creased with well-defined smile wrinkles. He was clean, dressed in a tee shirt, long pants, and construction-worker shoes. He put his arm around me, no longer to restrain me, but as a gesture of friendliness, and I relaxed a little, limping along side him to the street. As we approached the corner, I saw Chile; we locked eyes, and Chile followed cautiously behind.

The man led me to a restaurant. We went in and took seats.

"Order whatever you want," the man said.

"Have you decided?" the waiter asked.

I looked at the menu, and pointed to "shrimp pancakes," "curried pork and rice," and "ice cream."

"So you can read?" the man asked, looking at me with soft brown eyes.

"A little."

"How old are you?"

"Maybe eight."

"Do you usually steal to eat?"

"I *never* steal unless I have to!"

"Do you have a family?" the man asked, his brow wrinkling like the skin on his knuckles.

"No."

"Ever gone to school?"

"No."

"Does that tattoo mean anything?" he asked, pointing to my hand.

"Not anymore."

"You're not from here, are you?"

"No."

I grinned as the waiter placed several plates of food in front of me. I ate greedily with my fingers, while the man sat across the table watching me, smiling, slowly sipping coffee.

"Thanks for the food," I said, as the waiter brought purple *ube* ice cream.

"Would you *like to go to school*?" the man asked, all the wrinkles on his face smiling.

"Um, sure."

*What's the catch?*

"I'm in a bit of trouble with my wife," the man said. "She wants me to find boys to help out at home. The nearest orphanage is clear in Davao, so I was thinking of getting street kids here instead."

I glanced around nervously, until I saw Chile through the window.

"Would you like to live with my family? You'd never have to steal—you'd have plenty to eat."

I looked at my feet.

"I live in Tagum, which isn't too far from here. You could go to school there."

I looked up.

"I need two boys," he continued. "Maybe you have a friend who could come too."

I finally returned his smile.

"Is it a deal then?" he asked, knowing he must have offered the right incentive.

He extended his slab-like hand for me to shake, and I startled at the touch.

"I know my hands are rough," said the man pleasantly, "I'm a carpenter." Then with a twinkle in his eye, he joked, "I work with my hands, not with my feet."

He seemed to like me, and it was mutual.

*At least we'll have a place to hide... And maybe a family?*

⁓⁓⁓⁓⁓

Chile and I dozed in the back of his pick-up truck on the ride to Tagum, the warm breeze soothing our faces. We wakened abruptly as we pulled onto the gravel of his driveway.

The carpenter looked at us fondly, and gestured to the two-story stucco house in front of us, "I built it myself," he said, showing off what he could provide. "It's new. I just finished painting it." We glanced at the cream-colored walls accented by chestnut-brown framed windows on either side of the door, and the flowers flanking the walkway. Inside were a patterned sofa, lots of chairs, a television, and a player piano with family photos on it—the carpenter, his wife and two boys—all of them smiling.

His wife came in and said "Hello," with deliberate courtesy, but that was the closest she ever came to being pleasant. Her teeth were crowded and uneven, with pointed incisors, which formed part of her typically sour expression. She had scowl lines between her painted eyebrows, and soon proved as ornery as she looked. Maybe she was only happy in her photos. When she left the room, the carpenter said apologetically, "I don't have any children of my own. She has two boys from a previous marriage."

He called the boys in. They were both in their teens and not at all welcoming. The first had a perpetual frown, and the misnomer, "Baby Face." Gloomy and scowling, he continued through the front door, slamming it on the way out. The second, Li Li, was pigeon-toed, and his poor posture made him look like a hunchback. He glanced at us without interest, and left the way he came in.

Chile and I woke up before the others, did the dishes from the night before, and tidied the house. The carpenter hurried down the stairs, glowing when he saw us, "I'll be back next week when I finish my job in Butuan, then I'll set you up in school," he said, hugging us on his way out.

His wife came down in a gray cotton robe with black-scribble designs on it, recited our list of morning chores, made *champorador* for breakfast, and called her sons to eat. We came to the table, but she shooed us away, "You eat *after* the family."

Chile and I looked at each other.

When she left to drive her boys to school, we ate.

"It's good a good place to hide out," I said.

"Uh huh," Chile said.

When the woman, short and sharp-angled, returned downstairs in the late morning, she wore a yellow polka-dot swimsuit and flip-flops; her hair was pulled into a careless bun at the side of her head. After she recited an expanded work-list, she stood by the hall mirror putting on pink lipstick, and sat on a blanket in the back yard beneath a standing electric fan blowing at full speed, applying coconut oil at intervals. She read magazines, drank, and dozed outside most of the day, while we worked inside.

When the carpenter came home, he announced that Chile and I would start school the next day, and he'd drive us.

"Not until they've done their chores," said his wife, in a voice full of gravel.

We got up in the dark to do chores, and were eagerly waiting when he came down in the morning. He appraised us with a look of amazement on his face, "Those are the only clothes you have, aren't they?"

We nodded.

"We can wash them," Chile offered.

He laughed. "I'll take you shopping today, and you can start school tomorrow."

Our new clothes felt stiff and itchy, unsoftened by ocean salt, but we were proud to wear them on our first day. The principal asked lots of questions and took us to first grade, where the children sneered at us, teasing us for being so old and still in first grade. But their taunting ended at recess, when a bully from sixth grade demanded our lunch money, and Chile's quick kick to his crotch left him wishing he hadn't.

I liked reading, and was soon at the top of the class.

*When I find my siblings, I can help them more if I have a diploma.*

Chile did less well, barely enduring school, but we both advanced to second grade within a few months. The school schedule stifled us; we hated the bells. Every time it rang we had another class—one after another all day. And rules everywhere—we couldn't even go to the bathroom without permission. And given the chores we had at home, we couldn't do our homework. The teacher wasn't happy.

The clock had become a relentless boss, and bound us to its pace all day. "Stop wasting time," the carpenter's wife scolded when I exercised my knee. We always had to hurry to the next task. "Finish the dishes and get to the store," she said with her usual arrogance. She wasn't happy either.

The only good time was when the carpenter finally came home from work. "My boys, what did you learn in school today?" he said, always calling us "my boys."

"We studied maps. Here's my map of the Philippines," I said.

"Can you show me Tagum on the map?"

Chile and I both pointed out Tagum and other cities on the map.

"I'm so proud of you!" the carpenter said.

When our teacher praised our rapid improvement after only five months, he beamed. "My sons," he said with tears in his eyes, putting his arms around us. On Saturdays he always took us someplace special: the cinema, clothes shopping, hiking, or to buy ice cream. He bought us bikes and taught us how to ride them. Often he took us to his job, and taught us basic carpentry. He gave us all the coins he had, pulling them out of our ears, laughing at our amusement. We walked down the street with his arms around us, and we felt like a family of three.

Baby Face and Li Li were hardly ever home, for which we were grateful, but the woman was harder on us for it. When the carpenter paid us for weeding the garden, she was beside herself. She stood at the door, fuming, "You treat those filthy street kids better than us. You'd better pay more attention to me and *my* boys."

The carpenter was happiest when he came home to see us. He loved buying us candy, encouraging our reading, and going on outings. We began planning a fishing trip, but our excitement irritated his wife. Then one day we overheard him talking to his wife in the kitchen. He said he wanted to adopt us.

"Over my dead body!" she said, sucking air through her cluster of teeth.

"Now there's a thought," Chile said in a subdued Donald Duck voice, "Think of the possibilities…"

The next day she yanked us out of school. "You're too many grades behind," she said, "and way too stupid to catch up."

"We'll try harder," I said.

"No. I've made up my mind; you have work here. Do I make myself clear? You are nothing but *spoiled*," she spit out, looking like a vampire with her bite-ready incisors.

Chile and I glanced at each other. He mouthed, "We've got to get out of here."

A moment later, in our room, he said, "If we tell him about school, he'll be sad, and she'll yell at him."

I nodded.

"If we leave, she won't be so hard on him." He paused and lit a cigarette. "Too hard for everyone, if we stay."

"Let's go tell him." I said.

"She'll lose her temper…"

"Too late; it's already gone."

We both nodded.

"For sure, they'll get into a huge fight," said Chile.

"Maybe she'd lose?" I said.

"Doubtful."

"We could leave him a note…"

Chile nodded, tossing his cigarette to the floor, where it burned a small spot on the linoleum. I wrote a note thanking the carpenter for wanting us, and telling him how very much we loved him, and would always remember him. I drew a heart at the bottom, and tucked it in his tool belt, where *she* wouldn't find it. We left through the back door, glancing through windows as we passed through the garden. The last time we ever saw him, he was sitting on the sofa—tired, unlacing and dropping his work shoes to the floor. It hurt to leave him. The memory of his happy smile wrinkles, gentle voice, and words of encouragement lingered, and tightened my resolve to get an education some day. I wanted to make him proud.

We continued through the backyard, and I realized we'd forgotten to bring in the clothes from the clothesline.

"What do we care?" Chile said, ducking under the line. "Wait a *minute*," he whispered, running back into the kitchen. He came out with handfuls of something. "Hold open the pocket," he said, indicating the wife's gray robe on the line. He dumped in a mound of fish guts, "These should be ripe by the time she discovers we're gone and has to get the clothes down herself!" We both laughed, imagining her scrawny face twisting up like a dirty dishrag.

We found the bus station, but it was closed, so we sat on the bench outside and smoked. We looked at each other. Then Chile said, "Well, there are good families and bad families."

The posted schedule said the next bus for Davao would leave in the morning. "I have an idea," I said. "We could try the bakery. Maybe we could work tonight and earn some money."

"Okay." He paused and said, "Let's not get adopted again."

"What about an American family?" I said hopefully.

"Well, I like American music," and he began singing, "You ain't nothin' but a hound dog, cryin' all the time…" He smiled and sang, "and you ain't no friend of mine."

We made the mistake of cutting through an alley on our way to the bakery. All of a sudden, a few members of the local gang ambushed us. I never saw them, but I definitely felt the board from behind that knocked me unconscious. I wakened to the smell of wet rust and the clank of a lid falling off a metal garbage can, and staggered to my feet. As my vision cleared, I looked across the alley and saw a mangy dog licking blood off the ground. Then I saw Chile lying against the wall—with his face cut open. The cut extended from his temple to his mouth, and blood streamed down his face and shirt, pooling in the dirt. He wasn't moving. I ran over, kicked the dog hard, and knelt down by Chile.

*Dead?*

"Chile?"

*Not breathing.*

He groaned.

"You're alive!" I cried.

"Not so much," he said, wincing with the pain of moving his mouth. He tried unsuccessfully to brace himself against the wall, and nodded toward his arm, "Broken."

"Your face is worse. You need stitches."

The blood on his face was clotting. He tried sitting up straighter, but passed out.

I kicked a cockroach-covered crust toward the dog that waited at a distance for more of Chile's blood. Then I chased him down the alley, shouting, and landed a rock that sent him scavenging elsewhere. I made a lean-to of cardboard as a shelter and hiding place for Chile.

My head felt like a rock-hammered coconut. I was dizzy and disoriented. I tried to find help on the street, but early morning workers ignored me. Finally I had enough clarity to realize I'd have to steal what I needed: bandages, money, and medicine.

*Strategy: not from a store. Can't get caught and leave Chile alone to die. A house where no one's around...*

I ran limping to an upscale neighborhood and browsed, biding my time, watching for opportunities. Finally a taxi drove by and stopped in front of a house up the street. A couple with suitcases got in the car.

*Perfect!*

After they drove away, I circled the side of the house, looking through windows. A maid sat on a cream-colored sofa, feet up, drinking coffee and watching TV. I noticed a mop standing in a bucket of suds at the back, and slipped through the unlocked door without a sound. In the bathroom I pocketed a bottle of aspirin, stuffed a stack of white hand towels under my shirt, and tucked it in. Tiptoeing back into the kitchen, I swiped a stack of money from the counter, opened a cupboard, grabbed a bottle of rum, and edged out the back door, just as the maid entered the kitchen. I ran, anxious to get back to Chile, praying harder than I ever had.

*"Please, God, don't let him die; don't let him die. If one of us has to die, let it be me! I don't want to live without him.*

*Please, God, help Chile! And, God, if you are there, at least get these difficult things over with."*

I jogged back to the alley and up-ended the bottle of rum for Chile. Then I poured some on a towel and began cleaning his wound and the crusted blood on his face.

"Ye...ow!" said Chile, wincing.

Dumping out two aspirin, I downed them without liquid. Then I mashed some into powder for Chile's cut, and sprinkled it along his wound and over his abrasions as he took sips, then gulps of rum. I bought pillows and food, but Chile didn't eat much, staying drunk, throwing-up, and sleeping. When the rum was gone he begged, "Get some drugs!" He burst into tears, but then held back because the salt stung too much, "Pleeease."

Rushing to the street, looking for sellers, I saw two guys about twenty years old in white shirts, ties, and long pants— one Filipino, and the other white as toothpaste—both with hair cut above their ears. They were exceptionally clean and I supposed they were wealthy. I decided on heroin or cocaine, but when I asked, they looked at each other and laughed.

"So you want drugs, do you?" one chided.

"It's not for me; it's for my friend. He's hurt really bad—he has a lot of pain."

They had black plastic tags pinned above their pockets with printing on them. I read the first part, "The Church of Jesus Christ of..."

"Where is he?" the Filipino asked.

"Back in the alley."

"Maybe we can help."

They followed me into the shade of the alley, ducked under the lean-to, and were horrified by what they saw.

"What *happened* to him?" exclaimed the white guy.

"We got beat up," I said.

"Where do you live?"

"Here," I said, indicating the alley.

"Would it be okay if we offered a prayer?" asked the Filipino, kneeling down beside Chile.

"Sure."

"Elder, do you want to say it?"

The white guy nodded, they folded their arms, and he began in Tagalog: "Our dear Heavenly Father, We thank thee for all thy blessings, and especially that of serving here in the Philippines. We pray for thy blessings to be upon these boys. We ask for guidance in how to help them, in the name of Jesus Christ. Amen."

I said "Amen" when the Filipino did, not knowing quite what was expected.

"That wound is bad. We can carry him to the hospital," the white guy said.

"His arm's broken too." I said. "But we can't go to the hospital."

"Why not?" he said.

"It would put us in danger," I said emphatically.

"Okay. Well, we'll do the best we can," he said, examining Chile's arm. "We'll need a splint, antibiotics, painkillers, and butterfly bandages. We'll be back soon."

They returned with a big box of medical supplies and food. The guy with skin like toothpaste carefully splinted Chile's arm as he slept.

"How'd you learn to do that?" I asked.

"I was a Boy Scout."

"Is that a gang?"

"Not exactly," he grinned, carefully cleaning the wound on Chile's face, and closing it with butterfly bandages. "Here's the Polysporin," he explained, squeezing some across the wound, and taping two larger bandages over it. "It's better than aspirin, and won't hurt *nearly* as much." Handing me a small plastic bottle he continued, "Here's penicillin to kill infection. Give him one in the morning and one at night until the pills are all gone. And here's something for pain—two every six hours, with food, if possible."

I must have seemed uncertain.

"That's two pills three times a day," he said, looking directly at me with kindly blue eyes, "Two when the sun comes up, two in the middle of the day, and two before you sleep. Give the food and medicine at the same time."

The Filipino slid the box of food and supplies under the lean-to, and handed me a soda, "We thought you'd like a treat."

"Thank you. I could never repay you for all you've done, but I do have some money."

"Keep what you have. We're glad to help," the white guy said. He hesitated and said reluctantly, "We've been transferred to another area, and have to leave. I'm sorry we can't stay longer," he said biting his lip and looking at the ground. "Here's a little more money to take care of your friend," he said, digging into his pocket and handing me a few bills.

"This is all we have," said the Filipino, adding his money.

"We want to read you a scripture before we go," said the white guy. Then he opened his Bible, flipped through the pages, and read: "Therefore, cheer up your hearts, and remember that ye are free to choose for yourselves."

Then they put some oil on Chile's head, and with their hands on his head, said a prayer especially for him, blessing him that he would recover.

"He's going to be okay," said the Filipino, smiling broadly, shaking my hand.

"He's lucky to have a friend like you," said the other guy, pumping my arm vigorously, "God bless you."

"Thanks a lot."

As they walked away, I cataloged the details of their faces, their clothes, and their voices, committing them to memory, as was my habit with those who showed me kindness on the street.

A few days later when Chile felt a bit better, I ran to Mainit Springs where hot and cold springs converge into a river. I slid into the warm water, soothed by its flow over my body. For awhile I didn't think about anything, and felt a sense of peace. Then I recalled part of the scripture, "Be cheerful... free to choose..."

*I didn't choose this!*

~~~

"Am I really ugly?" Chile said a week later, fingering the scar on his face.

"Ugliest kid I know."

"Pretty scary, huh? Well, good, I'd like to scare some people."

"Not pretty, only scary. Actually, it's a good disguise. You look tougher than you really are."

"Think of the advantages," Chile said.

"And your breath could knock out a dog."

Chile gave me the cross-eyes.

"Are you eleven by now?" I asked.

"I might be." he shrugged, looking up in amazement, "I don't *remember* our birthdays!"

"Well, we could choose new ones."

"Maybe holidays, so we don't forget them."

"I'll take Easter!" I said.

"I want Christmas," said Chile. "How old are you?"

"Around eight, I guess."

"How old do you want to be?"

"I don't want to be eight any more."

There was a procession in Tagum with the Virgin Mary, and we realized it was Easter, so we decided to attend Mass in celebration of my birthday. We were bloodstained, dirty, and ragged, not to mention looking like casualties of war, with Chile's horrifically scarred face, and my limp. We made our way to the church, arms around each other for support, like war-weary soldiers returning from battle. Ashamed to go inside, we sat on the steps and listened to the choir.

"Maybe sometime we could make confession…" I said.

"The priest wouldn't have *nearly* enough time for you," Chile grinned crookedly, crossing his eyes.

"And then there's you!"

"It would take until *next* Easter!" Chile grinned.

"Well, there is *good* news," I said, looking at Chile. "Assad won't recognize you. We won't need to separate."

"No sacrifice too small," Chile said, pulling his hat down over his face.

At the end of the service, families fanned out the door. A small boy, flanked by his father and mother, holding their hands, squealed with delight as they stepped forward together, swinging him up over successive puddles. Someone handed us a few coins, and another a bag of candy; still another gave us combs, bars of soap and shampoo. One man took a double take on Chile, and dug more coins out of his pocket. Then all the parishioners left for home, having done their good deeds. I watched a kid skipping by his mother's side, holding her hand, and wished I could hold *my* mother's hand. I would tell her I loved her. She'd wipe away all my tears, hug me and say, "Happy ninth birthday, Mark!"

# CHAPTER 26

—⟶⟫⟫⟫⟫⟫⟵⟶—

Dark, distended clouds gathered as we entered Davao and walked toward the main part of the city. Night came suddenly. It was dark as pitch and the sharp smell of gasoline assaulted our nostrils. We ducked in a doorway as a fireball whizzed past our feet. Another fireball flashed across the street, zigzagging back and forth, and boys screamed with excitement as they kicked it. A fireball came toward Chile; he punted it down the street, and a volley began. Soon Chile and I were playing "hot-foot" with the locals, and we sharpened our reflexes.

Corrugated thunder rumbled over the sky; rain exploded with a crash. Oversized raindrops hit the ground like detonations, but the kerosene-soaked tennis balls fizzled in the street. We hunched through the downpour to the shelter of a covered market. As the strongest and toughest kids muscled their way to the best places, camaraderie reverted to caution for Chile and me. We separated from the others and found an isolated spot to sleep.

"We'll have to join a gang," Chile whispered, wringing out his tee shirt and wrapping it around his singed right foot.

I nodded.

"Davao is gigantic. There must be lots of gangs."

"What about joining here?"

"We should look around first."

A collective settling took place throughout the market. It was quiet, apart from the usual sounds of street kids. In other areas of the world, there might be freeway or airplane noise that people tune out. But street kids ignore snoring, scratching, stomachs growling, sobbing, moaning, and tossing provoked by restless dreams.

We wakened to pounding rain and stirrings in the marketplace. Water poured down tin roof groves in parallel rivers, combining into waterfalls and cascading to the street. When at last the rainfall subsided to a thud-splat, we ventured outside. Roof edges and palm fronds dribbled; trickle-paths etched down walls and plants, and water puddled and veined the muddy street.

We sucked in air swollen with moisture and headed for the Bangkerohan Bridge, where I'd had my first swimming lesson, toward Mt. Apo where we'd seen Bonifacio fight. While jogging along the muddy Ma-a Road, we came to a long driveway with the sign, "Boy's Town."

"I've heard of this place," Chile said, brushing back hair from his face.

"We could stay here until we find a gang."

"We need protection," Chile said, his long, pink scar twitching.

"Should we check it out?"

The rectangular stucco building was whitewashed, centered in a plot of mud and weeds. A boy opened the door and regarded Chile, staring at his wound. Children sat around battered brown tables, eating. A few boys glanced at us, and a plump woman with a dumpling sort of face came with a clipboard.

"Whatever happened to you?" she asked Chile.

"Just an accident," he said. "I'm okay."

"Where're you from?" she asked, her thick black eyebrows lifting.

Chile hastened to answer, "Tagum."

A boy about Chile's age motioned us to a table and put plates of salted rice and vegetables in front of us. We ate with enthusiasm.

Dumpling-face glanced at the tats on our hands, frowning, "Have you been to school?"

"Oh, yes," I said, "…a little."

Chile nodded, eating ravenously for the first time since the attack.

"You can attend school here," she said, "but you'll have chores."

"Okay," I agreed, wolfing down my vegetables. "Um, does the government own Boy's Town?"

"Oh, no," she said, biting on the pre-cancerous lesion on her lip. "It's privately owned. We have a few volunteers. Everyone works. You two can wash dishes and help the little ones hang out their clothes. After that, you can all play soccer. See that you hose off the mud before coming back in."

"Where'd you get that huge scar?" asked a gaping boy of five when we went outside.

"In a fight," answered Chile.

"Did you at least win?"

"Not that time."

We gave the woman with the clipboard new aliases, I became Lester and Chile became Mykeey. But that night Chile said, "She noticed our tats. We have to take them off."

After everyone was asleep, we went out the back door, through the dirt field, and down the road to the river. Chile lit up. He took a deep suck, pressed the cigarette into his tat and held it sizzling there for a moment, his teeth locked in a clench. The smell of burning flesh filled the air. He quickly relit and repeated the process until the diamond on his hand was obliterated. He thrust his hand, hissing, in the cool river for a few minutes. Exhaling as though he'd been holding his breath, he lit another cigarette, and passed it to me.

The next morning, we walked to school barefoot, with raised red welts on our hands and feet that were surprisingly painful. The tired-looking principal didn't seem to notice. She asked questions about reading and arithmetic and took us to second grade. "You'll start here, and when you're ready you can advance to third grade," she said, forcing a smile.

We went to the second grade barrack but, as in Tagum, the children were younger and smaller than us. The teacher took off her glasses and introduced us to the class.

"You guys must be *really dumb*," murmured one kid.

Chile got up to leave.

"Sit down!" the teacher said, whacking Chile's burned hand with a ruler, which really had to smart. "You boys have the same work as everyone else." She sat down at her desk, and put her glasses on, "Now, children, remember that education makes you grow."

Later I said, "Well, she's awfully short." We laughed, and I went on, "She has a face like a fish."

"And a shape like a frog..." Chile said, tittering.

A few days later, Chile paid a street kid to deliver some flowers to her during class, and she was eager to open the box. Her look when she lifted the lid was something to see. They were Stinky Passion Flowers, and smelled worse than rotten fish.

One whiff shriveled her face and convulsed her whole body with dry heaves.

Students were on the floor laughing.

"Class, class, settle down," she stammered, retching.

We laughed even more.

When Chile and I were alone, I said, "I don't think she suspected you, even though you laughed louder than anybody."

"She doesn't like to look at my face. Another bonus!"

<hr />

A knock on the door came to Boy's Town. A girl wearing a tattered blue dress rushed in carrying a little boy on her hip. "Can you take care of my brother?" she said in desperation, her brother clinging to her neck, sucking his thumb.

"Where are your parents, dear?" asked the dumpling-faced director.

"Soldiers killed them," the girl sobbed.

"What happened?"

"They came to the house, dragged my mother and father

outside… and *shot* them."

"Oh, honey. When was that?"

"This morning."

"I'm so sorry," the woman said, bending down, drawing the girl to her shoulder. "How old is your brother?"

"Almost three."

"He's too young for Boy's Town. We can't take him here."

The girl resumed crying, which in turn caused her brother to cry.

"Don't worry, we'll find a place," she said tenderly, rubbing the girl's back. "What's your name?"

"I'm Chesa, and my brother is Danilo."

"How old are you, Chesa?" she said, putting her ample arm around them both.

"Nine."

The woman nodded sympathetically. "I'll take you to a place where you can stay together. Wouldn't that be better? You'll be all right." Then turning to Chile and me, she asked, chewing the lesion on her lip, "Could you boys come and help?"

No air stirred the suffocating heat. The unyielding sun poured down like hot lava; sweat ran between our shoulder blades, and our clothes stuck as we walked the several miles to the *nipa* hut that had been Chesa and Danilo's home. At last, a volunteer in a rickety pick-up truck joined us, and we loaded the family belongings into the back—a plaster crucifix, bed mats, kitchen utensils, a few clothes, a machete, and a sofa leaking stuffing.

We drove to an orphanage centered roughly in the middle of a dirt field—a two story stucco the color of condensed milk—and churned across a gravel driveway to the cement slab that served as a porch. Pots of aloe vera bordered the door.

A nun in a tan cotton dress met us at the open door, smiling, her brown eyes soft with cataracts and kindness.

"Hello, Mother, how's business?" said Dumpling-face from Boy's Town.

"If my business is children, then business is good. I'm Mother Avita," she said to Chesa and Danilo, bending down to look at them, "And what do we have here?"

The orphanage teemed with more children than furniture. Shaky plastic tables with fold-up aluminum legs lined the room, but there were no sofas or chairs, only wobbly benches near the tables. A faded picture of the Virgin Mary hung on a crumbling wall, a crucifix on the adjacent one. Florescent lights sputtered on the tile floor, revealing a scarcity of toys.

A few nuns in matching tan dresses marshaled the orphans into long lines, and they left for a puppet show.

"You'll be able to go to school, dear," Mother Avita said.

"And won't that be fun," Chile muttered.

"You can sleep up here," Mother Avita said gently. She climbed the stairs in orthopedic shoes, motioning them to follow, "where the women and girls stay. Chesa, it might be best for Danilo to sleep with you for awhile."

Danilo clung to his sister while adults did the paperwork. Chile and I wandered around, and then went out through a small kitchen to the back door, past a *narra* tree, heavy with yellow flowers in bloom. We meandered through a garden of squash, carrots, corn, beets, sweet potatoes, cassava, and green beans, to a basketball standard, and shot hoops.

Mother Avita came out, caught an out-of-bounds ball, and

tossed it to me for one more shot. Her double dimples lifted her mouth into the kind of smile that lasts all day. "It's time to go," she said. "I hope you'll come visit."

Chile and I rode in the back of the pickup truck, our faces lifted to the warm breeze. Evening was approaching, and the cruelty had gone out of the sun.

# CHAPTER 27

ON SUNDAY A NUN IN A WHITE HABIT came to Boy's Town and took us to church. The sun was hot enough to cook a turtle in its shell. We sweltered through Mass and were raring to go, but the priest announced that candy would be given following a short meeting. All the kids from Boy's Town stayed.

A mustached man in a green shirt with long hair and a red headband, named Commander Tito, spoke: "I want you to know the truth about Ferdinand Marcos! He promised to eliminate poverty—by redistributing the wealth. He's done it too. He took our businesses and lands, and gave them to his relatives!"

The congregation shouted and applauded, and he continued, "And now we have martial law! Not only has he ruined our economy, he's taken away democracy!"

He paused until another round of applause ended. "He doesn't care about us. Within the past year, he's burned hundreds of homes, as you know. He's taking it all: our homes, our lands, and our freedom. What more does he want?"

He introduced successive people who told about friends and relatives who'd turned up missing, never heard from again, and people killed without cause even in broad daylight, including street kids.

"He's our country's 'strongman,' all right," the commander said. "He owns the cops, but it's time to take away his power!"

Everyone roared and stomped their feet.

"*Our* mission is to restore honor and goodness to Mindanao. We want to clean up corruption, and we need your help!" He raised his fist into the air and shouted, "We're called The New People's Army—the NPA—and we want you to join!"

Most everyone signed up, certainly all the children. A woman in a green shirt wrote down our names, Gani and Honesto, our newest aliases, and gave us the promised bag of candy. We walked back to Boy's Town, hurriedly licking chocolate as the melt ran over the sores on our hands.

"I wonder what the army will be like?" I said.

"Probably lots of guns, and no *panas*," Chile said.

"And we'll fight against the government—the soldiers and the cops."

"Uh, huh. The good guys against the bad guys."

The next morning, just as we assembled for prayers at Boy's Town, three men burst through the door, "Hide us," they said. "The soldiers are coming!" One man slid between two staff members, posing as one of them. Another attempted to hide his gun as a few soldiers crashed through the door, and shot him on the spot. The third man panicked and ran for the door, but as he reached the threshold, he was blasted with a bazooka, leaving a hole in his chest so vast we could see daylight through his body before he hit the floor.

"Where's the other one?" asked a soldier, shoving the muzzle of his gun into my temple.

"Ran out the back," I stammered, feeling the fugitive trembling behind me, my face burning with the expectation of a bullet.

"Sorry for the inconvenience," said the officer, pointing two of his men to the back door, stepping over the gore at the front. "We'll be back tomorrow and purge this area of NPA rebels."

The soldiers were clueless—everyone in the room probably belonged to the NPA. They dragged the two bodies to their truck and drove away, leaving us to clean up the mess.

⁓⁓⁓⁓

Chile was in detention after school the next day for getting into fights three days in a row, so I walked back to Boy's Town alone. On the way, a pregnant woman stumbled toward me. She was bruised, battered, and bleeding profusely from a cut in her forehead, and both eyes were black, blue, and swollen nearly shut. She was crying and couldn't see her way. Stopping for a moment, she wiped her face with her hands.

I rushed to her. "Let me help you," I said, sliding under her arm to support her. "Where are you going?"

"There, to the pharmacy," she said, pointing with bloody eyebrows.

A man ran across the street toward us, his walrus-jowls flapping with each step.

"It's okay, he's my brother," sobbed the woman.

The man caught his sister under her other arm to lend support, her blood smearing across the shoulder of his white jacket. When we reached the pharmacy, I washed the blood off her face while her brother prepared butterfly bandages. When the wound was bandaged, I filled rubber gloves with ice scooped from the soda chest, tying the wrist ends like you'd tie a balloon.

The man looked at me appreciatively and laughed, "I'm Chico. My wife calls me 'Cheeks,' and so do my friends," he said, patting his walrus jowls. This is my sister, Marta. And what's your name?"

"Um, Honesto," I said.

"Can I pay you something?"

"No, no. Glad to help," I smiled.

"Would you like a drink of *guarapo*?"

"Thanks."

"Haven't seen you around here before."

"No."

"But you live here now?"

"Yes."

The man regarded me thoughtfully, and said, "There's an NPA meeting tomorrow night at my house. Maybe you'd like to come?"

"Maybe."

"I'd like you to come very much—we live in the tan house next door. Come early, and my wife will make you dinner."

But I didn't go. Chile had located Commander Tito and had volunteered us for an assignment the next day.

"I don't want to sleep at Boy's Town where they tell you what to do and when to do it—when to sleep, and when to wake up," Chile had said. So we slept in the field where duty would call the next day.

Ordered to monitor activity on an incoming road at dawn, we were in place as the first sunlight splintered through the trees. We lit our bonfire. Soon we felt a low rumble in the distance, looked through the wet air to the misty horizon, and saw government trucks. As the trucks came nearer, we heaped mounds of green plants onto the fire, changing the smoke from gray to black. That was the signal.

Knowing the NPA waited in ambush only a few miles away, we ran toward them through the field, positioning behind trees, ahead of government forces. Sweat gathered in our elbow creases and behind our knees. The trucks roared by, a few soldiers straggling in their wake. Chile and I low-crawled through tall grass at the side of the road, and came up behind them. One of the soldiers stepped in back of a tree to relieve himself, but as he squatted, Chile eased behind and smashed a boulder over his head. The guy went down like a felled tree. Chile grabbed the gun, and I slid the ammunition belt up over the bloody head and handed it to him, felt along the man's ankle, pulled the knife from its sheath, and tucked it in the back of my shorts.

Further up the road, where several hundred NPA soldiers waited, a downed tree blocked the road, halting the trucks. Suddenly the first truck exploded into bits and pieces. Simultaneously, a staccato burst of bullets shot from the forest. Chile fired successively, killing or wounding perhaps five soldiers.

Close by, I maneuvered behind a soldier and kicked him in the back of the knee. When he stumbled, I grabbed him by the hair, yanked back his head, and slit his throat. As I rose, I saw Commander Tito glancing my way. He gave me the upward nod of respect and confirmed, "No prisoners!"

It was over quickly. We guerrillas scavenged the area and killed the wounded. Chile helped gather weapons, stacked them, and passed a gun and ammo belt to me, keeping a good knife and ammo belt for himself. Three captured trucks, now loaded with bodies, were driven to a well-hidden base camp where the dead were stripped of their shoes and clothing, driven to a remote area, and dumped for the insects and buzzards.

San Miguel beer flowed freely in the town square, after which the townspeople, who made up most of the guerrilla force, went happily back to their homes with newly acquired weapons. Chile and I walked toward Boy's Town, totally pumped. Chile hefted his gun, running his fingers along the muzzle, and said suddenly, "I want to join a gang."

I stared at Chile's scar in the moonlight, thinking it looked like a seam, "Okay."

"I hate living at Boy's Town, and I hate school. I'm suffocating with rules—I can't breathe."

"Where should we go?"

"You should stay, and go to school. You can make it, but I never will. Don't worry, I'll find you."

"Chile?"

"Work hard and you may even get to third grade," Chile said, giving me a playful punch in the arm. "Don't worry, I know where to find you, and I'll visit all the time. Might even send flowers for the teacher."

We walked together for awhile with our arms around each other's necks. But then Chile abruptly patted me on the back, "Might as well go now—I'll come and see you." He flashed a nod of respect and broke into a run.

# CHAPTER 28

I WALKED ALONE THROUGH MUD RUTS. It was late, and dark as an ant's eye. The dull, permanent ache flared in my heart. After a while, I wondered if I was on the right road, but it didn't matter. My beginning tears were interrupted by the grind of an approaching jeep. I wiped my face as the jeep slogged along side, and Commander Tito called out, "Where're you going?"

"Boy's Town, sir."

"Hop in. I'll give you a ride."

"Yes, sir."

"We did well today," he said, twirling his mustache.

I nodded.

"How old are you?"

"Not sure. Ten or eleven."

"You're darn good with a knife."

"Thanks."

"Well trained."

"Yes, sir."

"I need your help."

I lifted my eyebrows.

"Some of us must hide out for awhile, but there's something I'd like you to take care of."

I looked up.

"There's someone who must be killed quietly. Will you take the assignment?"

"Yes, sir. A cop?"

"No, it's a man who lives near here. He's one of ours, but a tremendous liability. He's been warned, but he's an out of control drunk—with a bad temper; he's nearly killed his wife. The thing is, he drinks and talks too much, putting us all in danger. Unfortunately, he's risking our lives; he has to go."

<hr />

I sat outside the bakery most of the night, waiting for my victim to exit the bar across the street, but I got drowsy and nodded off. The rough kick of a policeman wakened me.

"Where's the money?" he snarled, grabbing the knife from my waistband.

"What money?"

"Empty your pockets!"

I turned out my pockets.

The cop shouted, "Where did your friends take the money?"

I didn't reply.

"Let's go," the cop said, as he cuffed my hands behind me, and shoved me into his car.

In the interrogation room, he kept it up: "Why's there blood on your shirt? Where are your friends who robbed the bakery?"

When I said I didn't know anything, he slapped me repeatedly.

"What were you doing outside the bakery?"

"I just slept there."

"You were the lookout."

"I don't know what you're talking about."

"You're lying."

"I'm telling the truth."

"What's your name?"

"Honesto."

"Oh, right. Where do you live?"

"Boy's Town."

"Then why were you at the bakery in the middle of the night?" he asked.

"I told you."

"You're hiding something!" he shouted, picking up a baseball bat.

"I just fell asleep," I repeated.

The cop glared at me. "I know you were the lookout. I want to know where your friends went."

"I don't know anything about it."

"Explain the blood on your shirt!"

I pursed my lips.

The bat caught me on the temple—not a hard blow, but sufficient to knock me to the floor.

I stayed down.

The cop took out his gun. "Get up," he said, grabbing me by my shirt, checking under the neckline for a tat on the back of my neck.

I pulled away. *Not yet.*

"I know you're hiding something, and I'm going to find out what it is."

I slumped into the wooden chair.

"Stand up!" he yelled, taking three bullets out of his gun.

He walked behind me and grasped my still-handcuffed left hand, jammed the bullets between my fingers, and with both hands compressed my knuckles until I shouted, "Stop!" He squeezed again, and I screamed, falling to my knees and begging, "Stop. Pleeeease, stop!"

Suddenly the door burst open, and I caught the drift of just-ironed fabric. A policewoman in a crisp blue uniform came in. "You're way out of line," she said to the cop through clenched teeth, calling another cop to come in.

I stared at my assailant and memorized his features: puffy face, downward wrinkles, a fat ugly mole on his forehead, and a hanging paunch. His beady eyes met mine, and I looked at him defiantly. His eyebrows rose briefly, then flat lined.

*You just put your first foot in the grave, mister. And I'll kill you when you least expect it.*

The policewoman took me to another room and gently cleaned my bloody hand and fractured knuckles. She gave me a bag of ice, and pills for pain. Compressing her lips, she said, "You can go; we caught the ones who did it. You'd better go to the hospital; you can take a jeepney; here's some money," she said, digging a few pesos out of her purse. She looked the other way while I slipped my knife off her desk and tucked it in my waistband.

Whatever she gave me for pain didn't help much, and the memory of my knee pain returned to compound my agony.

*Will I ever be able to fight again? At least this won't stop me from killing Uncle Anton and Aunt Ana. I really only need my right hand, and my knife.*

# CHAPTER 29

ASSAD EASED INTO HIS FERRARI, and slid his sunglasses from the top of his head down over his eyes. He chastised himself for neglecting loose strings. Three contracts vaulted to the top of his list: Dameana, her husband, and Mark. As for the first two, he'd do it himself, on his return to Manila.

Business had kept him busy. There'd been little time for personal vendettas, or even thinking about them. What he knew for sure was that he never wanted to see his house in Forbes Park again. Without doing any research, he'd put it on the market, furnished, and told his agent to sell it immediately. She did, at what Assad knew was an enormous loss to him.

*What do I care? The whole thing is best gotten rid of. Gone. I'll never make a mistake like Dameana again.*

She'd pay though. He considered the best revenge.

*A quick death won't do.*

He drove faster, heading south to Calamba; his heart raced, and he thumped out a rhythm on the steering wheel with his hands.

*She'll get a combination punch—first I'll kill her husband. She'll still be reeling when I bring on the next punch—the baby. One day, when she leaves the brat with a babysitter, I'll be there. I kill the baby and the sitter. Blood all over the place.*

He smiled.

*Then for sure she'll suffer. She'll say, "I should have been there" a thousand times. I'll let her wonder how such misery came to her. Guilt and loss—double tragedy.*

He ground his teeth.

*Then the triple tragedy. I could join her church. I could play that part. First, I'd win over the priest. How hard could it be with a donation? After the priest brags about me, I'll run into her by accident, win her over with profound sympathy and sincerity. She'll be vulnerable. She'll depend on me, and then I'll have the supreme satisfaction of dumping her.*

Assad sneered, accelerating at the apex of every curve, taking them with a practiced sense of cool.

*When the time is right, I'll tell her how she brought it on herself, just before the power punch—her permanent knockout.*

He headed toward Lake Taal, stopping at roadside shop to buy a few flip-open, butterfly knives for some of his recruits. He sped out of the lot, shifting gears, spewing gravel in arcs, high on horsepower.

*On second thought I couldn't stand her that long. Just kill her. But draw out the satisfaction... Film it? Hum, that could be interesting!*

He pulled into a favorite restaurant. The dining room was empty, but the waiter was excellent, and recommended *tawilis,* a delicious fish only found in Lake Taal. Assad took pleasure in every morsel.

*She should have the slow go down. Small knife cuts... death by a thousand cuts?*

He spent all afternoon lingering over food and wine, delighting that he could afford the best of everything. He read several newspapers over successive cups of coffee.

*Batangas coffee. Hard to beat volcanic soil for producing great coffee beans.*

He drove up to Tagaytay Ridge, parked, and walked along the edge. The scene was glorious: the greenery of surrounding mountains broken only by occasional flowers spilling down to the lake below; the sky virtually cloudless—a ready canvas for the saffron, melon, and purple of the setting sun. The crystal blue lake was massive, and magnificent, and out of its center stood the Taal volcano—erect, and smoldering.

*I am* power; *I can do anything I want.*

He'd once planned to bring Dameana here. A cool, flower-scented breeze recalled her fragrance. He had often fantasized about how she'd look on horseback, riding along the ridge with perfect posture. Her silky hair would glisten with the sun's last light, spreading in the wind.

*Catching in a vortex.*

He'd planned a picnic; something put together by Sonia's Secret Garden Restaurant, with fruit and cheese, caviar, and the finest wine.

*Her graceful, long-fingered hands caressing the goblet.*

They'd dine by the lake, served by a waiter with a white linen napkin over his arm. The table would have lace cloth, gold-rimmed china, Baccarat crystal, golden flatware, and red roses.

*Of course, I could still do it. If I could bear the sight of her. Might be worth it. A velvet box with diamonds for that soft neck of hers... put them on her.*

His hands curled and tightened.

*Hands around her neck, adjusting the diamonds...*

A passing truck honked as it rounded the bend, disrupting his thoughts. He looked across the lake at the smoking volcano, and thought of the seething red magma inside.

*Or take a* banca *across the lake and hike up to the crater together. Stare down into the heat. Then...*

He slicked back his hair, and lit a cigarette.

*Then tell her how much she disgusts me, jiggle the necklace and tell her it's made of glass. Cheap, like her. She'll cry, and I'll get pleasure from every tear. Then the power punch: one push ought to do it.*

He pulled back onto the road, spewing gravel beneath his wheels, and headed for The Palace in the Sky, one of the Marcos country mansions. There he'd pick up assignments for Davao, and a great deal of money.

*When I return to Manila, I'll kill the husband and kid, then decide which combination punches to use on her.*

Assad considered more ways to spend his upcoming infusion of cash.

*A home in the Tagaytay Highlands, another in the South of France, another Ferrari...*

He switched thoughts to the business at hand in Davao. There'd be at least two assignments there, and then...

*The hunt will begin. Mark isn't in Ormoc City, so he's in Davao. The gang must be hiding him, with orders from Bonifacio. The fun will be in tracking him down.*

Assad licked his lips and smiled at the surety of besting Bonifacio.

*I could give the assignment to one of my recruits, and take bets on the outcome. Then again, I'd hate to deprive myself of the pleasure.*

# CHAPTER 30

I LEFT THE POLICE STATION, my bloody fingers curled in my palm, crooked and swelling. I cradled in the bend of my right arm. Looking up and down the street, I was dizzy and disoriented. Two prostitutes, maybe fourteen or fifteen, with red lipstick, short skirts, and open-toed high heels came up to me.

"We saw you get arrested," said one, "We know the cop."

"He's not human," said the other, staring at my hand.

I stumbled forward and they caught me. Threading their arms under mine, they supported me as I walked.

"We'll help you," the first one said tenderly, "We have something for pain."

They took me to a pink, two-story stucco house, and helped me upstairs. The last thing I remembered was red toenail polish. I came to, barely feeling the prick of a needle in my arm, and had no idea what they'd given me, and didn't care. I shivered and felt a wave of nausea as the room spun around. One girl placed my head in her lap, continually wiping my forehead; while the other put my hand on a pillow, brought ice, and prepared splints.

*Red fingernail polish...*

The first girl began rocking gently, rhythmically, singing like a mother to her child. Sleep embraced me like a soft blanket. The girl was still humming. I had the most pleasant dream; I was flying above rooftops with Chile. We flew all over Davao, laughing, seeing everything from the air, and exploring the streets. The girl rocked back and forth, back and forth, and the melody of her song lingered on.

*Heroin. No wonder Chile likes it.*

I offered no explanation when I returned to Boy's Town a few days later, and no one asked. My fingers were in splints, and I wore a sling, but the swelling was down. Although my knuckles throbbed painfully, I forced my fingers to move every day, and my hand slowly improved.

While school stayed open, I worked hard, borrowing books and reading late into the night. But the aftermath of the NPA ambush struck hard—Ma-a became a war zone. The school was shut down. Many villagers were killed, and many disappeared. Soldiers and cops automatically shot anyone not in uniform with a gun, including children. I stayed at Boy's Town, but was bored and antsy.

I decided to fulfill my commitment to Commander Tito. This time, I waited outside the victim's house after dark, and finally the guy staggered along home through the vapor of moonlight, drunk, not noticing me—conspicuous though I was with a sling.

It was easy, just a quick stab and slit. The man shouted out and fell to the ground dead. His wife came running and dropped on the body, sobbing. She didn't see me.

*I need to lay low for awhile, and change my name; no more Honesto. I need protection.*

I returned to Boy's Town where I dug up my gun from my hiding place, tucked it out of sight, and left without saying goodbye. With no destination in mind, and not knowing how to navigate the huge city of Davao, I found a street that spidered off in many directions, and chose one at random. Eventually, I found myself in the heart of Davao, and began to explore, looking for the best gang to join. In a matter of days, I found three: the Agdao, the San José, and the Bangkerohan. After careful consideration, I decided on the San José gang: the area was wealthier, the kids seemed to dress and eat better, and besides, weekly fights were held there, in case I could ever fight again. That was my best option. But I didn't do it.

Paradoxically, I reached San José and kept going, like a train unable to make an unscheduled stop. I had momentum that required me to continue on to where I thought Chile might be, in Bangkerohan.

My heart leapt when I found him—in the middle of the action, of course, surrounded by kids in animated conversation. I wove through the crowd and caught his eye, and we ran to each other and hugged. He pulled me into the circle, smiling broadly, "I see you're playing hooky."

"That would be it."

"You came at a good time—we're about to have some fun."

Retaliation was brewing against a University of Mindanao student who'd made the mistake of berating gang members. A few boys had shadowed him and knew his routine. Now they lay in wait, standing around smoking.

"I missed you," Chile said, hugging me again. "Come and watch."

When the student's class ended, four or five boys, including Chile, walked toward him as he crossed a crowded intersection, abruptly bumping him, as two others unzipped his backpack and stuffed in a sausage string of firecrackers, leaving the fuse trailing out. Another boy lit it. When the firecrackers started exploding, the poor guy thought he was being shot, and hot-footed as if a machine gun was firing at his feet, jumping all over the place. He fell to the ground screaming, rolling through the dirt and oil of the street. When he realized the shots came from his backpack, he tried desperately to yank it off, but the straps were tangled with those of his fanny pack. He fumbled frantically, twisting up the ties even more. Meanwhile, people gathered around laughing—a good many of them members of the Bangkerohan gang.

When the excitement cooled, I found the gang leader and asked to be initiated.

"Got money?" he asked.

"No, but I'm a good fighter, and I can get some," I said.

"*Hay naku!* That's great, but I was kidding. You don't need money. We don't even have initiations."

I lifted my eyebrows, looking at Chile, who nodded confirmation and shrugged.

Life was much more fun away from Boy's Town, and the gang much different than the *Tibays*. At night, Chile and I roamed the San José area with our new gang, lacing strings of firecrackers through the toes of sleeping boys, dipping the long ends in gasoline, lighting them, and watching the fun.

Sometimes we could only imagine the results of our pranks, like when we found boys who sleeping soundly, usually ones who were stoned, and shaved bald spots, or something even more imaginative on their heads. Then the other thing: once we managed to slip a few drops of methylene blue in their drinks. I wish I could have seen their panic when they discovered their urine was blue!

At night we hunted rats with *panas*. Our four-inch nails were marked with distinctive colors so we could count who shot the most. Our finest moment was when Chile and I raised our slingshots simultaneously, and nailed a cat-sized rat in mid-air, our colors side-by-side.

〰〰〰

Physical therapy paid off: I found that by stretching and strengthening the lateral and medial muscles surrounding my injured knee, that I had total mobility with only a slight limp, and very little pain. My fingers finally healed, although with knobs where the fractures had fused.

Eventually I felt able to fight. Chile and I went to gym in San José for the weeklies where each contestant fought successively until only one was left standing. We entered and won. From then on, we entered every week, and our combined winnings paid for training with a master. We were back.

But one night as I slept alone on a street corner, I sensed someone approaching and abruptly opened my eyes. Bonifacio was standing there. I felt a surge of confidence in his power, certain he'd come to protect me. He motioned me to follow, put his finger on his lips signaling silence, and we eased past sleeping kids, through shadows, and hurried along a dirt road up a hill. His stride was lengthened, and I anticipated an emergency. We came to a small house, and I followed him inside with some urgency.

"You're in danger," he said. "Assad's in Davao—he's come for you."

"Why does he care so much about *me*? I'm *nobody*!"

"The contract."

"It's been a long time."

"Irrevocable."

"*Still* after me?"

"The word is, he'll get you no matter how long it takes."

"But I move around so much..."

"If I can find you, so can he, just not as quickly. Of course, it's hard for anyone to keep up with your aliases. Now that he can't find you at school or Boy's Town, he's looking on the street, but his connections to the government make him unpopular; street kids won't talk to him, and that slows him down."

"Do you think Chile's safe?"

"Since you've changed names again, and Chile's unrecognizable, I think he should be, especially if he isn't seen with you. But you *must* split up."

"What about Ormoc City?"

"There's a whole network watching for you there."

"How does Assad even know I'm alive?"

"He knows you're in Davao. When he heard about the stabbing of the NPA guy, he started poking around, asking questions. The killing was done in his style, and he thinks you did it. Also, you were seen with the guy's wife."

"His wife?" I laughed, "Not possible."

"Assad thinks it was you."

"It wasn't."

"The way I heard it was you helped her get away from her husband," he continued, looking at me intently.

"Not me."

"You took her to Cheeks at the pharmacy?"

"Oh, that. I didn't even know her. She was all beaten up. I only..."

"This means they're hot on your trail. You've got to leave quickly. I've got clothes for you."

"So that guy was *her* husband?"

Bonifacio nodded.

"Where should I go?"

"There's only one safe place. I'd suggest hiding for two or three monsoons, and if he can't find you in all that time, hopefully, he'll think you're dead."

"An island?"

"You should stay with the Ibo Tribe in the mountains."

"The cannibals?"

# PART TWO:

# HIDING

# CHAPTER 31

EVERY FILIPINO KID LIVES IN HORROR OF CANNIBALS, but I'd heard things on the street that would terrify anyone. It's said they like their meat fresh; they keep a person alive as long as possible, cutting off one body part at a time. While live victims slowly became quadruple amputees, the torsos are maintained to keep major organs alive. Even then, they only cut off what's required for the next meal. Naturally they prefer the softer flesh of children.

Yet trusting Bonifacio's judgment, I set out with a guide he hired to navigate the nearly impenetrable rainforest, deep in the mountains of Mindanao, where tribes still live isolated from civilization.

*I'm really quite brave.*

It was a slow go; we chopped through difficult terrain for perhaps ten days, one plodding step after another. The guide didn't say so much as a word, communicating only with a few gestures. He was of mixed descent, more tribal than Filipino, and was inexhaustible. He was tall and thin, and all sinews. I had just the view of his ropey calves as we climbed.

*His only fat must be in his earlobes.*

Day after day, we slashed and climbed, sleeping but briefly in our hammocks at night, not stopping to eat. Every so often he cut a length of water vine, coiled it, and placed it high in my backpack, with an end draped over my shoulder so I could sip at will. Periodically he chucked a hunk of dried meat or fish over his shoulder, or handed off fruit, or a bunch of begonias to eat.

We'd crossed a river and had just scaled a steep bank when I first saw the cannibal chief. There he was—standing on the ridge, blood running out of his mouth, dripping down his chest. He looked at me and spat a wad of flesh on the ground, grinning with bloodstained teeth. I panicked, and glanced toward my guide. He was gone.

*Alone. With the cannibals.*

I trembled from head to foot. The chief broke into a long belly laugh, patted my back, and prodded me up the hill. I glanced around and considered my options: I was significantly outnumbered, and I knew I couldn't find my way back without a guide.

*They've got me.*

It took several days to reach the village, mostly uphill. We went through a wet gully lined with tree ferns, where mosquitoes whined through the air, their legs trailing long and straight behind them. I pulled myself up mossy waterfalls, grabbing Cogon grass that shredded my hands. Between the grass and thorny vines of the forest, my body had cuts all over.

*And mosquito bites.*

I must have been eleven or twelve. I have no idea what year it was, but monsoon season was due. We hiked through a swampy area and climbed a muddy bank. My knee was painfully swollen. Exhausted, I sank to the wet ground, the cannibals sitting on fallen logs around me. My legs began to sting, and I slapped them, as though swatting mosquitoes, but was repulsed to feel slime on my hands. Two-inch leeches covered my legs—burrowing into my flesh. They'd come out of the ground anticipating the monsoons: brown, slick, and hungry for blood.

*Mine at the moment.*

Instinctively I tried to pull them out, but it didn't work; they just stretched thin, or broke off. The chief laughed. He came over and poured salt on them; then the fat slimers backed out.

*Fat with my blood.*

The chief continued to laugh.

*Still plenty for him.*

The chief was in a state of celebration.

*Thinking of me for dinner.*

We kept walking, but I was burning hot, and worn out. I slumped down on a fallen tree trunk. The children were curious and stared at me, often giggling. The chief's machete slashed down on the trunk next to me; I saw it coming, and rolled to the ground. The chief chuckled, and then hacked to the center of the rotted wood, exposing thousands of grubs. The kids scooped them up with their hands and shoved them into their mouths.

*Appetizers.*

The chief looked at me and laughed again, as though reading my mind. We resumed hiking on a path I couldn't make out, but that was clear to them. Only adrenaline kept me going. The chief motioned to a jagged rock twenty feet away, and the children pointed to a cobra that was making pass after pass against the rock, scraping off its shed. We moved in slowly and saw its cloudy-gray eyes, blind until the old eye-scales pulled away. It was hungry, not having eaten during the molting process, and flicked its tongue, searching for food. A rat scurried nearby, while a long, skinny snake slithered over the rock. The cobra went for the snake, swallowing it headfirst.

*Preferring to eat its own kind.*

I plodded ahead, feverish and faint, mechanically putting one foot in front of the other. I staggered a little and someone took hold of my arms to support me. I don't remember what happened next.

***

Hundreds of hungry cannibals surrounded me, drooling blood. They grinned with orange-brown teeth, salivating over my body parts, sliding their rough hands and arms under my back and legs, and under my neck and head. I struggled but couldn't get away.

*Where are they taking me? Why do they keep dunking me in water? Washing me before putting me in the pot!*

Terribly thirsty, I tossed around on a sweat-soaked mat. A woman knelt by me, pouring water from a coconut shell into my mouth. She wiped my forehead, and poured cold water through my hair.

*They're making a cut in my skull, to keep me alive as they eat my brain—scoop by scoop.*

Water flowed over me, and I was trussed up in a net. I thrashed around trying to get the net off, but then felt cold. My teeth chattered, and I couldn't stop shivering. I was wrapped tightly.

Then I got hotter. I was dripping sweat, extremely hot, and my head was exploding. My eyes were hot rocks ready to pop out of my head.

*I'm being roasted on a stick. I'll be dead soon.*

I heard someone moaning.

*Did I kill my aunt and uncle?*

There was a *carabao* (our word for water buffalo); I climbed on his back and rode to the top of the canopy. Mama was in a clearing, waiting with outstretched arms. She held me, told me I was safe, and sang the old lullaby: *"Sana'y di nagmaliw ang dati kong araw, Nais kong matulog sa dating duyan ko, Inay, Oh! Inay."* I melted into the silky bliss of her arms.

I woke up in a hammock, covered with blankets, feeling good. A woman funneled sweet liquid into my mouth with a leaf; another trickled liquid from the cut of a sweating branch into my eyes. A little dog snuggled under my arm, nuzzling and making puppy sounds. I had on a hemp tunic, and it was dry. All the cuts from Cogon grass and thorns had healed, and my knee felt better than usual. My hair had grown, and my fingernails were longer than they'd ever been. I was thinner.

*I'm so hungry.*

Three women smiled down at me. I smiled back. Confused, it took some time to realize that I'd had malaria, and the chief's wives had cared for me. I'd picked up a few words during recovery, and when they brought me soup, I managed to say "thank you" in their dialect of *Manobo*. They were delighted, giggling and petting me, and from then on competed to see who could feed and teach me the most.

They led me to an enormous, round, communal hut lit by resin torches. The tribe sat around a fire in the middle—dressed in brightly colored tunics of cotton or hemp, and barefoot. They wore beaded necklaces, bracelets, nose rings, and multiple earrings. A good-natured old man was talking in a soft, singsong voice, and everyone laughed at what he was saying. Children with stained teeth smiled at me, and were delighted when I nervously smiled back.

Women passed out betel nuts, and everyone chewed them. The introductions began, and I soon felt more at ease. Each person said his name and I repeated it. But I couldn't pronounce their word for "chief," and every time I tried, they laughed. The chief danced around imitating me, and the more I tried, the more they laughed. Finally the chief said, "Always call me that—because, oh, yes, it makes us full of joy."

For some reason, they called me "Ti," which was a private joke with them.

*Might be a recipe.*

Udol was the oldest of Chief's many children, probably a little older than me. Tall and muscular with shiny black hair down to his shoulders, he was good-natured and smiled constantly, like his father. "Udol, you will be helpful to Ti," Chief told him.

# CHAPTER 32

I HAD DOUBLE WORRIES: that the tribe might eat me: and that I couldn't navigate back to Davao on my own.

*Better make friends.*

I opened my backpack. Everyone was intrigued with the zipper, crowding around to watch as I demonstrated how it worked, laughing as I said, "zip," and "unzip," their language apparently not having a "z" sound. Fascinated with the sound, they buzzed around like bees, and all practiced zipping and unzipping my zipper.

I got out the balloons I'd bought in Davao, and blew them up for the children. They'd never seen any, and stood in line for them. Several kids came multiple times, but it turned out they were sharing with adults. They had a hard time blowing them up, so I usually did it for them. Amazed at the colors and shapes, they rubbed their finger-pads across them, enthralled with the squeaking. Then they poked them, making dimples that disappeared. The first time one popped, everyone jumped back, and stood open-mouthed, laughing nervously. So I blew one up, popped it, and laughed, and then they did too.

I rubbed Udol's balloon over his hair a few times, raising it arm's length over his head. His hair stood straight up. It was a pretty good trick, and they were duly impressed. After that, I blew up a balloon and didn't tie it—letting it fizz all over the place. Both children and adults ran around in crazy circles, imitating the action and the sound.

Afterwards, I got out Chief's tribute—a 12 oz. can of Coca Cola. I popped it open, making another new sound for them, and made a drinking motion. Chief shook the can slightly, and bubbles frothed over the top. He stared at the foam and extended the can to arm's length, showing it around. He took a small taste, lifted his eyebrows, and swished the liquid around in his mouth, fully savoring it, and swallowed, smacking his lips, grinning with pleasure. Then he passed the can. Each person took just a tiny sip, so everyone could try it.

It was dark now, and resin torches lit the sleeping huts and the perimeter of the round communal hut. Large copper pots hung over the fire in the center, and something was simmering. I glanced at the closest pot.

*I could fit in there.*

I peeked over the edge.

*Full for now.*

Using a combination of words and gestures, Udol told me we were having monkey stew. He looked at me and laughed, along with quite a few others.

Suddenly rain poured over the thatched roof in torrents— the monsoon had arrived. Since the perimeter wall was only three feet high, with open-air above, the communal hut became the core of a massive surround of crashing water, and we were inside a magnificent waterfall. We shouted as loud as we could but couldn't make ourselves heard through the thunder of water. I thought of Ben and PP shouting behind the waterfall during my first boar hunt, and wished they could see this one, especially how beautiful it was with the torch lights from surrounding sleep-huts streaming through.

Nights were unexpectedly cold because of the high altitude. Udol came and draped a brightly colored blanket around me, curled up in a blanket with two of his sisters and their pet monkey, and sat next to me, reminding me of Ben, surrounded by his sisters, riding down the stairs on a pillow. My reverie was interrupted when the little puppy pounced me, licked my face all over, and burrowed under my blanket making circles and settling, unknown to everyone but me, like an ace in the hole. I named him Ace.

Everyone was affectionate: children and adults constantly kissed and petted each other, huddling around the fire, cocooning in blankets with babies and young children. Girls caressed each other's hair, finger-combing it for hours. Mothers breast-fed their babies or someone else's. A few women took mouthfuls of water from *carabao* horns, and held newborns to their lips, so the babies could suck water from their mothers' mouths. Women with fingernails black from dyeing cloth sometimes continued their work in this cozy setting: picking seeds from cotton, combing and twisting cotton into yarn, or weaving colorful designs on their handlooms.

The monkey stew was served in coconut shells and scooped with seashells. It was actually quite good. But what I loved, and could never get enough of, was fried flatbread, made with manioc flour, dipped in honey—the best of comfort food.

Then the storyteller began. He told stories almost every night, with many repeats, which helped me learn their language. Here's one of the tribe's favorites:

"Once a young man from a low-valley tribe entered our camp carrying a large bag of rice. After chewing betel nuts, as was the custom, introductions were made, and the traveler presented the rice tribute. He had quite a story to share. Many seasons ago, while hunting far from home, he saw a group of women gathering stones from a river. As he watched, he noticed one in particular. She was incredibly beautiful as she looked up at him and smiled. He decided to visit her tribe.

"He took a wild boar as tribute to the chief and stayed many days, because his mind was set on taking the young girl to wife. At last, he asked her father what the bride price would be, and was told that no fewer than four heads were required. The young man was appalled, as headhunting had been abolished in his own tribe for several generations. He offered alternatives to no avail. He even appealed to the young girl, offering colored beads and a *carabao* hide in place of the heads. To his amazement the girl refused his offers. She stood firm. In fact, she even began to shout insults, taunting him in front of the whole tribe, making slurs on his manhood. He was driven out of the village with stones thrown by the girl's family.

"Two days later he found the girl alone in the forest. He called to her, and when she saw what he carried, she hurried to him. He presented her with a heavy bloodstained sack, which she quickly accepted. She was filled with anticipation, extremely proud that he had wanted her *that* much, and she pulled open the sack with great ceremony, thinking about her moment of glory when she'd repeat the motion in front of her whole tribe, especially her family. She grabbed the bottom ends of the bag and emptied it—and out rolled the heads of her father, mother, and two brothers!"

Upon learning enough *Manobo* to understand the story, I laughed along with everyone else. With repeated telling the story became even funnier.

There were, however, shrunken heads topping the entry posts to the village, which were more scary than funny.

*If Uncle Anton and Aunt Ana could see me now!*

Udol had a twin named Udelen, who had been on a salt-harvesting expedition. His party had located and harvested a particular type of bamboo, burned it, covered the ashes with water, and waited for it to evaporate, leaving a residue of salt. This was such a long process that monsoon season came upon his group unexpectedly, and they stayed with a lowland tribe until the rain let up. So Udelen was gone for the best part of six months, and during his absence, I became good friends with Udol. This was to cause me some grief.

They were identical twins with opposite dispositions. Udol was cheerful, usually smiling like his father; Udelen was cranky, and almost never smiled, especially at me. He certainly didn't look kindly on what happened the first time we went spear fishing:

All three of us headed for the river, but Udol and I took the lead, rushing to our favorite spot, automatically falling into our routine. Udol waded through a section of water, driving fish toward me, and I speared them as fast as they appeared, seldom missing. We had a comfortable rhythm. Sometimes we tossed ripe fruit across the surface, and as fish jumped for it, we speared dozens and dozens in synchronized movement. Our baskets were brimming, enough fish for the whole tribe, with many more to salt and dry. With an unspoken gesture Udol and I packed up our catch and headed back to the village, arms around each other, laughing.

Meanwhile, Udelen was left to his own devices, and had pitifully few fish in his basket. Udol and I reached the communal hut, and saw Udelen trailing behind. He glared at me with such intensity that I knew we'd gotten off to a very bad start. I climbed the steps behind Udol, and as he reached down to give me a hand up, I swayed a bit to the side, just as Udelen threw a rock at me. It grazed my head.

Udol kicked at Udelen as he climbed up, inadvertently making contact. Blood gushed from Udelen's nose; it was broken. He jumped backwards off the steps, and stomped off, holding his nose.

"I'll go help him," I said, jumping down off the stairs.

Udelen's tracks were disappearing in the trailing bits of monsoon rain, but I saw that he'd gone beyond a near-by sleep-hut. As I rounded it, he clobbered me with a soggy log, sending me to the ground. I awkwardly rolled over and got to my feet, slipping and sliding in the mud. He threw a weak punch, and I reacted with a quick triple-combination, knocking him out.

*Not helpful for his broken nose... or his jealousy.*

Rain brought him around fairly soon, but I decided to give him time to cool off, and went back to the hut. He followed shortly after, scowling, keeping his distance.

After dinner, Belayum, the fortuneteller, began predicting futures with betel nut spittle.

He looked at mine, and said, "There is big tragedy."

"For me?" I said.

Udelen came closer.

Belayum signaled, "wait" with his hand. Concentrating, he said, "Death..."

Udelen moved in.

Belayum's forehead creased, "but not yours."

"Do you know who?"

"Maybe, it's hard to know, maybe someone close to you, but not you."

"Where will I live?"

"I will look."

"Possibly with us?" Chief asked hopefully.

"Oh, quite possibly, Chief. Let me see," Belayum continued, stirring the spittle. "It is not certain."

The old man continued, "but you will get very, *very* old!" pausing and nodding his head.

The tribe clapped.

Then came the punch line: "It is because you will have only *one* wife," he said.

The men who had multiple wives laugh hysterically.

"*Pobrecito*," Chief said to me with mock sympathy.

Udelen hissed.

Linguistically skilled, Chief couldn't get enough of being taught new words and phrases in Tagalog, mixed with words and phrases of Cebuano, Spanish, Visayan, Letenio, and a little English. He delighted in keeping the jumble of language that I spoke, just between us, like a secret code. As much as we enjoyed this bond, Udelen hated us speaking in language that excluded him.

~~~~~~

Sometimes we had rats for dinner. Hunting them was one thing, eating them quite another. I only liked the hunting part. Ace and I were a team: he would sniff them out, and when he chased one into its hole, I got a kick out of shouting "Ace in the hole!" which was also a private toast to my dead poker-playing friends—Juan, Soft-Serve, and Ben.

Over Udelen's objections, since it used to be his job, Udol asked Chief if we could trap roosters. Chief grinned, "Oh, yes, Ti likes chicken more better than rats," and he winked at Udol and said to use the rooster I'd named Cockscomb Crowsalot. We leashed him, found a clearing, tied him to a tree, and set up snares around the perimeter. Of course, Crowsalot didn't like being tethered and almost crowed his head off. When the wild roosters heard him, they came to fight, and were caught in the snares, and for awhile we had roasted roosters, and not so much middle-of-the-night crowing.

# CHAPTER 33

UDOL SHOWED ME A SELDOM-USED WATCHTOWER on high stilts at the
perimeter of the village, and I began sleeping there. Too small
for more than one person, Ace and I went up alone, sometimes
even during the day. I enjoyed time alone, but also hoped that
if the twins were together more, that Udelen would get over his
resentment.

I tried to restrict my time with Udol, but he made it clear
that he preferred me to Udelen, and he persisted in honoring his
father's request to look after me. Udelen countered by disre-
specting me in small ways, usually under the radar: he'd hide
my spear, blame me for something he'd done, or even spit on
me when no one was looking.

Chief always made an effort to insure harmony. If one of his
wives was out of sorts, he found a way to make her laugh, even
by pulling funny faces or doing silly dances. He settled disputes
among the young ones with playful wrestling. Almost every

night he danced around the fire, dancing circles around me, laughing as I tried to learn. He must have noticed some friction between Udelen and me, but probably chalked it up to Udelen's petulant nature. He encouraged everyone to dance.

Then came the talent shows. Especially during the monotony of monsoons, everyone participated in shows with songs, impersonations, body painting, beading, and quite often weaving. One night, one of Chief's wives displayed a beautiful orange blanket, blushing as she eagerly shared credit with her husband, since the dye was made from jackfruit roots he brought home. Then one of Udol's sisters showed the shed of her pet tarantula—the shed proving her spider had been well fed. A few children sang while someone played a nose flute.

Then an uncomfortable silence settled, and all eyes were on me. "I don't have any... talent," I protested, thinking how cool it would be if Chile were here to imitate Michael Jackson and do some moonwalking. But Chief and Udol elbowed me forward, so I clowned around, balancing a coconut shell on top of a bamboo pole, hopping around the fire.

Just as they thought I was finished, I handed the pole to Chief. Everyone gestured approval, apart from Udelen who walked past me growling, "He's not *your* father!" I continued, "Keep it steady for a moment," and Chief made a big deal of balancing the coconut shell. I pretended to walk away, but then with a spinning back kick, knocked the shell across the room and outside so fast that no one knew what happened. They wanted an encore, so I did it again, slower, and followed with a martial arts demonstration.

My new assignment was teaching kickboxing to all males, and Chief quickly released me from all other responsibilities.

Even three-year-olds lined up to learn. I taught everyone to bow with respect at the beginning and end of each session, as they would to a proper master, and they loved the ritual, except of course Udelen, who refused to bow, at last drawing a response from his father.

"Udelen, you should bow."

Red-in-the-face, Udelen dared to defy him, "No."

But Chief shouted: "Udelen, show respect to Ti!"

Udelen grudgingly bowed.

*Better not teach* him *too much.*

The only time Chief seemed allied with Udelen was when I got teased about cannibalism: they were both entertained by my discomfort, as was the entire tribe. One night, though, I learned what I needed to know. We were sitting around the fire when an old man recalled the time when the Philippine government decided to enforce laws against cannibalism:

"Food scarce and tribe hungry. We travel to Davao and ask permission to raid other tribe, 'just this once.'

"Davao say, 'No.'

"We invade other tribe anyway."

The old man smirked as he continued, "Something surprising, Davao never punish us…" He looked at me, closed his eyes, and moaned with pleasure, "If you think boar meat good," he said, licking his lips, "you *love* human meat!"

I must have been on the anemic side of pale. Udelen flashed me an especially hateful look, and whispered something to the kid next to him. Everyone looked at me.

I shook my head, and shuddered.

*My muscles would be tough and chewy, not a bit good.*

Everyone laughed at my distress.

Later they passed around betel nuts, and everybody chewed all evening. I began to feel strange. My face went kind of numb, and I felt high. For the first time I paid attention to the blood-like saliva dribbling from their mouths, and occasional spitting.

*It's not blood I've been seeing! It's betel nut juice. And what they spit out isn't flesh, but chewed-up pith!*

Observing my epiphany, Chief rocked back and forth with deep belly laughs, almost shaking the whole mountain. I think all the highland creatures knew his laugh. Everyone realized I wouldn't be frightened about being eaten anymore. I laughed from relief, and the others because they'd kept my fear going for several years.

---

Chief bragged about my talent, frequently relating the story of the time Udol and I were cornered by a boar. Told around the fire many times, it's quite certainly a legend by now. This is how Chief told it:

"We went on hunt up-river. Udol and Ti, they chased Lina's Sunbird, and followed it long time. After they lost sight of it, they decided to find place to sleep until tribe caught up.

"They hiked under vines to flat lava rock by river, which seemed like good spot. But there was surprise: from out of no place, boar charged Udol and almost came to rip him open. Oh, yes.

"But just in time, Ti fancy-kicked boar, and knocked him down. The boar fell on its back, trying to run with its feet in the air. Udol had time to use his spear."

Everyone laughed and cheered.

But Chief had the last word: "We need weapons, but Ti, he can just kick him to death."

~~~~~~

When game became scarce in the mountains, we hunted in the lowlands, this time without Udelen. We reached our destination, and settled for the night.

Curious about my family, Chief wondered why I didn't live with them. "Where is your father?" he asked, easing into his saggy hammock.

"He's dead." I shifted in my hammock, which hung next to his. Then to my astonishment, because I never talked about it except to Chile and Bonifacio, I confided, "he was murdered."

"Oh, yes... Mine too," said Chief, "near to here."

I was embarrassed—so caught up in my own tragedy I hadn't considered that he might have one too.

He went on, "Killed by Moro (ethnic Muslim) soldiers. Their training camp is two days from here. I was little boy and my father took me hunting in lowlands. They ambushed us, and killed everyone right away. Oh, yes."

"How did you escape?"

"I was chasing a sailfin lizard up-river in pond, when I heard shots. I hid under bushes and wet leaves."

"How long did you stay under the leaves?"

"Too long. Oh, yes. Until dark. I was finally coming out, but then smelled tobacco smoke, and covered back up. The only thing I saw was orange light of cigarette through leaves. A soldier sat on log near me, smoking. Insects tortured me, but I was not moving. After a long time, soldier threw cigarette down. I started scratching, and wanted to run. But soldier lit up again, so I stayed. Insects pretty much eating all of me. After very long time, man left. I crawled to pond to relieve itching self, and heard something big sliding down tree... coming to ground. It said my name... I put my head underwater, and held my breath. But when I came out, I heard my name again."

"Ay."

"It was old man from tribe who was in tree before Moros came. When he heard guns, he stayed up there. And, Ti, I was *most* glad to see him."

I turned in my hammock. "And you probably needed him to guide you back to the village. Could you have found your way back by yourself?"

"Of that I am uncertain. Maybe no. I wanted to go quickly, but old man said we needed tokens of our dead."

"Everyone else was killed?"

"Oh, yes. We snuck back down river. My father had holes in chest, and there was plenty of blood. I took his spear, and his blowgun, and darts. Then I took off his necklace. I cried many times looking at his face. I wanted to go after soldiers and kill them right then—my life didn't matter. But old man said, "You Chief now.""

"Are you wearing your father's necklace?"

"Oh, yes, Ti. I wear it always," he said with pride. He slid his hand under the necklace and shook it slightly. "Tomorrow I show you."

"I know it. It's made of *carabao* bones, and it has black seeds, red pods, and green feathers."

"Oh, yes!" Chief said, pleased that I knew it so well.

"Then what happened? Could you bury your dead?"

"That bad thing. We could not risk tree burial because soldiers too close. I cried until we got to village. Then I was Chief, and could not show tears."

"Did you want revenge?"

"Oh, yes. Moros deserve to die. They shoot tribal people for sport."

"What if all the lowland tribes joined you? Maybe an ambush at night..."

"Lowland tribes are big problem too," Chief said. "They fight with Moros because they take Muslim belief."

"What if some of the high mountain tribes banded together?"

He mused, "One time five tribes struck Moros at night, but lost quickly." He squirmed around in his hammock. "Moros have guns, and they good fighters."

"I know what you mean. In my tribe in Davao we fight bad leaders. We like to recruit Muslims because they fight well and aren't afraid to die." Tossing scat into the fire to drive away mosquitoes, I asked Chief if the tribe wanted revenge.

"Revenge is tradition. Oh, yes..."

"Would they go against you?"

"When I say no, they obey. I am *Chief*."

"Haven't any other tribes tried to get revenge?"

"Oh, yes..." Chief said. "The tribe of Sanduku captured ten Moros and ate them," he chuckled with satisfaction. "But maybe only a story..." He shook his head and clicked his tongue as if to say, "Too bad."

We both laughed.

And then becoming serious he said, "Revenge is not good thing—our tribe would be destroyed." He paused, and then continued with authority, "This is better way. At present time, I have peace in heart, and people happy."

〜〜〜〜

The first night after our return, Ace's barking startled me from a deep sleep, just in time to see a snake slithering toward me. It was a pit viper, and extremely deadly. I jumped up, grabbed it by the middle, and tossed it over the side. Someone was descending the rope ladder with a basket, and then ran; it looked like Udelen. My resin torch only lit the top part of the ladder, so I could have been wrong, but I doubted it. I couldn't go back to sleep. For the rest of the night I patrolled the small platform of the watchtower, shuddering with the prospect of the snake climbing back up. Ace patrolled the perimeter, sniffing every inch. That species of snake was not indigenous to this elevation, and when it got light I found Udelen's lidded basket near the bottom of my rope ladder. Now I saw Udelen as a real threat. No longer satisfied to disrespect me, he wanted to kill me.

# CHAPTER 34

———⟫⟫⟫⟫⟫———

IT WAS A CURIOUS THING. I loved being a part of the tribal family; yet the very happiness I experienced with them also exacerbated my sense of loss. My own family was elsewhere, or what was left of it, and I felt increasingly empty. I felt a mounting urgency to return to Davao and reunite with my brothers.

*Has Assad figured out that Chile and I are brothers? Probably.*

I knew Assad could ultimately find him. Chile's appearance was altered all right, and he was sure to have an alias, but his habits were unlikely to change. He had many friends, some of them casual, and one could inadvertently give out the very scrap of information that would give him away.

Thankfully, Bonifacio was extremely hard to get to. I knew he'd protect Chile if possible, although he wasn't in Davao often—only occasionally for the monthlies. But then I worried that his frequent checking up on Chile might backfire, exposing both of them to danger. Of course, if something had happened to Bonifacio, it would be my responsibility to lead the *Tibays*, a thought I didn't want to consider.

I chafed at the postponement of killing my aunt and uncle. My thoughts gnawed and gained dimension. Theirs would be a different killing than happened between gangs, in wartime, or for Assad. They weren't a threat. Their murders would be premeditated, motivated solely by revenge, poles apart from what I'd done before.

*But I* will *do it.*

After about three years with the Ibos, I assessed my position. I might need to hide in the rainforest once again to evade Assad, or even to lay low after killing my aunt and uncle, and now I had the survival skills to do it.

My body had changed: I was taller, and muscular in a different sort of way—longer and leaner. My mothers had applied poultices to my knee; I'd stretched and worked it daily, and my limp was completely gone. Hopefully, I'd become someone Assad wouldn't recognize.

I craved a competitive fight, but was no longer fit for martial arts. Apart from teaching moves to the tribe, I hadn't trained, used weights, or done any serious sparring. Although I had walking and climbing stamina, I wasn't a good bet for a series of fights. I desperately needed to train.

*Time to go back.*

I was conflicted. I was comfortable and happy, cared for and nurtured, adored and respected. Chief was my surrogate father; I loved my mothers, and Udol was very much my brother. On the other hand, the escalating threat of Udelen, missing my family, and wanting to take care of unfinished business with my aunt and uncle, were strong motives for leaving.

*I want to stay, but I have to go.*

So I did the difficult thing quickly: I told Udol and Chief that I planned to leave early in the morning, and then immediately went to my watchtower so they'd have no chance to protest. I slept very little.

I wakened to see everyone gathered for a farewell. My mothers took multiple turns hugging me, crying, and loading me with food for the trip. The whole tribe followed me to the edge of the village, decked in their most colorful clothes, jewelry, and beaded headdresses, singing, playing nose flutes, and drums. There was a moment of silence as men and boys bowed their respectful goodbyes to their martial arts master. Udelen refused to bow. But he did smile.

Chief made a great ceremony of presenting me with a *carabao* horn, and said I should remember my mountain family whenever I drank. He gave Udol the honor of escorting me to Mt. Mindol, and tearfully patted my shoulder many times, holding Ace so he wouldn't follow. My heart was heavy as we started out, especially when Chief tearfully called out, "Oh, Ti, Ti... Goodbye, my son!"

I backed away from the village, waving and weeping. Udol put his hand on my shoulder and we began hiking downhill, accompanied by a small hunting party. The tribe resumed singing, and their voices stayed with us, lingering in my heart.

We traveled through miles of rainforest all the way to Mindol Mountain that we'd climbed the year before. "This most important place," Chief had said. "From top we see many places. We call it name of my father, Mindol." He'd pointed to where we'd been, and to where we were going.

Udol and I separated from the hunting party at the base of the mountain and began our ascent. Apart from the usual birds and simmering of insects, the climb was quiet. Relaxed with our friendship, we didn't need to talk. As we hiked, a cool breeze sighed across our path. It was one of those perfect days: the air was fragrant, clean and refreshing, and we were both energized and content. Time was irrelevant, and there was no threat, absence of food, sickness, pain, or worry of any kind to spoil it.

It didn't last. We came across a wounded Moro officer who'd wandered for days in the rainforest, having been separated from his unit during a field exercise. We found him sitting on a ledge, gazing at the ground, hopelessly lost. Without water and enough food, he was thin and suffering from loss of blood, altitude sickness, and delirium. His exhausted eyes looked like open sores. Udol and I applied a poultice to the wound in his side, gave him dried fish and water, indicated a course to the river, and sent him on his way.

We hiked in a switchback pattern before stopping to eat. Somewhat later I was napping before undertaking the lava scramble at the summit, when a subtle disturbance of air jolted me to full alert. Then I heard the same soldier's voice talking to Udol, who couldn't, of course, understand him. It seemed the officer was lost again, suspicious of our directions. His voice became increasingly loud, angry, and hostile. "Stupid infidel!" he shouted, fumbling at his gun, aiming at Udol.

But he didn't have time to pull the trigger; my poisoned spear was already in the air.

"You can be useful," Udol exhaled moments later.

I grinned at him. Then I bent down, yanked out my spear, tore a patch off the soldier's uniform, took the knife, gun and ammunition belt, a wad of money from his pocket, and then rolled the body over the ledge for the forest to swallow. Udol watched with his jaw dropped, and shook his head, amused to see this side of me.

When we at last reached the summit, we sat down and looked around on all sides, back in the direction of the village, and forward toward Davao, not speaking, enveloped in a sense of love and harmony. I handed him my spear, on which I had burned the names of my siblings: Isabel, Bonifacio, José, Francisco, 2 Tall, Chile, and Segundina.

"I want you to have this; I won't need it anymore."

"Maybe until you reach lagoon?"

I patted the soldier's gun tucked in my waistband.

Udol leaned back, "Maybe gun shoot your foot," he said.

I showed him how to load and shoot. Having plenty of ammunition, we chose targets, and Udol finally overcame his trepidation and had some fun shooting. Postponing our parting, we used the whole gun belt of bullets.

"Give this to Chief," I said at last, handing Udol the patch torn from the officer's uniform. "Tell him it's small revenge for his father."

"Will you please to tell him yourself?"

"No, my friend."

It was time. I knuckled Udol's arm, not looking at him. I turned abruptly, and began chopping a path with my machete to the stream on the other side of the mountain. I knew he watched until I was out of sight, and then I let my tears flow freely. But after a while, I smiled, thinking about good things, like the time Udol and I found a mountainside of smooth rock, with sun-warmed water flowing over it; the round soft sound of running water cascading into a swimming hole where we'd swum and played for hours. We'd gone back many times, one time being more memorable than the others: women of the Nubu tribe were bathing, using ashes for soap—but it wasn't the ashes that were amazing. It was the first time I'd actually thought about women being naked under their clothes.

Recollections flooded my mind—the scent of frangipani, the smokiness of the communal hut, the magnificent waterfall, and the cool mountain air. I missed water-vines, cyanide centipedes, grub-filled logs, betel palms, and the challenge of climbing mossy trees. I craved the comfort of flat bread and honey. I felt like sitting under fig trees where monkey hunting was good, surrounded by the superlative colors of birds, frogs, and flowers. I could hear the clear river rush, the soft padding of soggy leaves underfoot, the puff of a blow gun, the wobble-wave of a spear in the air, bird songs, the rasp and creaking of crickets, the chime of tree frogs, and Udol's little sister singing to her baby monkey, rocking in her hammock.

Then there was Chief's laugh—I imagined his great belly laugh reverberating through the hills. "Follow river to the lagoon," he'd said. "Crocodiles will be hatching soon. They be making sounds like 'Umph, umph, umph,' before they come out of their eggs, so they all hatch together, and some will live after predators come."

Every night I made a fire, tied my hammock, and slept fitfully. After several weeks I finally reached the lagoon. It was evening and bats looped and soared overhead, eating moths, mosquitoes, flies, and gnats in full flight, their shrill sounds echoing all around. A mother bat skimmed across the water, drinking as she went, holding her baby in the pocket of her curled tail. I felt lonely.

Daybreak came with the sun's slanting rays over the next hill, and I set my course toward it—east—toward Davao. But then I dawdled.

*What's the hurry?*

Dew evaporated from flowers, and leaves followed the sun. I sat, leisurely drinking water from my *carabao* horn, and thought about Chief, Udol, and my mothers. Absently, I touched the underside of a nearby leaf, and felt dozens of soft grape-sized eggs just beginning to hatch. Tiny caterpillars chewed out of their shells, then ate the rest of the shell, needing the strength of their home before going out into the world.

# CHAPTER 35

———◆·⋘⋘··◆———

DAVAO HAD CHANGED, or maybe it was me. Clouds of gnats buzzed around my head. I felt vulnerable in the open spaces of rice paddies and cornfields, uneasy without the safe surround of forest. The sun glared without benefit of shade, and the air hung heavy with insecticide. Shanties with corrugated steel roofs appeared in the distance, separated by muddy lanes, and dirty children lined up at a hosepipe to drink. Before I even got near I smelled the stink of poverty and violence.

*How can people live like this?*

The honking of horns grated my nerves, warning me to shift awareness. My radar was set to monitor the threat of insects, poisonous plants, boars, and cold. Now I had to worry about people.

*I've come to a savage place.*

Abruptly I turned my back to the city. The fragrance of flowers called me to my tribal home. I longed for the safety of mossy mounds made fertile by hundreds of years of volcanic eruptions, and the security of mountains. I yearned to hide and nestle in the warm cleavage of hills.

*Are my tribal mothers crying for me?*

Distracted by the "bek-bek-bek" of a giant Philippine frog, I reacted as a hunter-gatherer, reaching into the crevice and catching him. He was stocky and green, with little yellow flecks and warts all over. His wide mouth curved upward, creating the illusion of a smile; yet he peed in fear, and turned dark in my hand. I walked over to a large sun-spangled pond, put him near the water, and watched him change back to green. He leapt in, and concentric circles spread.

I dove into the center circle—disrupting the pattern—and swam across the pond. Mushy mud squished through my toes as I got out and sat at the edge. I rinsed off my feet, turned from the beckoning arms of the forest, switched thoughts, and walked with resolve toward Davao.

I entered the city cautiously, staying away from Bangkerohan, and everywhere else I'd known well, avoiding people, not speaking unless I had to. I eavesdropped everywhere, but didn't learn anything about Chile, and knew that looking for Bonifacio in Ormoc City was out of the question. While this strategy kept me under the radar, it didn't help me find my brothers.

*First I need a job.*

I applied for work at the first nice restaurant I came across, owned by Roy and Wuta Tsuya. "I'm an orphan, a good worker, and don't require much money," I told them. They smiled and asked me to come on a trial basis.

By that night my job was permanent. I liked them immensely, and the feeling was mutual. They had heavy epicanthic folds above their eyes, giving them a venerated aura of wisdom. Roy was short and slim, with a preference for white shirts, like my father. Wuta was shorter than her husband, petite actually, and had short black hair that curved forward on her face, covering her large pearl earrings. She was soft spoken and mild mannered, easy to overlook. I only noticed her when she shook her head, and the unexpected luminosity of her pearls caught my eye.

The couple worked well together but they'd never had children, and ran the restaurant with inadequate help. Adding me to the business was the remedy. I worked smart and hard, and their business increased. They gave me many responsibilities and more than reasonable pay. Soon I was assigned produce shopping, which necessitated driving. Roy enjoyed teaching me to drive on little-used dirt roads and empty streets at night, and also schooled me in car repair, as time permitted.

The car was a battered blue four-door, and a few more dents wouldn't have made much difference, but I felt honor-bound to take good care of it. The traffic of the city was scary. I was nervous, and the stress of screeching brakes, swerving, and cars veering onto sidewalks kept me alert.

I felt well disguised in the car with my hat and sunglasses, and fairly safe. During the next few months I got into a shopping routine, driving to the bakers at dawn, continuing around the city until late-morning, always keeping an eye out for Chile and Bonifacio. But there was not so much as a hint of them anywhere, and I was losing hope. I looked down San José Street at the mirages of water on the asphalt, iridescent as a Lina's Sunbird, and just as fleeting—traffic soon wiped them out.

*Is the goal of finding my brothers an illusion?*

I heard a bird cooing to my right and smiled: to the Ibo's, a bird cooing from the right was a good omen.

*I just need to know exactly where to stand.*

I had just finished shopping and was loading my groceries into the car, which was parked on the sidewalk, when I happened to glance up the street. A familiar limp caught my attention. The man was just ahead of me, moving briskly.

*That's—it has to be—Master David?*

In my excitement I called out in the Ibo dialect of *Manobo*, but the man turned anyway, adjusted his glasses, and I looked into the welcome face of my master.

〰〰

We heard the music clear down the street—the Bee Gees were singing, "How Deep Is Your Love?" The door opened, and there stood Bonifacio, sweating, a towel around his neck, and just past him, Chile, bench-pressing double his body weight. We rushed into a huddle-hug, heads touching, with our arms around each other's necks.

"We thought..." Chile began, but apparently thinking better of it, said, "It's good to see you!"

"You were gone so *long*," said Bonifacio, wiping his cheeks.

"You turned out all right—even handsome, you dog!" Chile said, checking out my body.

"Lookin' good," Bonifacio confirmed, feeling up my abs.

"I can't stay," I said, hesitating as they clung to me. "At least tonight... I have a job. In fact, I have to go. They need me."

"We're training for the monthlies, and I'll be here for several months. Chile too. Come stay here," Bonifacio said. "It should be safe."

They followed me to the car, talking all the way.

Master David didn't stop smiling, but as man of few words, said only, "Your limp is gone!"

"Assad isn't around," Bonifacio said, "He's usually in Ormoc City or Manila. In fact, I haven't seen him here since you've been gone. He avoids Davao, having cut his ties to Islam and his family. There's a rumor his mother still walks the streets of Davao looking for him; she still can't believe he just left..."

I opened the car door.

"You keep getting better looking," Chile said in his Donald Duck voice.

I started the car, smiling, and pulled away from the curb.

They followed, still throwing out bits of news.

"PP's been in Davao for the past year. He stays at the orphanage, but we hang out..." Chile said.

"Come back tomorrow..." Bonifacio said.

"Quit your job!" Chile shouted, running alongside the car.

I drove through the city, weeping, tremendously relieved knowing my brothers were alive and well, and thinking what a good friend Master David was. I hurriedly finished shopping and drove to the restaurant, reliving memories all the way, energized and excited. As I unloaded the groceries, my thoughts turned to PP.

*He must be fifteen or sixteen by now, hard to imagine.*

My lips pursed; I smiled and shook my head.

*Of all the surprising survivals—the frail, sickly one.*

I considered how to quit my job.

*If I could train someone to take my place it wouldn't be so hard on the Tsuya's. If only... PP? Now, there's a happy thought: PP, terrified, driving through downtown Davao, shakin' like a wet dog...*

⁓⁓⁓

He was taller, still skinny as a twig, with jaundice-yellowed skin, and noticeably fewer freckles. He ran across the dirt yard fronting the orphanage and jumped into my arms, his legs around my waist, weeping without shame, smiling and sobbing, putting his scrawny arms around my neck, "I missed you!" We climbed the steps to the porch, two-at-a-time, arm-in-arm, as though no time had passed.

"Ay, I've been here before," I said, glancing at the potted aloe vera plants on the front porch.

"Did you live here?" PP asked, holding his arm down for Mano.

"Only visited."

"Everyone's gone to the cinema, and they won't be back for awhile."

"The nun," I asked, "what's her name?"

"There are five or six of them, depending on the day."

"Is there someone in charge?"

"You probably mean Mother Avita."

"That's her. I met her."

"She's been here the longest."

"Is there a girl named Chesa? She had a brother..."

"Chesa died several years ago, but Danilo's here."

I nodded.

"You look thinner," PP said. "Are you going to muscle-up for the monthlies?"

"I don't know… I want to train, but first I have to find someone to take over my job. I work at a restaurant. Would you like a job? Of course, you'd need to learn how to drive."

"I need a job, and I have restaurant experience… Um, drive?"

"*Oy*, it will be just like when you were boar-bait. You'll be bug-eyed and pale as a *gweilo*, entering a five-way intersection with a gasp sounding like your last—astonished to get through alive."

"When you put it like that…" PP laughed.

"Hey, you don't cough anymore."

"Whatever it was, I seem to have outgrown it."

"That and your freckles," I said with affection, putting my arm around him.

Mano jumped onto my shoulder, checking for lice and chattering, doing his bit to catch up.

*

PP was hired on my recommendation, and I showed him the ropes, but he worked hard and soon exceeded expectations. He especially tried to please Roy and Wuta, and they loved everything about him: he was without guile, uncommon for a kid who grew up in the streets, and had his funny ways that made them laugh.

It was only a few months later that Bonifacio, Chile, and I all celebrated PP's sixteenth birthday at the restaurant. Wuta was exultant handing him their gift—a paper tied up like a diploma. PP couldn't imagine what it was, and held it for a moment without opening it. We urged him on. It had a stick figure drawing of Roy, Wuta, PP, and even Mano. PP dutifully admired the artwork, and his eyes wandered to the note at the bottom, which he read out loud, "We want to adopt you. Will you be our son?" Before he finished reading it, he choked up, and continued to sob every time he thought about it—officially joining a family—people he loved, who loved him! "At my age!" PP said. The hooded eyes of Roy and Wuta teared up. It was the best kind of party. We all practiced saying "PP Tsuya," and told him he was Japanese now, and really should learn the language.

〰〰〰

I moved in with Bonifacio and Chile; we changed apartments, and I joined them for intensive training. Motivated to work hard, we set up a rigorous schedule. Before breakfast was long-distance running, this time with a pacer-dog running behind us, nipping at our heels. Later we lifted weights, and did sprints up and down the stairs to disco. We ate, napped, and then practiced martial arts with Master David in the evenings.

Master David remained the paradigm of fitness, as disciplined as ever, which was contagious. He still wore his favored white tee and pants, and his hair in a ponytail. Graying at the temples, he wore a strap around his head to keep his glasses in place. His movements remained precise and graceful.

Bonifacio was an incredible fighter, and credited his success to Master David. I'd never seen anyone better and told him so.

"You can write my epitaph," he smiled, and changed the subject, "Chile will fight this month. He has a gift—he's naturally big and strong and comes on like a bulldozer—his opponents have to be able to take a punch."

I nodded, "And *he* can take a punch." Then, quoting from "Rocky," as was common on the street, "It's about how hard you can get hit, and keep moving forward."

"That would be Chile, alright," Bonifacio said, "He routinely comes back from the dead."

Chile did a zombie-walk into the kitchen, and pulled sodas from the fridge, "Wait 'til they see my little brother!"

We sat around the table, drinking sodas, and Bonifacio said, "Mark, you should plan to enter soon. I'm pleased with your progress—you've become much stronger, and have exceptional speed and strategy: strength, speed, and strategy—a trifecta to bet on!"

There couldn't have been better motivation for Chile and me. "We're going to rock the monthlies!" Chile said, and we hit knuckles.

Bonifacio said, "You know, we should do some hiking, take a little vacation. Why not climb Mt. Apo?"

Chile and I raised our eyebrows.

The climb took four days, but our pace was slow and relaxed, and we enjoyed the time together. The greenly fragranced air became light and cool. When we camped, Bonifacio demonstrated his knife-throwing skills, holding the blade between his thumb and index finger, some times even flipping the knife in the air before hitting the target.

"You'll see when we get back," Chile said. "He can take fifteen knives hidden on his body, and hit fifteen bulls-eyes in a minute's time."

"Could you teach me?" I asked.

"It's just a matter of practice," Bonifacio said, demonstrating another throw.

Without doubt my several years of spear chucking helped, because I was a quick study, soon throwing with speed and fairly consistent hits. Chile was content to watch.

"Could we add knife-throwing to our routine at home?" I asked.

"We'll have to find a secluded spot," Chile said, already anticipating the entertainment.

"Too bad we can't go back to the Palace of the Toads," I said.

Chile smiled his crooked smile, and I hardly noticed that half his face was badly scarred.

In the late afternoon I taught them how to make off-ground shelters with bamboo poles tied with shredded palm-pith, none too soon, as snakes would be coming out to hunt. Bats flapped their leathery wings in pursuit of mosquitoes; we heaped our fire with whatever scat we could find. After a while, other nocturnal animals stirred—rodents, frogs, and a rare tarsier.

Bonifacio knifed open a can of beans, which we shared, passing it between us. "This will give us something to do to-morrow…" Chile quipped.

"Oh, goody, do I get to be trail sweep?" I said.

We made a fire, then coffee, and lapsed into silence, contentedly sipping, taking pleasure in the bond of brotherhood we had to deny elsewhere.

# CHAPTER 36

—◆∙∙∙∙∙∙∙◀—

ASSAD HAD LOOKED FOR A KID WITH A LIMP at every place of illegal kickboxing he could find, and he'd offered a substantial reward for anyone knowing Mark's whereabouts. He'd hired private investigators in Ormoc City and Manila who turned up nothing.

He'd worked with police in Davao investigating all murders done in his style within the last three years, and had identified fourteen such murders, but Assad had commissioned them all. No one with Mark's description had a left leg limp, and most amazingly, no one had come forward with *any* information about Mark, not so much as a false lead, despite the reward.

Three years ago, Assad had questioned many, but all he'd found was the *possibility* of a link between Mark and the killing of the pharmacist's brother-in-law. Everyone he'd interrogated seemed unaware of the details, apart from the police, who had meticulously described the knife wound in their report, which was consistent with Assad's method.

His detective in Davao had heard a *rumor* that Mark was seen with Bonifacio in Davao two or three years ago, but not since. His final report concluded that Mark was probably dead.

Assad didn't believe it.

He knew people often lied to him, and he was certain someone was hiding Mark. Gang loyalty was nearly unbreakable, and he resented the fact that he couldn't buy it. Convinced that Bonifacio was involved, his jealousy mushroomed. Yet the search was at a standstill.

*He can't stay hidden forever.*

<hr />

Assad switched to his next bit of unfinished business. His investigator in Manila gave him a well-researched report on Dameana's husband, and he was astonished to learn that her husband was Chinese, and thirty years older.

*What could he possibly have that I don't have?*

The guy owned an import-export business, and along with Dameana, traveled frequently between London and Manila. She was currently at their London apartment with their son, and he was in Manila. Assad's red Ferrari was too conspicuous, so he rented a ten-year-old black Lincoln and drove to find their house.

*Forbes Park, of all places, not that far from the house I bought for her.*

He drove past the security kiosk after another car, waving to the driver as if he knew him, and accelerated up the hill, disappointed by the diminished horsepower. Different. He had a sudden realization: killing Dameana's husband would be different also, not just another job. He tried to calm himself.

*Don't think about who. Just how.*

According to the report, the guy had exacting habits when Dameana was gone: he left his office at the same time, had dinner with his in-laws, and was home by nine o'clock without fail.

It was eight-thirty. The street was quiet, dark, and misty, without a moon. Assad parked the Lincoln near the top of the hill, walked leisurely down the path, and slipped over a wall into the unlit backyard. He banged his shin on a swing set, tripped over a soccer ball, and swore under his breath. He found the back door and picked the lock.

The draperies were drawn, and a few lights were on. He glanced around, and looked at the piano. It was a small, somewhat battered upright, and couldn't compare to the black lacquered grand that he'd bought. He sneered. A framed photo of the family at the beach was on the piano. The husband looked even older than expected, with fully gray hair. The kid had Dameana's looks. In the photo they were all laughing.

*Not for long.*

Assad rifled through a roll-top desk, pulling out a checkbook.

*A half-million dollars in checking. Not that much.*

He tucked the checkbook in his shirt, and then found receipts for regular hundred thousand dollar deposits to two other banks, but the account books weren't there.

*Maybe he keeps them at the office. I'll find a way to have the government confiscate their money. A domino in the Dameana go down slow..."*

He climbed the stairs, and found himself in a small sitting room, then a wide hallway. He entered a bathroom with a blue bathtub and a bin full of water toys—a pirate ship, rubber duckies, and bathtub finger-paints. On the rim of the tub were bottles of No Tears Shampoo, children's foam soap, and bubble bath.

He found the kid's room, painted pale blue and decorated with airplanes. There was a full bookcase, filled with well-thumbed children's books, and a bulging basket of toys. The chest of drawers was covered with stuffed animals, and a giant teddy bear was on the bed. Taped on the wall were crayon-scribble pictures.

He wandered back into the hallway and saw family photos all over the walls, dozens of them. He looked carefully at Dameana's husband, and was puzzled.

*So much older. And so involved with the kid—in his arms, on his shoulders, together in a bubble bath, side-by-side at the piano…*

Assad glared down to the end of the hall: *the master bedroom.* He went in, and saw the king sized bed.

*Where he sleeps with her. Touches her.*

He clenched his jaw, felt for his knife, and rushed downstairs as he heard the turn of the key. The front door opened, and he was face-to-face with Dameana's husband, who jumped back upon seeing the intruder. He was shorter than Assad, gray-haired and wrinkled around the eyes. He wore an expensive suit in silver silk, a yellow pima cotton shirt, and a bright yellow and silver silk tie. He composed himself, and looked carefully at Assad.

Assad said, "Do you know who I am?"

"You're Assad, Dameana's former boyfriend. Why are you here?"

"Curious to see who she thinks is better than me."

"It's not like that."

"You moved in on her pretty fast."

"She was afraid of you."

Assad stiffened, "So you took advantage…"

"She needed help, and I helped her."

Assad was red in the face, and the veins in his neck stuck out. He shouted, "You're old enough to be her father!"

"I'm an old family friend. Look, Assad, you left her in a bad way."

Assad rushed forward, "Now it's my fault? You *filthy* hypocrite!" He plunged in his knife and raked it upward, "*No one takes what's mine!*" He wiped the bloody knife on his victim's pants, and tucked it back into his waistband. Dameana's husband fell, gurgling out his last words, "The child is yours."

Assad lingered, staring at the dead man in disbelief.

*My baby?*

*So that's why she married so fast…*

*Why didn't she tell me?*

*Well, I don't want it…*

*Or a family…*

*Or her!*

# CHAPTER 37

—━━◆◆◆◆━━—

BONIFACIO WAS IN GOOD FORM—strong, quick, and confident. His veins layered over his well-defined muscles like filaments of lightning. His first two fights were easy and didn't take long. The third fight was more of a challenge, and he got cut along his right eyebrow, but Master David stopped the bleeding, and Bonifacio fought the fourth contender, winning decisively. The audience cheered.

The fifth fighter was scary at six-foot-three, at least five inches taller than Bonifacio, with a fifty-pound weight advantage, a longer reach, and fists the size of grapefruits. He came on strong, but Bonifacio dodged his blows. The match was fairly even for the next fifteen minutes, and both fighters remained uninjured, although they were shooting sweat like dogs shaking off water. Those betting were tense, each cheering for their champion. Bonifacio landed a lucky combination punch that stunned his opponent, and advanced with a rapid-fire finish. The crowd roared, encouraging him to go for another. Master David signaled with an even hand for "you decide."

"He's getting tired," Chile said.

"His cut hasn't reopened... He's going to take another one!" I said.

Bonifacio smiled at the audience, raising his arms in victory. His hair hung wet against his back. Glistening with sweat, his pumped muscles were impressive; he danced around the ring, excited for another fight.

His sixth opponent was strong and fresh, but Bonifacio's adrenaline had momentum, and he beat the guy, although it took thirty minutes. Now he was exhausted.

Master David rechecked the cut over his eye, gave him water, and made preparations to leave. The next contender, who had approached trembling like a high wire in the wind, was ecstatic that he didn't have to fight Bonifacio, and happily made his way to the ring for a lesser challenge.

Bonifacio looked at the crowd. They were chanting his name, stoked by six good fights. It was the middle of the night. Suddenly he spat out the water, climbed back in the ring and thanked his fans, glowing with success, and shouted that he'd fight one more. The crowd roared. He shouted, "Seven's my lucky number!" and rolled his shoulders.

Perhaps not seeing Master David's "thumbs down," indicating he shouldn't fight, Bonifacio nodded to the other fighter in recognition. His opponent was mediocre; Bonifacio must have thought it would be quick and easy. The challenger paled; we could smell his ulcers from ringside.

Bonifacio hit him hard in the face, knocking him down, and then smiled and danced around the ring. The guy staggered to his feet and threw a weak kick that knocked Bonifacio down.

"Enough. Stop!" Master David, Chile, and I shouted in unison, alarmed that such a soft kick had sent Bonifacio down.

But he probably couldn't hear us over the roar of the crowd as he jumped up, "No one can beat me tonight!"

And then came the moment in time that changed everything. As soon as Bonifacio was on his feet, his opponent threw a roundhouse kick. Bonifacio saw it coming and moved back slightly, but the kick was fast and the guy's foot caught him on the chin. Bonifacio's neck snapped… and everyone heard it.

The sound echoed throughout Mt. Apo's vast cave and carved a place in history. A tremor shook Bonifacio's body, and he fell to the mat. The other fighter was dumfounded. A hush fell over the crowd as though the whole world had stopped. They were dazed—no one could believe what had just happened: Bonifacio was dead.

I reacted, jumping into the ring to finish Bonifacio's fight.

*I'll take over; I can win!*

But that's not the way things work at the fights. Bonifacio's guards stopped me with guns to my head. Chile had the same idea and was also restrained. We both desperately struggled to get to him.

Master David quickly put his arms around Chile and me, gathered us close, and whispered, "You can't be here; you're in tremendous danger. You must get out, *now*!"

"We have to bury him!" Chile said.

"You can't."

"It's our right."

"I know," said Master David.

"*Naku!* Then you know we have to take care of our *brother*," I said in his ear.

"Listen to me! You'd be killed! Is that what you want?"

"Of course not…" Chile said.

"This is what will happen—rival gangs will strike like cobras. They'll assassinate *Tibay* leaders, and everyone with *Tibay* tattoos."

"That means war," I said.

"They don't want war. They'll avoid it by disabling the *Tibays* quickly—through *assassination*," he repeated for emphasis.

*He was right.*

"You must completely disconnect from him—don't even mention his name."

"Can we…?"

"Go! And change apartments!"

"Ay!" Chile cried, looking up at Bonifacio's body in the ring.

As though reading his mind, Master David assured him, "I'll bury his body—no one will find it."

Distress quivered through the crowd; Chile and I pushed through, pausing only once to look back. Master David somehow seemed smaller; his glasses hung by their strap around his neck. He cried freely as he lifted the body of his friend from the ring.

〰〰〰

Within ten minutes Chile and I gathered our belongings: money, weapons, music tapes, my *carabao* horn, and clothes from the apartment, tossing them into the Tsuya's car that we had for the night. Chile had gone back for the weights when I saw a car a few blocks away turn off its lights, still moving, slowing as it got closer. I started our car, edged away from the curb with the lights off, and pulled around the corner into the dark alley behind the apartment before they pulled up in front. I left the car running, leapt from the car with two loaded guns, and pulled the master power switch on the outside wall. A shot was fired. No sign of Chile.

I eased through the back door, gun drawn, as Chile pulled himself along the floor by his forearms and scrambled to his feet. I fired into the dark, handed a gun to Chile, and we positioned on either side of the door. There were maybe four or five of them stumbling across scattered equipment in the dark. We fired, aiming low; one guy cried out, then another. Chile motioned me toward the car and kept shooting. I jumped in, leaving the door open. Chile dove in after me, and we took off like a shot.

"Thought they got you," I said when we were safe, my hands trembling against the wheel.

"I distracted his aim with a kick to the crotch... You're timing couldn't have been better. You cut the lights just in time."

We were lucky to find a new apartment at night; a manager happened to have a baker son just going to work, and so the family was up before dawn with their light on, like a beacon. We quickly made arrangements, and moved our stuff in. While Chile set up things in the apartment, I drove the car across the city to the restaurant and left it in back.

⌇⌇⌇⌇⌇

The stars had paled and retreated, and the morning sky was the color of wet cement. I walked to the beach. The sand bore impressions of someone recently there, but crashing waves came to wipe them out. When the sea took back its water, I aimlessly wandered in, but was soon slammed by a great wave that dumped me back on the shore.

As I sat on the sand, it seemed like the very earth was in mourning. Clouds like shredded tissues streaked the horizon. The air hung wet, as though filled with the collective tears of Filipino street children everywhere. Everything was dissonant and blurred; the plaintive cries of seabirds were more off-key than usual; dimension and color had drained from the earth: gray sand merged into gray ocean; gray ocean became gray sky at the horizon—blurring into nothingness. The sun had deserted the world, leaving everything empty—except for the eagle claws that raked my heart.

⌇⌇⌇⌇⌇

Like everyone else, I thought Bonifacio was immune to injury or death. Many children now realized that death would come for them too, *and probably soon.*

In the newspaper for weeks following were headlines of Bonifacio's death and ensuing events:

*"Gang leader killed during fight in undisclosed location... killings throughout Davao. In other news, Ormoc City was scene of widespread gang violence..."*

Within a week the *Tibay* gang was wiped out. The cops claimed credit, of course, and used the killings after Bonifacio's death as an excuse to shoot street-kids everywhere. With the breakup of the *Tibays* in Ormoc City, and the random killing of other street kids, hundreds of children were left unprotected. Many joined lesser gangs; pimps took some; others came south to Davao, and the orphanage overflowed. I was crippled with grief.

Chile and I had grown up idolizing Bonifacio. Could I have led the *Tibays*? I couldn't imagine it. There never was, nor could there ever be, anyone like him. I recalled his handsome face clearly, unchanged, and as unscarred as the face of Oscar De La Hoya, despite hundreds of fights. For Chile and me the world was upside-down. Of the many fights we'd seen, no one had died in the ring. It was beyond comprehension.

*How could such a thing have happened? Maybe to a lesser fighter, maybe to a lesser person, maybe to someone else. But Bonifacio was invincible!*

Sadness held me down. I could never cry as much as I needed. Sometimes I held my eyelids closed to hold in the tears. Our *brother*, but we couldn't bury him—we never even learned where his grave was. There was no place to commemorate him, where we could go to feel near him. He was like a great tree felled and taken away, leaving no residue.

*Just gone.*

I drank successive cups of strong coffee, and wandered aimlessly through the city. When I ran out of coffee, the caffeine inversion hit, and I slept through fitful dreams, waking with a massive headache.

*When I take revenge, it will be for you too.*

~~~~~~~

We changed our names yet again, this time Chile became Rodel, and I became Jay, but we didn't know who we were anymore. We took refuge in training, and worked to exhaustion, trying to eclipse our misery. If anyone asked who we were, if we answered at all, we would say, "Kick boxers."

The sting of death was ever-present and it was a challenge to work through our depression: most of our friends were dead, and many of our enemies. When we read about deaths in the newspaper, names weren't listed, and we wondered about kids we'd known, but as time went on we thought we were the only ones left.

*And we're sure to bump up the death statistics soon.*

Ultimately I exploded, "I'm sick of this; I need to fight!"

"What about Assad?" Chile asked.

"I *have* to fight."

"What about Assad?" Chile asked again. "Why don't we kill him?"

"It would be too difficult; he's well protected."

"Not impossible."

"Even if we got to him, it would be a trade—our lives for his."

"Not ideal."

"We shouldn't go to Ormoc City or Manila. Mindanao's still the safest."

"He probably thinks you're dead."

"Almost certainly."

"But we should keep our heads down."

A few months after Bonifacio's death Chile chanced the month-lies. His posture in the ring had changed: he'd begun to fight with his head down, like Gene Fullmer. He seemed more defensive than assertive, and boxed more than kicked, which confused his opponents. He fought and won two fights without much trouble, collected his winnings, and left in a hurry.

The next month we both entered, won, and left quickly. We didn't see anyone we knew, but of course we weren't looking. We kept a low profile outside the ring, and were convinced no one followed us, or knew where we lived. We had money from our winnings, and didn't need to fight for awhile.

*But we are kick boxers.*

The fourth month, we both fought and won. Unfortunately, during the last move of Chile's third fight, his ankle twisted, tearing ligaments. I collected our winnings and helped Chile into a waiting taxi. Our purse was good, and we craved celebration. The taxi dropped us near a pharmacy. I bought an Ace bandage, and then went across the street for groceries, while Chile bought cocaine—"to *really* celebrate."

We had an unusually great dinner—beefsteak, vegetables and rice, and durian ice cream. Chile played "Bad, Bad Leroy Brown," "Black Magic Woman," "Rock You Like A Hurricane," "If You Leave Me Now," "Don't Stop 'til You Get Enough," and "Who'll Stop the Rain?" We kept the music going and played it loud enough to crack walls. Chile snorted a line to the lyrics, "If you wanna hang-out.... You gotta take her out ... Cocaine!" We danced around the room, or rather, I danced and Chile hopped.

Then Eric Clapton was singing, "I shot the sheriff... but I did not shoot the deputy..." which we thought beyond funny. We laughed freely for the first time since Bonifacio's death.

I said, "I wonder if PP likes to dance?"

"That would be something to see," said Chile.

"Probably thinks we're dead."

"We should remedy that," Chile said, "Wouldn't it be fun to sneak up behind and scare him?"

I laughed, "I wish..."

"Me too."

"It's probably safe by now."

"Let's go!"

"Sure, no one will even notice you hopping like a kangaroo."

Chile settled comfortably in his chair, and lifted his ankle to the table.

"I'll go." I said, packing Chile's ankle in ice.

"Might not need that," Chile said, snorting another line. "Could you put on the ELO tape?"

As I walked out the door just before sunrise, "Roll Over Beethoven" was blasting from the speakers. The painting on the wall was bouncing.

I came back with PP hours later, and just in time. Chile had apparently ridden down the banister, rolled over the railing and hit the bench press, fracturing his femur. His broken bone poked through his skin, and the rug underneath was blood soaked, squishing like a sponge when we stepped on it. A workout band was tied above the fracture, and the bleeding had stopped, but he was unconscious. His lips were blue, his breathing shallow. PP and I made a makeshift splint out of the broom and the mop, padded with towels, and dragged him onto a yoga mat, straining to avoid unnecessary movement. Fortunately he remained unconscious as we hoisted him into the back seat of PP's car.

We pulled into the emergency entrance and I found orderlies to bring a gurney. Before Chile knew what was happening, a flurry of personnel appeared, his leg was packed in ice; he was given morphine and blood, and finally his femur was repositioned, a cast applied, and he was taken to a room with soft music and a comfortable bed.

But he didn't wake up happy, and every time he wakened, he asked for morphine.

# CHAPTER 38

MASTER DAVID DISAPPEARED, and to our sorrow we never saw him again. He left a note, but we didn't find it until months after Bonifacio's death. We'd finally gone to our forest stash: a buried metal box full of knives, guns, ammo, and money. Master David's note was there, saying he'd been honored to do what we couldn't. Under the note was an envelope full of Bonifacio's winnings—thousands of dollars. But we weren't interested: it belonged to Bonifacio! We couldn't get past that; only *he* had the right to spend it: it was *his*.

I fought several more times in the monthlies, usually winning, making enough to pay for Chile's hospital bill, food, and rent. I set aside enough for a trip to Ormoc City, and still had enough to donate to the orphanage, all without touching Bonifacio's money.

*As soon as Chile's well enough…*

Chile lived in the apartment for awhile, but the siren call of drugs beckoned, and he began to go out often—cast, crutches and all. He made new friends, went to the movies, played pool, drank and drugged, and sadly, slipped into complaisance. He returned to sleeping on the street.

〰〰

On PP's afternoon off, the two of us visited the orphanage, planning to donate money. As the car bumped over the dirt yard through the heat-haze, we saw an overflow of unattended kids—dirty, crying, with runny noses. We made our way inside, stepping around children younger than we remembered, taking stairs three at a time. There were some sleeping mats, but now most spaces were marked with chalk lines on the floor, perhaps forty to a room. We turned toward the women's and girl's section, and caught a glimpse of Mother Avita through a cracked door. She was kneeling, praying, and weeping. She cried, "Oh Father, how can I possibly help *all these children?*"

My heart softened. I shoved my money through the door, and PP contributed his. We looked at each other. Then I took the sock of Bonifacio's money, which I had planned to stash near my new apartment, and pushed it through her door.

*Bonifacio would approve.*

But that night I was troubled. The desperation in Mother Avita's voice remained with me, and I paced the floor, feeling her sorrow.

*"God, are you there? She's so good, why don't you help her?"*

PP brought Chile to see my next fight. There was a surprise: while they watched me down my third opponent, Chile broke concentration long enough to lite a cigarette, and as he glanced up, his gaze locked on a face across the room. He jolted.

PP came to warn me. Skinny enough to slide through the crowd like an eel, he made his way to the ring with rounded eyes, his few remaining freckles rattling. The look of terror on his face easily persuaded my master, and a quick thumbs-down was given as my fourth opponent was called. Puzzled by the decision, I looked down to see PP mouth: "Assad!" A quick conference propelled my master in one direction, and PP and I in another.

Assad followed my master to the dressing area, no doubt expecting me to come for my winnings. I didn't. Instead, PP and I made a quick exit to the car where Chile was waiting with the car started, and we were speeding downhill before the next fight started. We chose new names; PP dropped Chile off at the covered market, and I moved to yet another apartment. We never saw my master again—and learned much later that he'd disappeared.

Now I was at a loss. Fighting in the next monthly seemed too risky: Assad would stake that out. I'd hoped for a quick trip to Ormoc City, but now lacked money. Maybe Chile could sell one of the guns, and I wanted to convince him to come back to the apartment I'd already paid for. I needed him.

I put on my hat and sprinted to the Bangkerohan Market, but he wasn't there. I searched the streets all night hoping to find him, and thought of asking if anyone had seen him, but didn't know which of his aliases to use. Finally I realized I should be asking about a guy with crutches, and just before dawn, I found him in a warehouse, snoring like a freight train.

I roused him, "How ya doin'?"

His swollen eyelids fluttered and blinked. "Well above average," he slurred.

"Let's go home."

"*This* is my home."

"Come on. I can help you."

"Then bring coke!"

"Chile..."

"Don't you know?"

"What?"

"I can't fight anymore!" he shouted, boring through me with bloodshot eyes.

"You'll feel better after you sleep it off..."

"I can't *ever* fight again!"

"Chile..."

He staggered to his feet, but his eyelids drooped, and when he slumped back down, his eye sockets retook their shadows.

"I'm not good company!" he said to end the conversation.

I tried to help him up, but he sucker-punched me.

My breath backed up in my lungs. I straightened up, and gasped, "You still pack a punch!"

Chile leaned against the wall with clenched fists, "I'm *not* coming!"

"I *need* you, Chile."

"You're safer without me!"

"Chile?"

"No!"

"Well, if you want me," I finally said, "PP knows where I live."

His face flared with light as he lit a reefer, and receded into darkness as he smoked.

I decided to return home. But what was home without Chile? I could barely remember where my newest apartment was, or my current alias. I kicked a rock down the street until it disappeared on the rough side of the road. My eyelids took turns twitching with fatigue. Sitting at the edge of a poorly maintained fountain, I stared at decaying leaf-skeletons float on the surface.

—————

Hunchbacked crows were the only ones watching when I left for my next fight, and they didn't have much to say. It was late afternoon, and the streets were uncommonly empty. PP was working and couldn't come, and I didn't ask Chile because if he was drugged out, I didn't want to add that to my list of downers. I was alone.

*If Assad* does *find me; maybe he'll end my misery.*

I was bound to lose with this attitude, so I grasped for something to hang onto, something with meaning. I dug up my revenge addiction and raked it to the surface, and became energized, ramping my mood by thinking of the purse I'd win. Most of the money could go to the orphanage, which would be cool. I only needed enough for the trip to Ormoc City.

But before the first punch was thrown, whistles blew throughout the cave, and cops surrounded the crowd, cuffing all fighters, sponsors, and anyone associated with us. The government had recently squeezed promoters for a larger piece of the action, and was retaliating because they weren't getting it.

*Really bad timing.*

Jail was jammed; we were packed tight as teeth. The strongest and toughest secured sitting spots from time to time, but most stood for hours without food, water, or bathroom privileges. I stood because it didn't seem worth fighting for a place on the floor. Fights broke out, though, and ultimately five prisoners died—none of them kick boxers. Unable to place responsibility for the deaths, authorities sentenced all kick boxers to ten years in prison.

*Government in action!*

Of course, there was no place to put us, and some fighters were quite young, so in the end, we were given three choices: prison, Boy's Town, or the orphanage.

*Prison's out of the question. Tried Boy's Town. The orphanage it is.*

# CHAPTER 39

—◆—▬▬—◆—

I RESISTED LIVING AT THE ORPHANAGE; it was incredibly boring, but I was stuck. Not only was Assad a threat if I left, but now the government had official license to kill me, whatever that meant. So I went to school, and again took purpose in my progress, trying to think of how pleased Bonifacio would be.

I began to venture out gradually. Assad was less of a risk, probably having returned to Manila or Ormoc City after scavenging the streets without success; he wouldn't have suspected I'd live in the tedium of an orphanage. I doubted the cops would recognize me, or even care enough to notice. So I began to help Mother Avita with errands. Sometimes I got medicinal plants from the forest—especially cat's claw for kids with diarrhea, and bamboo pulp for asthmatics to chew. Occasionally I risked a trip into the city for her to round up run-aways from the orphanage. Of course she was unaware that she might be putting me in danger; she never knew about my life with Assad, and I wouldn't have burdened her with it.

Many kids left the orphanage because of harsh discipline. Unlike Mother Avita and a few others, some nuns and volunteers were unsympathetic, severely punitive, or blatantly sadistic, all under the cloak of forcing children into becoming obedient Christians.

Danilo, the little boy Chile and I helped move to the orphanage six years earlier, along with his sister Chesa, ran away after she died of malaria. Chile found him on the street, stabled as a prostitute. He was only five. Chile beat the pimp to a pulp, which gave him great satisfaction, and he took Danilo to Mother Avita.

By the time I got to the orphanage, Danilo was nine. He had become resigned to living at the orphanage, but was poorly socialized and sullen, and understandably scarred, angry, and often belligerent. Once he shouted, "No matter what you do, I won't say it!"

"Danilo, you're making it hard on yourself. Just *do* it," said a nun with a posture as rigid as her rules.

"No."

"What's so hard? Say the *words*. Just say, "Christ is my Savior."

"I'll *never* say it!"

At that the nun dragged him outside, poured salt on the sand, and shoved him to his knees.

Danilo's eyes watered, and his nose ran, but he refused to cry as the salt chewed away at the open sores on his knees.

"Hold your arms out to the side!" the nun shouted, whipping him until he complied.

Mercifully, Danilo fainted, and that was the end of that particular session.

Chile summed up the problem of punitive punishment at the orphanage: "Why would I want to live in the orphanage? If I get beat up on the street, at least I can fight back!"

The cruel discipline was difficult, but the unyielding schedule, unbending rules, and expectations of both the orphanage and school were also hard. Most kids preferred the freedom of the street. They couldn't see education as relevant to them. Although I tried to convince them otherwise, I didn't think it right to force them back.

It became my lot to deal with unruly children at the orphanage. Empathizing with their emotional wounds, I listened to their stories, protected them from violence, and advised them. When they helped me with my schoolwork; I praised and encouraged them, much as the carpenter had done with me. Often the young ones wrapped around my legs like roots, and called me "*Kuya*," which means, "honored older brother."

Danilo was my assistant. He mostly straggled along by me as I supervised other children assigned to planting, watering, weeding, and harvesting the garden. But he was keen on the chicken business, which we ran together. He fed them and gathered eggs; I did the slaughtering, and within a year we built it into a steady revenue-producer. We relished killing the old red rooster that habitually raked our legs, and putting him on the table. I got a kick out of hearing Danilo laugh with every bite.

When I visited a nun many years later, she told me how frustrated they'd been in those days: buried under governmental red tape, packed beyond capacity with almost no financing, forever burdened with fund-raising to supply mere necessities.

Mother Avita constantly thanked me for my help. She

worked long days and always saw to the children before caring for herself. My admiration for her grew—she was incredibly hardworking, patient, and kind. I loved her.

One day she said I had an old friend waiting on the basketball court. I looked out the second story window and saw a man with a German shepherd watching kids throw hoops, and realized it was Cheeks, of the walrus jowls, from the pharmacy! I walked toward him and shook his hand.

"How did you find me?"

"I've known Mother Avita a long time—she's very protective of you. I thought you were probably dead, but decided on taking the long shot that you might be here," Cheeks said, removing his sunglasses. "You've grown a lot."

We sat on the step like old friends. The dog came and licked my hand; I scratched him on the soft spot behind his ears, and he licked my face all over.

"I was so grateful when you helped my sister," the man said, "and I always wanted to thank you properly. Then I didn't see you and worried. Later there was a guy asking questions; he wanted to know if you were NPA, and if you knew my sister. He said you were always changing your name, and the way he talked made me suspicious, so I've wondered about you these past few years. Bonifacio and I were friends; he asked about you too... I'm so sorry about his tragic death."

"Thanks..."

"Hard times."

"Yes."

"Death everywhere."

I nodded. "Um, how long ago did the guy ask about me?"

"Three, maybe four years ago. I hadn't seen him around

until last night, when he came looking for you again. He doesn't wear a red scarf, but I think he's Muslim. I was wary, and told him you were most certainly dead. Yet *hoping* you were alive, I wanted to warn you, and called Mother Avita on the off chance…"

I took a deep breath and sighed. "Glad you did. It's good to see you. Um, how's your sister?"

"*Gracias a Dios*, her husband died several years ago, good riddance! Best thing ever happened to her," he nodded. "She and her little boy live with us."

I didn't say anything, but I might have smiled.

"We're moving to Japan," Cheeks continued, his fleshy face lifting into multiple curves. "That's another reason I wanted to find you. I'd like you to have my dog."

As though he understood, the dog put his head on my feet. I roughed his back, and his tail went into warp speed wagging.

"He's a great companion. He's smart and loyal—he'll protect you with his life. We've always called him 'Dog,' because that's what my nephew calls him. You could name him. What do you think?"

"Um… How about 'Rumble?'"

<hr />

I'd missed Ace after leaving my tribal family, and was glad to have Rumble. We became the best of friends—he slept with me, ate with me, stayed close to the garden while we worked, and carried on a crusade against presumptive crows. He was the fastest and most enthusiastic soccer player at the orphanage, though it was hard to know which team he was on. Aside from being unhelpful with the chicken business—he'd rather eat than herd them—he understood and obeyed my commands, and was a great companion. When I was at school, he waited outside the door. When I cried at night, he tried to comfort me, and didn't require an explanation.

Not so with Mother Avita. One night she heard me crying, and took me aside. "What *is* it?" she said, expecting an answer.

I finally told her about Bonifacio's death in the ring, and then I really cried. She sat with me for a long time without talking. After a while she said, "You know sometimes when the tide goes out, how you find beautiful shells on the shore?"

I nodded.

"There are many beautiful and worthwhile things left for you to discover."

We sat without talking for a moment, me still sobbing.

"You will have opportunities," she continued, "but you have to make wise choices."

"I want to fight."

"Didn't it scare you to see your brother get killed in the ring?"

"He made a serious mistake; he should've stopped when he got tired. I'm good, and I know when to quit. I want to take over where he left off."

"Listen to me. Bonifacio's dead, and that part of your life's over." She put her arm around me, "Isn't it?"

"A lot of it," I said, my chin quivering as I thought about the annihilation of the *Tibays*.

"The important thing is not that Bonifacio died, but that he lived, and goes on living elsewhere. You must live your own life, and Bonifacio wants you to be happy. What advice do you think he'd give you right now?"

"I don't know… Probably to get an education."

"Do you want that?"

"Yes."

"Can you continue with school, catch up on what you've missed, and still train and fight?"

I took a deep breath, "I haven't thought of it that way."

"You might do both, but not do well at either one. They say if you chase two rabbits, they'll both get away."

I smiled.

"He'd be proud to see how much you help the children."

I kept smiling, "He would."

"Will you promise me, at least, to give up monthly illegal kickboxing?"

Thinking about it later, I couldn't believe I'd said yes.

It was an odd coincidence though, because soon after, the government permanently shut down illegal kickboxing at Mt. Apo. Rumor had it they still couldn't get the payoff they demanded. The official claim was that "promoters used up and discarded fighters—if a fighter was too injured to rehabilitate, he was thrown in the river to drown." It was true, that had happened, but according to greatly exaggerated newspaper reports, the river was "clogged" with dead bodies of discarded fighters.

Mother Avita struggled to feed everyone. The overflow was significant and there was never enough food. A new orphanage was under construction, but progress was slow. She prayed a lot. I desperately wanted to win a big purse to help, but those times were gone, so I dedicated my time to building up the chicken business, expanding the vegetable garden, and training children to work with me. I established a hierarchy of assignments, and after a while delegated most of the work.

I had become a leader of sorts, and now I concentrated on getting through school. I worked hard, got help from other kids, tested out of some courses, and finally got into the equivalent of high school, where I immersed myself in studying.

*The carpenter would be pleased.*

I was elected Class President, and one of my jobs was enforcing penalties imposed by the teacher. On a day hot enough to fry lizards and humid enough to steam them, I had to make students stand in the sun because they were noisy at their table. A pretty girl named Celestina, who had liquid brown eyes, and was a breath away from perfect, came outside humming a song I'd never heard before, until the brutal heat wilted her energy and muted her voice with thirst. When the required half-hour was over at last, I motioned the sweating and dehydrated kids back inside.

Celestina glanced at me with wounded eyes, and glared as she passed me.

"I don't make the rules," I said.

"You don't mind inflicting them," she whispered.

"Look, I'm sorry. That was really hard. I'll get you some water."

"You're from the orphanage, aren't you?"

"Why would you think that?"

"You know a girl named Kim?"

I nodded.

"She's a friend of mine."

I nodded again, and started back to class.

"Do you like her?"

"Sure."

"I mean…"

"What?"

"Well, she has a crush on you…"

I opened the door, blushing to my toes.

# CHAPTER 40

CHILE LIKED THE STREET. Despite a badly scarred face and pro-
nounced limp, he was popular: Activity Central, in fact. He had
a cheerful girlfriend named Liberata who adored him, called
him "Chile One-Dimple," and said *that* dimple was worth more
than two on anyone else. She was just taller than Chile, willowy,
and moved with the grace of a ballerina. Best of all, she was
kind-hearted and loved a good joke.

Sometimes Chile and Liberata dropped by the orphanage to
visit. They played soccer with us a few times, and one time
brought surplus food from a party they'd helped cater. Of
course Danilo always regarded Chile as his personal hero, and
the two of them often shot hoops while Liberata read to some
of the others.

Once Chile and Liberata went with and Danilo and I to the
beach, along with Rumble. Gulls streaked the sky and came in
for a landing, but Rumble soon cleared the coast. Chile and

Danilo tossed a ball around, and we took turns throwing a stick in the ocean for Rumble to fetch. He pounced the stick in the water, tossing his head, and ran back across the sand, ending in an impressive nose dive at our feet, his hindquarters sliding forward under his front legs in a mass of quaking, whole-body enthusiasm, his tail keeping time with his joy, dropping the stick at our feet, and sneezing a few times. This scene replayed all afternoon. He slept for the next two days.

On weekends I sometimes worked construction at the new orphanage, along with occasional volunteers, but money had run out, and construction dragged. Much of the time I was alone, which suited me. The work was fairly intuitive, although I often wished the carpenter were around to help. I did my best, hammering nails and sawing boards most of the day, which didn't require much thought. My mind wandered, and I wondered about God.

*Who is God, and what is he like? Why did Christ have to die on the cross? Why is there so much* violence *in the world? Does God* care *about kids? Why does he let little children suffer so much, and most of all, why doesn't he do something about it?*

Rumble was my constant companion, loyal friend, and security guard at the site. One day, he barked at someone's approach. It was Liberata, and he ran to lick her face, but she ignored him, which was odd. I was hammering on the second floor, and jumped down the steps. She ran to meet me, sobbing.

"Chile's in the hospital, and he's so sick!" she said.

"What's the matter?"

"He had terrible pain in his stomach—he was in agony, and *so* thirsty. He had a bloody nose, and we couldn't stop it. I got some friends to carry him to emergency. It was awful!"

We ran, not talking, but when she stopped to catch her breath, I asked, "Has he been using?"

She shook her head, and panted, "not for weeks."

When we got there, no one knew about Chile, and emergency was busy with a childbirth. We hurried through the hospital, asking every one we saw, and at last found a doctor who provided some direction.

"Look in the west wing," he said, chewing the end of his pen.

"Which way is that?"

"Do you know where the waiting room is?"

I nodded.

"Just past it, there are a few rooms where patients are held before admitting; just ask at the desk."

We waited in line to speak to the woman in charge, thinking she'd tell us where he'd been taken. She paged a doctor. When we asked the responding doctor about Chile, he said, "Oh, you must mean the food-poisoning in 106-B. Are you relatives?"

"I'm his brother, and this is his girlfriend," I said.

"And your parents?"

"We're orphans."

"Come with me," the doctor said, grabbing a clipboard, "he's in the room at the end of the hall."

The doctor motioned us to follow, his rubber-soled shoes squeaking on the linoleum ahead of us. He looked over his shoulder, "I'm not exactly sure what was going on, but his symptoms were consistent with food poisoning."

"Has he been admitted yet?" I asked.

"We did everything we could," he said, walking faster.

"Is there medicine for food poisoning?" Liberata asked.

But I don't think he heard her. Neither of us realized what he was saying until he continued, "Before we could pump his stomach, he was gone."

The room was empty, apart from a gurney in the corner. We stood at the door, and looked at the doctor for an explanation. He stepped over to the gurney, and then we noticed a pale green sheet covering a body. The doctor pulled back the sheet, and there laid Chile, on his back, his arms motionless at his sides.

*Wait. This isn't him.*

Liberata burst into tears.

I stared at the body, and felt my heart drilled through with a jackhammer. There was the scarred face I loved so much. I stroked his hair, and finger-combed the length of it. I placed my hand over his scar, softly, as though I had the power to heal it. He was still warm, and I shook his shoulders, "Chile, Chile. Don't go!" His eyes kept opening, and the doctor closed them several times.

"Why do his eyes keep opening?" I asked the doctor.

"Sometimes they do that," he said. "The surrounding muscles relax at death, causing them to open."

*This can't be.*

Liberata held Chile's hand, and kissed it repeatedly, her head hanging like a bird in the rain.

I looked again at his face: his dimple was gone, forever. Unbidden tears streamed from my face to his; whatever I was about to say was choked off by spasmodic sobs.

"I'm so sorry," the doctor said. "I can help make arrangements for burial, if you want."

"I'll come back and get him," I stammered.

The doctor tilted his head, "Are you sure? Well then, I'll leave you two alone with him," he said gently.

"I don't want to see him buried," Liberata said to me, her chin quivering, "I couldn't take it; I want to remember him how he was."

"I'll take care of it," I said. We held each other in a moment of profound grief. "I should go."

"Me too," she said, turning and resolutely walking through the door, not looking back, curled over like a willow in the wind.

She walked down the hall, and I never saw her again.

I stumbled through the pewter-colored day, crying all the way to the orphanage. This couldn't be real. I'd seen and touched his body, but how... *Dead?* I looked for him to come around the corner.

PP, Danilo, and I went through the motions: we made a box for a coffin, drove to the hospital, carried out his body, and found a place beyond the city to bury him. Each of us took turns digging, our tears mixing with every shovelful of dirt.

*If only I had something of Mama's to bury with him.*

We lowered the box into the ground, covered it with dirt, and stood looking down. I hated putting dirt on him. Almost in unison and without conversation, we pulled up nearby orchids and transplanted them onto the grave. We sat around the mound, lingering without words. I made a cross and carved the top. It said only: "Loved."

~~~~~~~

I'm not certain if I slept that night, but I remember being astonished that the sun rose, and angry that it did.

*How can things go on, just the same, as though nothing's changed?*

I couldn't conceive of life without him. He was the epitome of vitality. *Dead?*

A whiff of marijuana came around the corner, and I called out, but no one answered. I saw him moonwalking—but it was someone else dancing to "Beat It." I saw him walking along the beach with Bonifacio, their arms around each other's shoulders, but there was only the emptiness of sand, and the melancholy sea. I squeezed my eyes shut: his image was there, but he was gone.

Suppressed grief revived; my feelings were tangled, and it became painful to think at all. I felt like a savagely pruned tree that would never be the same—cleft and hollowed. I tried to bargain with God—I'd do anything to have my brothers again. Or, if time could be turned back, I'd go instead of them. But they no longer existed—I had nothing, no one, no reason to live. I felt deader than them. I *wished* I were dead. Not even vengeance was worth living for; indulging in hatred no longer gave me energy. Even Rumble dragged along behind me with a hangdog expression.

*Ugly past, dead-end future.*

A shell of sadness enveloped me, and closed me off to everyone. Mother Avita tried to help, but I avoided her; I wouldn't talk about it. When she approached I wouldn't listen. PP came; I turned him away. I couldn't pray—couldn't think of anything to pray for, and besides no one was listening. I couldn't imagine why God allowed all this to happen.

*Well, why wouldn't he? I'm just a dirty street kid. I'm nobody—worse than a nobody—I'm an assassin, the worst of the worst. Why would God care about me?*

Then one day an out of control fight broke out between two boys at the orphanage. Mother Avita asked me to break it up. But I had the ache of inactivity, and zero energy for problem solving, so I shut them in a room to fight it out. After a while I realized it was a case of bullying—a bigger boy full of pain, taking it out where he could. I stepped in and broke it up.

Mother Avita thanked me sincerely, put her arm around me and said, "He loves you."

Puzzled, I asked, "Who?"

"God," she said. With that I cried for hours, and she let me.

# CHAPTER 41

—◆ᗯᗯᗯᗯ◆—

ACCORDING TO THE NEW BIRTHDAY CHILE AND I HAD SET, the one listed in the orphanage records, I was about six months away from turning seventeen when he died. Since returning to Davao, events had set me off course—the death of Bonifacio, jail, work at the orphanage, school, Chile's death, and despair. As I dragged through my routine in the chicken yard, I noticed a stagnant pool of water laden with mosquito larvae, and hacked it apart.

I had to kick the blues. I mustered focus and reclaimed my revenge goal, once again starting to actually crave satisfaction. I knew how to kill them, no thought required. Chile's death was yet another to chalk up to my aunt and uncle.

*So what's keeping me?*

The cops wouldn't bother me now, and Assad would never suppose I'd be stupid enough to come back to Ormoc City. It was time. I'd find odd jobs and work my way there. I decided to leave the next night, after the children were asleep. Tucking the photo of my father in my pocket, I went across town to Bonifacio's stash box, and checked out the guns. There were some good ones, and I picked a .45, loaded it, but then put it back. There might be a time when I'd need it, but not for them. I tucked the best knife in my waistband.

⌇⌇⌇⌇

I took some of the children to a matinee the next day, enjoying our fun time together. But I returned to a buzz at the orphanage—rumor had it that an American couple wanted to adopt a boy. Mother Avita was waiting on the porch to tell me they'd chosen Danilo from a photo. The problem was he wouldn't leave me. He said he'd go if I went too; she hoped she could talk the couple into adopting us both. I stammered something to her, not fully registering what she was saying. She smiled, put her arm around me and said she'd get back to me. She handed me a package left by Liberata—"Something of Chile's," she said.

I rushed outside where I could be alone. Inside the package were Chile's knife and gun, and our family Bible. Tucked within its pages was a note to Chile from Master David saying, "Bonifacio would want you to have this."

*Is this all that's left of Chile? The sum of his life?*

I sank down in the discarded blossoms of the *narra* tree, and turned to the front page. I saw my parents' names, and the names of the children written boldly in the blue ink of a fountain pen, probably by my father: "Isabel," "Bonifacio..." Suddenly I couldn't stop the tears, crying from the core of my being. After a long time I wiped my face with my shirt, and through sore eyes read: "José," "2Tall," "Francisco," and then "Miguel" (Chile). I looked at my own name, "Mark," a little taken aback to see it after all the names I'd had. Below my name was "Segundina."

I walked around as though in charge of my body, but cried uncontrollably. My face stung with salt, and my eyes felt raw and exposed, like an onion with too many layers peeled away.

*I must avenge my family; I owe them that.*

I ran hose water over my head and hurried to tell Sister Avita I couldn't be adopted, but she met me at the door, "They want both of you!" She clapped her hands, and added, "and they're coming tomorrow morning to meet you."

I was speechless.

"It will be such an opportunity for you, and I know Danilo will be all right with *you* there."

"Mother, I…" She was so full of joy at the prospect; I didn't have the heart to say more.

"You'll have a much better life in America," she said.

I couldn't imagine what that meant. It certainly didn't change my mind. But she kept on talking, "I've been worried about Danilo, now I trust you to look after him. I love you so much!" she said with tears in her eyes, "I can't tell you how grateful I am you have this opportunity for happiness. I've been praying a long time for this!"

And with that, I gave in. I couldn't hurt her.

On my mat that night, I thumbed through the Bible and read an underlined passage from the Book of Revelation: "And God shall wipe away all tears from their eyes; and there shall be no more death, neither sorrow, nor crying, neither shall there be any more pain: for the former things are passed away."

*I could start over... leave the past behind.*

I held The Bible in one hand, and hefted Chile's knife and gun in the other.

# CHAPTER 42

ASSAD CHANGED HIS MIND. When investigating their holdings he found that Dameana's assets only looked good on paper. Their money had gone to buy inventory, much of which had been destroyed by an earthquake. Their import-export business was already sinking. Then there was the other thing. Knowing she had born his child softened his animosity. She hadn't really betrayed him: she married to protect his son's reputation. That made a difference. He remembered how he'd lost his temper in the restaurant and how quiet and afraid she'd become as he accused and berated her.

*How could I have been so out of control? I've got the coolest head in town. Business depends on it! Yet where she was concerned I lost it.*

Assad ground his teeth.

*Maybe she'll stay in London, and our paths won't cross. No more gut-wrenching ups and downs.*

As he walked down the street toward the lot where his Ferrari was parked, he impulsively kept going. He passed his tailor's shop, a laundry, and a favorite restaurant. It was a magnificent day—hot, but he never minded the heat.

*She can have the kid.*

Impulsively he turned into Dameana's bank, and deposited the equivalent of several million dollars into her account.

*My son won't go without like I did.*

∼∼∼∼∼

Business was booming and he restricted his contracts to those paying the most, or those of particular interest. He seldom took out cops or ordinary citizens. It was all about politics now. He briefly considered diversifying, mostly for the excitement of something new. Kidnapping Americans for ransom in Mindanao?

*Americans—such high maintenance.*

He'd already scaled down his business, retaining only three boys, planning to faze them out eventually. He could live well for many years on his sizeable investments. He could relax for awhile.

*Maybe become a professional racecar driver.*

As he sat musing by his pool, sipping a glass of *Veuve Clicquot Brut Rose*, he realized he had no immediate jobs. Suddenly bored, he reflected on his prospects for work. He frowned and plunged into the cool water. When he got out the phone was ringing. He answered it, and instantly perked up—a lead on Mark!

*Oh, yeah!*

His old jealousy of Bonifacio resurfaced, and the veins in his forehead pounded. He chewed on a *pili* nut, spitting the shell across the room.

*Doing his brother will be* such *a pleasure.*

He took the next flight to Davao and was met by his bodyguard with the misaligned pupils.

"What did you find out?" Assad asked, as he climbed into the car, maintaining his distance with dark sunglasses.

"It's him all right; now he goes by 'Rocky,' but it's him. He's the one I tracked from the hospital to the orphanage."

Assad took out a cigarette, which his bodyguard was quick to lite. He filled his lungs, "So the hospital thinks Chile died of food poisoning?"

"That's what it says in his chart."

"How do you know this guy's his brother?"

"I watched him bury the body."

"What else?"

"The girl took Chile's belongings to him."

"Did you get any information from the nuns?"

"Not a word."

"What about tattoos?"

"No."

"On the right hand and foot?"

"No tattoos."

"A limp?"

"No."

"You *sure*?"

"I've seen him running and walking. Absolutely no limp."

"I want to see this guy myself."

They turned down the street to the orphanage.

"Wouldn't it be best to get him at the new orphanage? He's usually alone there."

"Probably. But remember, he's mine."

"I'll get the mutt."

But Assad wasn't listening. They continued in silence for awhile, and then Assad said, "No. I want the world to know that nobody crosses me, no matter how long it takes. Make it the old orphanage."

"What about the nuns?"

"What about them?"

They drove without conversation. Finally Assad continued, "Better yet, we'll go Sunday after Mass. Everyone will be there; we'll have a big audience, and word will spread."

They made a u-turn.

# PART THREE:

# FOUND

# CHAPTER 43

—◆▬▬◆—

I HAD TO REINVENT MYSELF AGAIN. I didn't sleep the night before meeting my prospective parents, wondering how I'd have to adapt. My new family didn't know much about me, and if they found out, they sure wouldn't take me. I never gave out personal information, and Mother Avita wouldn't divulge a confidence, not even that Bonifacio and Chile were my brothers.

I'd heard a tape made for Danilo and me by the American couple, with missionaries translating. The man and woman sounded sincere and kind, and said things like, "We're so excited to have you join our family in the United States!" Still, meeting them was a shock. I put my arm around Danilo, and we put on our best behavior, saying as little as possible. "Father" was a medical doctor. They were tall, thin, blond, blue-eyed, and *extra* white. And they were Mormon! I'd heard terrible things about Mormons: they didn't believe in Christ;

they had many wives, and their missionaries brainwashed people. Worse yet, they had horns.

*Well, I'll adjust.*

〰〰〰〰

A government official was assassinated at the hotel where my prospective parents were staying. No big deal to me, but they were frightened and desperate to leave. The timing was auspicious, because according to the orphanage records, I'd be seventeen in a week, and ineligible for foreign adoption. So everything was rushed.

I merely waved to Mother Avita and a few kids on the porch as our taxi pulled away. I didn't get to say goodbye to PP, and never saw him again.

*Mother Avita will have to tell him.*

I left Rumble snoring on the porch, one hind leg twitching, no doubt dreaming of running. A wave of sorrow overtook me; my eyes watered, and I choked back a sob. I couldn't disrespect my new parents by seeming ungrateful, so I held back the floodgates of an enormous dam.

*How I wish I could take PP and Rumble with us.*

I looked out the back window as we drove, and saw the orphanage diminish, becoming a dot, then disappear altogether.

We spent almost a week in Manila doing endless paperwork, where my name again became Mark. For some reason the DSWD, the Department of Social Welfare and Development, wanted to make certain I wasn't being kidnapped.

*Who says the government doesn't care?*

We flew through a crystalline brilliance of clouds to Hawaii, rented a car, and checked into a Marriot Hotel. Here I was, suddenly in America. Honolulu wasn't so different from Davao—hot and humid, rainforest-beautiful plants, and soil steamy with new growth.

*Now I would be an American.*

We did things that tourists do—shopped for clothes, visited The Polynesian Cultural Center, saw the Mormon Temple, viewed the islands by helicopter, hiked to waterfalls, flew to Maui and drove the coast to Hana, and hung out on the beach, where my parents got major sunburns. We finished adoption formalities in the nick of time—I was on the very edge of seventeen—two days before my Easter birthday. It was a good time for us, and I felt exhilarated. Mother Avita had said to hug my parents, and I did.

The night before leaving I sat on the hotel balcony in Honolulu looking out over the expanse of sea. Currents flowed in two directions, but the incoming waves seemed like a succession of smiles. I took several deep breaths, and promised myself that someday I'd return to Hawaii where I'd been happy for an entire week. I was relaxed, optimistic, and felt entirely safe. Those feelings were premature.

# CHAPTER 44

---

I WAKENED EARLY THE NEXT MORNING FOR A SUNRISE SWIM. As I made my way through the hotel gardens, and past curved swimming pools with waterfalls, the fragrance of plumeria floated through the air. Up-lights illuminated cascades of hibiscus spilling down to the beach: yellow close to the hotel, pink near the pools, and white at the walkway curving past the patio, towel hut, bar, and bistro tables. Soft saffron-colored street lamps lit the sand and surf.

I walked along the beach, sucked in familiar salty air, and appreciated the balance of having energy within relaxation. Yesterday's footprints had been washed away by the tide, and the sand was smooth and clean. I immersed my feet in the silky bubbles of ebbing waves, waded out to incoming waves, jumped through the curl of larger waves, and swam beyond the breaks out to sea.

The sun poured over the horizon like liquid butter melting the morning mist. The water mirrored the sky, which slowly emerged in shades of gold and blue. I floated until it was light, almost relaxed enough to sleep, without a thought in my head. The waves undulated, as soothing as a rocking cradle.

I swam back to shore, and strolled back toward the lifeguard station, wondering vaguely when it would be manned. No one was around, and the only sounds were the slap and shush of the ocean, bird chirps, and beginning mists of rain. The beach was warm and blissfully serene. I eased into a sense of unaccustomed security.

Yet as I neared the empty lifeguard station, I became unsettled. I stopped and listened, but heard nothing unusual. Rain was falling in droplets now, and I shivered almost imperceptibly, though not from cold. Something was wrong. The hair on the back of my neck stood up. Instinctively moving away from the lifeguard station, I glanced toward it. Assad stood in the shadow, knife in hand. I froze. He carved the air with his knife, and smiled maliciously.

The sudden increase of rain didn't change the expression on his face, "Think you'd be safe in America? You can't *ever* get away from me!" He stepped toward me, his head forward like a fighting cock's.

My heart was thumping like a rabbit in a bag, but my instincts were intact, and I shot a hard roundhouse kick to his right arm, knocking the knife away, cutting my foot in the process. He elbowed me hard across the face and sent me to the ground, but I grabbed a hand-full of sand and tossed it into his eyes. Pretending no injury, he backed away, casually wiping his eyes.

"So," he said with a nasty grin, "Bonifacio was your brother!"

I ignored him, thinking only of strategy. In a split second I rose to maximum clarity—knowing I was fighting for my life. He was far superior in weaponry, but I could beat him in martial arts.

*Disable and down him fast, before he gets to his knife.*

His nostrils flared like those of a horse and he stepped closer, "I hated Bonifacio's guts... which is one more reason to kill you."

We advanced towards each other like the assassins we were. He stared with determination, disregarding the sand in his eyes; I ignored his psychological baiting, staring with resolve. We closed the gap, exchanging punches.

*This has to be fast.*

I moved the action away from where the knife had fallen, and got in my best eight-combination punch that left him unprotected, immediately following with a hard left kick to his sternum. He struggled to catch his breath, drooling blood. I sent him down with quick successive kicks, and body-slammed his chest.

I jammed my thumbs and the tips of my middle fingers into his neck and the hollow behind his ears, applying pressure to compress his arteries. He struggled hard, but I pinned his arms with my legs and leaned forward using my weight to hold him. Oxygen starved, his black-marble eyes rolled back in his head. I let go. There was a profound silence, apart from the hammering of my heart.

"Remember," I said in his ear, "*I let you live.*" He couldn't have heard me, but when he regained consciousness he'd have the sour realization that I could have killed him, and would be amazed that I didn't.

The outburst of rain slowed to a drizzle. I got up, picked up the knife, and walked back to the hotel, glancing back only once. He hadn't moved. There was a long trail of blood-soaked sand between us, beginning to dilute in diminishing drops of rain.

*Safe! I'll be on the plane before he finds me, and he doesn't know where I'm going. It would never occur to him that he'd fail to kill me... He has no plan B.*

The knife wound on my foot bled profusely under the outdoor shower, and for the first time I noticed the pain. I cleaned out the sand, shaking, but managing to hold the cut together, binding it with a small towel from the bistro, and tying it with a scrap of plastic bag. I ditched Assad's knife in a dumpster, and was fairly composed as I hopped back to my room, where my father had just come to collect me. Noting my foot, he said, "What happened, son?"

I shrugged, "Just cut."

My father stitched up the wound, and we headed for the airport.

# CHAPTER 45

—◄———————►—

WE HAD SEVERAL LAYOVERS before reaching our city, which here
must be unnamed, and then a long taxi ride. Our two-story
house was white and looked like a huge bodega, mostly rectangular with an entrance in the middle, set far back in an enormous front lawn, newly mown. Wind swished across the grass,
bending the blades nearly to the ground; flowers danced around
the front and sides, and a river ran through a shimmering forest
to the north.

We entered through a vast garage, which to my amazement
was nearly empty. I wondered briefly if this was where Danilo,
now called Dan, and I would sleep. We went up a few stairs and
entered the house. It was perfect: air conditioning, nice furniture, and everything organized. We were taken upstairs and
shown a room with two beds—ours—and *we* could decorate
the walls "with things that were important to us."

*I wonder what that would be?*

~~~~~~~

Different bird songs wakened me, and it took a while to realize where I was. Knowing almost nothing about America, I played some of Chile's favorite songs through my head.

I've heard it said that it's better to travel hopefully than to arrive. Despite our fantastic family time in Hawaii, the feeling that I'd finally eluded Assad, and the idyllic first impressions of our house, we had indeed arrived, and it was time to begin adjusting.

Unpredictably, one of the biggest challenges was the food. There was meat we weren't used to, and too much of it. Casseroles were absolute conundrums. Rather than fresh vegetables and fish, we now had canned or frozen vegetables and seafood. Fruit was not sufficiently ripe and of poor-quality.

*In the Philippines we'd have fed the fruit to the pigs.*

Restaurant food was disappointing, mostly because we never really knew what we were getting. We learned to order rice, and mother decided to serve it at home with every meal, including breakfast. She constantly tried to please us, but didn't quite know how, and we didn't know how to tell her.

I was enmeshed in the past, day and night. The deepest cuts of my childhood festered, possibly because I was now in a safe place and time, surrounded by support. I grieved for Bonifacio and Chile incessantly, and a flood of conflicting memories bounced through my head like a pinball. I recalled their victories in the ring, and relived their greatest fights, blow-by-blow, sometimes adding moves of my own, which helped me fantasize that they could win battles even after death. Yet I knew I'd never see them fight again; I'd never see them coming around the corner, arms about each other's shoulders. They were gone, but my sorrow stayed.

My heart seemed locked to the conflict-ridden beat of the Philippines. I missed the chaos—the excitement, the adventure, the uncertainty. I craved a fight. I missed PP and Rumble; I longed for Mother Avita. I needed the ocean.

Remaining withdrawn, and always carrying the feelings of inadequacy that street kids do, I kept to myself, which made me seem unfriendly. Of course, my training as an assassin had taught me the ultimate clam-up. I only spoke when absolutely necessary, always guarded and suspicious. People approached me with warmth, yet I cut short their questions, avoided social interaction, and almost never initiated communication. I resisted learning English as an excuse to stay isolated.

Dan and I were undoubtedly a challenge for our parents, especially since they didn't know our backgrounds, beyond that we were orphans. They sent us to therapists, but I wouldn't have confided in anyone, let alone some strange white guy, and Dan felt the same.

They were frustrated with our reticence. There were three older adopted children whom we avoided. And yet they persisted in working to unify our family of differing races, religions, and genetics, not to mention the diversity of childhood experiences—ours being off the charts. They got me a job in a grocery store, and I had a great boss who trained me, thanked me often, and treated me with respect. Despite my poor English, he said I was his best employee; I responded by working hard, and learning enough English to get by.

But my aunt and uncle remained unpunished, and I wallowed in resentment and hatred. For the immediate future, I channeled my energy into one goal: to save enough money for a quick trip to Manila—a turn-around flight to kill them. I had unfinished business.

~~~~~~

Adoption protocol stipulated we be raised as Catholics, so our parents sent Dan and me to the local cathedral, although we didn't like it. The priest was nice, but the congregation wasn't friendly, and our peers didn't accept us.

Feeling rebellious, I invited dad to come with me. I thought since he's Mormon, he'd be angry, but instead, he pushed away from his computer and said, "Hold on, son, let me get my jacket—and I'll invite mom too."

My parents were sociable and told people they were just visiting, happy to support their sons. They were well received.

*Because unlike me, they're white, well educated, and respected.*

During the following weeks our parents went to Mass in the morning with Dan and me, and to their church with the other children in the afternoon. One Sunday mother invited me to with them to their church. Exceptionally annoyed, and not good at expressing myself, I slammed the door in her face. I already disliked mine, and certainly wasn't interested in theirs.

She came back to apologize, and said she had just wanted me to feel included. In my room I thought about her kindness.

*If she could go to my church, why couldn't I go to hers? A family thing.*

I apologized, gave her a hug, and said I'd go. My father nearly fell off his chair.

The Bishop welcomed me; people introduced themselves, and since they knew my parents, they were aware of the adoption, knew my name, and were quick to shake my hand. I liked the friendliness. When I got home, though, I became pessimistic.

*All that warmth is faked.*

"I don't want to go again," I said the next week.

"Okay, son," my father said, unable to hide his disappointment.

But I got ready after they left, and rode my bike to church, wanting to see how I'd be treated without them. The missionaries were staking out the front door, so I snuck in the back.

I'd barely crossed the threshold when a tall kid called to me, "Hey, want to play basketball on Saturday?"

"Maybe," I said.

"Okay. I'll call you."

I figured I was off the hook until he said, "Don't worry, I've got your parent's number."

A cluster of talking and laughing members clogged the chapel entrance, and babies were all over the place. People seemed eager to talk and shake my hand, and one baby wanted to goober my face.

Just then the Bishop gave my hand a shake, "Good to see you, Mark."

*What's with all the hand shaking?*

Then came the missionaries to pump my arm for awhile.

*Well, no one has horns.*

I was rescued by my parents who were thrilled to see me, and motioned me to sit with the family. Everyone sitting around us smiled and nodded. A child in the pew in front of us kept playing peek-a-boo, hiding behind his mother's shoulder, and then looking at me; I winked and curled my tongue to amuse him.

Before leaving the building, I'd joined the basketball team, and had decided to attend church with my family. And yet, I had two separate compartments: one for church and family, and the other for revenge.

By the time I applied to the university, I'd been promoted to manager of the grocery store, and had saved enough money for my trip. It was summer, and I wanted to clip the nagging loose ends of my life before starting college. I had a two-week vacation from work—my father had arranged for me to attend a youth enrichment program at Brigham Young University during the first week, and I'd bought a round trip ticket to Manila for the second.

I was impressed with what I saw at BYU: the campus was gorgeous and clean, the students remarkably wholesome, friendly and accepting, and I loved being around them. They didn't smoke, drink, swear, or have sex outside of marriage. There was constant focus on achieving worthwhile things, and in doing service for others.

*Refreshing.*

But I could never be like them. I was quite different—merely an observer—having seen and done things everyone should be protected from, and I definitely wasn't *good* like them.

# CHAPTER 46

THAT WAS MY MINDSET AS I FLEW TO MANILA, and then traveled by land and sea to Ormoc City. The old obsession returned with the frenzy of maggots on rotten meat. I searched for my aunt and uncle, frantically skimming phone books covering a radius of thirty miles from Ormoc City, and within a day I was on their street. The house was the color of old chewing gum, and smaller than I remembered, but it was the one. I pounded on the door.

He was older and balder, but cranky as ever, "What do you want?"

"Is your wife at home?"

"What business is it of yours?" he said, sour-breathed.

"Oh, I'm here for both of you." I shoved past his beer belly through the door.

"Where do you think you're *going*?" he shouted.

I sat in the most comfortable chair, and crossed my legs. "Who *are* you?"

"Get Ana."

"How do you know my *wife*?" he said, red in the face.

In a split second I jumped up and twisted his arm behind his back, "I said, *Get Ana!*"

"She... she's not here."

"Get her."

Anton was sweating. I let go of his arm and pushed him down the hall toward the back of the house. He had patterned baldness on top, tonsured like a monk, but there was nothing pious about him. Ana stumbled toward us. She was thin and bony, with gray stringy hair. Her dress was wrinkled from napping, and her face wrinkled from time, smoking, and most probably chronic meanness. She plunked her atrophied bundle-of-sticks-self down in an upholstered chair and fumbled for a cigarette, coughing.

I punched Anton hard, and he fell back on the sag-bottomed sofa. I stood looking down on him.

"Who *are* you?" he wheezed.

"You don't recognize me?"

That got Ana's attention. They stared at me and looked at each other, puzzled.

I took out the photo of my father, and threw it in his lap.

He gasped, and finally croaked, "Where did you get this?"

I squinted, and stared.

"Who *are* you?" he said yet again, looking pallid.

"It's pay-back time. You killed him."

"Who?"

"Your own brother."

"I don't know what you're talking about. Get out of here!"

"The thing is, that's my father."

"Impossible."

"I'm your nephew."

"José?" he said weakly.

"Guess again."

"Francisco?"

"No."

"Not 2Tall!"

I shook my head, "But you're getting closer; they're my brothers."

Anton attempted to get up from the sofa; I shoved him back down. "You're not Bonifacio," he said, "and Chile and Mark are dead."

"I'm Mark."

"You couldn't be, unless you're a ghost. There was a funeral."

"What do you mean?"

"There was a funeral at the church. Chile and Mark drowned in 1991, after the typhoon in Ormoc City."

"Nope."

"Isabel put gravestones in the cemetery. Go see for yourself."

"Where *is* Isabel?"

"Don't really know," Ana said, her goat-face drawn forward in a ruminative look.

Ignoring her, I leaned toward Anton, feeling the warm assurance of the knife-handle against my back, tucked in my waistband. But I didn't go for it, yet. Instead I grabbed his arm and twisted it, hard. He cried out in pain, "I don't know!"

"This is for Chile!" I said, still twisting. Then I yanked his arm until I heard it break. "That was for Bonifacio."

Anton cried out, tears streaming down his cheeks. He wiped his face with his good arm, took in a shuddering breath, and assumed a look of terror now that he realized I really was Mark.

I turned to Ana. She was petrified, her face bloodless.

"Now it's your turn," I said. "Where is my *family*?"

"Not here," she croaked, with the deep voice of a smoker.

"*Gracias a Dios por eso*. Who took them?"

"Nobody," said Anton.

I grabbed his broken arm.

"I mean, the relatives didn't take them," he whined. "Isabel put up too much of a fight—they all went with her."

"Where?"

"To Manila," Ana said quickly.

"Do they work for the company?"

"We don't own the sugarcane company anymore. A big conglomerate bought us out," Anton said, "a long time ago."

"That must have brought in a lot of money. I suppose you gave my family their share?"

"Ay… There wasn't any profit after all the debts were paid."

I scowled, "Sort of like my family's house in Manila?"

"We, um, owed money."

"What are you going to do with us?" Ana begged, shrinking in her chair, her cigarette shaking between fingers stained brown and yellow like roots of rotten teeth, clicking her BIC lighter frantically without success.

"What's the sentence for murder and extortion?"

"No one will believe you," Anton said. "After all this time…"

My eyes bored through him.

"You wouldn't hurt…" Ana began.

I grit my teeth, "Wanna bet?"

"The neighbors would be here in seconds," Anton said quickly, glancing toward a window.

I raised my eyebrows. "Doubtful."

"Isabel works as a dress-maker," Ana said desperately, "in a shop."

"And the others?"

"We don't know. Please don't hurt us!" Anton sniveled, looking mournfully at his broken arm.

"Who would know where they are?"

"We don't keep in touch with anyone anymore," Ana said, her hands shaking, still unable to lite her cigarette.

"What's the name of the shop?"

Ana and Anton shook their heads.

"Where's the shop?"

Ana shrugged.

"Is Isabel married?"

"We don't know!" Ana cried.

I stood regarding them for a moment. They were both shriveled in their chairs, fidgeting, beads of sweat glistening on their foreheads. I grabbed Ana's cigarette and lighter, and she winced as if about to be hit. I lit her cigarette and handed it back to her. She took it with a trembling hand, and took a deep drag.

Anton stammered, "Would you... um... like a drink?"

I shook my head.

"Mind if I have one?"

"Help yourself."

Anton rose unsteadily and crossed the room, quivering with the pain of his broken arm, which he held in the crook of his other arm. He awkwardly poured a liberal amount of rum into a glass, spilling quite a lot, then filled it to the brim and gulped it down. He poured two more, struggled to hand one to Ana, and then sat shaking, guzzling his drink, slopping on his shirt.

Finally he said, "Why are you here?"

I drew my knife, "To kill you."

# CHAPTER 47

———

I DIDN'T REMEMBER EVER FEELING SO GOOD. That part of my life was now officially closed, sealed, done.

*And Assad thinks I'm in America!*

I took a deep breath and boarded my flight home. Home. I couldn't wait. I thumbed through the flight magazine, found Hawaii on the map, and thought of how happy Dan and I'd been there with our parents. I remembered the impressive Banyan tree in Lahaina—a single tree that covers *two-thirds of an acre*—its widespread branches dropping extensions to the ground that grow into new trees, forming a forest around the parent tree, like many generations of one family.

*I have a family now. Even an extended family.*

I thought about my parents showing us our new home, and then "as a treat," taking us to a restaurant. They'd been incredibly patient and kind to Dan and me. They'd helped me get a social security card, prevailed on their friend to teach me the grocery business, helped me with English, admission to college, and countless other things. Now I felt eager to help Dan with his homework, attend church with my family, and get to know my other siblings and extended family. I was excited about being a key team player in our upcoming basketball game.

I spent all five hours of the Hong Kong layover walking and thinking. Most of my life had been dedicated to revenge: it was the force that guided me into training as an assassin, and for a long time, my reason for living. My addiction.

*It's finally over.*

Since yesterday I'd begun to think of revenge as a curved knife that kept me wounded. The energy I'd gotten from hatred had fizzled. It was very like cooking in old grease, and I didn't want it anymore. Fortunately the realization came before it was too late. I'd stood there looking at my aunt and uncle, knife in hand.

I do *have choices. This is not what I want.*

I'd gazed at them quivering in their chairs, entirely helpless, and suddenly felt no rage. Something Chile had said resonated in my mind, about them living in a hell of their own making. I didn't even want that, and was somewhat amazed to find that I actually wished them well. Placing my knife on the table next to the liquor, I'd said goodbye to the astonished couple, and walked out the door, not looking back.

Chile would have given me the cross-eyes, but he'd have respected my decision. If he were here, though, before we went to sleep at night, he'd say something like, "At least we should send them a dead skunk in the mail!" and we'd roll on the floor laughing.

~~~~~~

Next Sunday in church, I had an epiphany: the guys I'd asked for drugs after Chile and I were beaten up in Tagum, the ones who splinted Chile's arm, and his face back together with butterfly bandages, and bought us food and medicine, and gave us all the money they had—they were Mormon missionaries! I felt a rush of gratitude, thinking of their kindness to my brother; I still remembered their faces, although I never knew their names. I felt like properly thanking them, but knew I couldn't find them.

I decided to honor them by listening to their message through someone else, and made an appointment with the local missionaries. They arrived within the hour. I listened intently to what they taught, and felt their sincerity. When we prayed together I felt a connection to a deeper part of myself, and agreed to have further discussions and to read The Book of Mormon.

Reading was a real challenge in English, so at first I only registered for two night classes, one of which was a class on the Book of Mormon, held at the Institute of Religion. Energized by reading the scriptures, I could hardly put them down, praying for help every time I read and studied. One particular passage inspired me: "And when ye shall receive these things, I would exhort you that ye would ask God, the Eternal Father, in the name of Christ, if these things are not true; and if ye shall ask with a sincere heart, with real intent, having faith in Christ, he will manifest the truth of it unto you, by the power of the Holy Ghost."

My prayers were answered with surety that Christ's teachings are true, and I felt overwhelmed with love. I read and reread both The Bible and The Book of Mormon and found that they both testified of him. Things I'd known in my heart, so long eclipsed by hatred, began to surface.

An issue that had long tormented me—why Christ had to suffer on the cross in such a barbaric way—was answered by the prophet Alma: "And he will take upon him death, that he may loose the bands of death which bind his people; and he will take upon him their infirmities, that his bowels may be filled with mercy, according to the flesh, that he may know according to the flesh how to succor his people according to their infirmities." Now I understood. Christ experienced the depth of pain and suffering so he could understand every adversity we suffer. I realized that he knew of my life and had suffered right along with me.

*Could I be forgiven?*

When I told the Bishop about Ben, he cried with me. When I told him about killing cops or politicians when I was seven, he reminded me that I had only been a child. The responsibility was with those who commissioned the assassinations. He made it clear that acts of war are different in the eyes of God than murder, and that when I was older and in the New People's Army, it was indeed a time of war.

He explained that I was not alone in my challenges: many veterans of war return, having known and lived hatred and killing, some for many years, having participated in the ugliest of atrocities, often under orders. For veterans of war, adjustment is extremely difficult, and most civilians can't relate and don't know how to help.

When the Bishop told me he could not absolve me of my sins—only *God* could, I was crushed. "*You* need to restore your relationship with God," he said. "You must truly forgive all who have caused you harm; forgive yourself; look forward, and concentrate on doing good in the world. God's greatest desire is for your happiness; he knows you well; you are his child, and he loves you beyond your imagination. His son, Jesus Christ, is your *Kuya* (honored older brother), and is holding his hand out to help you. He is your advocate, and he understands what your suffering has been."

"Your brothers are in a place where they can progress," he said, and you *will* see them again. They'll be proud of what you make of your life, and will be interested in hearing all you've accomplished. You'll have much to tell each other."

The Bishop showed me a great deal of love as I went through the steps of repentance. As I continued to study, ponder, and pray, I tried my best to follow the commandments, and felt relieved of the heavy burden I'd carried for so long. Childhood wounds and feelings of retribution no longer defined me. The certain knowledge that I am loved, overwhelming gratitude, and an attitude of good will have replaced the burden of hatred.

My father baptized me when I was twenty-one, immersing me in water, as though I were buried. When I emerged, I felt clean, reborn, having symbolically washed away my past life. I realized that the Savior, my *Kuya*, had made this possible. We are now partners, and I need to do my part.

# CHAPTER 48

---

THE SCRIPTURE SAYS, "Where much is given, much is required." I prayed for guidance, and decided to serve a proselytizing mission for the Church. School friends tried to dissuade me: "Why *ever* would you drop out of school, give up a good job, and donate two years of your life that *you* have to pay for?" But my course was set, and I worked to earn money to finance my mission.

I had doubts about my usefulness as a missionary—my education was limited; I was a relatively new member of the Church, and I wasn't as prepared to teach doctrine as others might be— maybe I'd do more harm than good. But my desire to serve God was strong, and I knew he'd help me. I prayed for hours, and promised I'd dedicate every moment of my life for the next two years to his service. I asked for help in being happy, enjoying my mission, and to watch over my family while I was away.

I began my assignment at the Missionary Training Center (MTC) in Provo, Utah. It was more difficult than training for the monthlies. I couldn't have imagined a more rigorous regimen of unrelenting study. On the other hand, I had great advantages: first-rate instructors, lectures from spiritual giants, and numerous uplifting experiences.

I felt like a *Kuya* at the orphanage again, being several years older than the eighteen-year old boys, and packing a whole lot more life experience. Some boys had never even been away from home. Usually I was able to help. When my roommate said, crying, "I'm going home; I miss my girlfriend too much," I took his photos of her and locked them in my drawer. He was livid, but I didn't give them back. A week later, and for the six weeks following, he said, "I can't thank you enough." He became a strong missionary.

My mission was the finest two years of my life. I felt as close to my Savior as promised: "And whoso receiveth you, there I will be also, for I will go before your face, I will be on your right hand and on your left, and my Spirit shall be in your hearts, and mine angels round about you, to bear you up." Having his spirit, I was able to help others change dramatically, and find meaning in their lives, which gave me immense joy.

Near the end of my mission someone asked if I had a girlfriend waiting for me at home. The only woman I'd ever thought about in that way lived in the Philippines. I'd never corresponded. It had been six or seven years, and I didn't even know if she was married. But after my mission I wrote, then called. Finally I went back to the Philippines to court her.

I married Celestina—the girl that as Class President, I'd made stand in the sun for half an hour. *Go figure.* She's beautiful, petite, and graceful, with delicate features, warm brown eyes, and a smile that reflects goodness. I also gained her family: her father accepts me as a son; her mother is so good that I take her hand in mine and bow my forehead to touch it—a gesture of respect in the Philippines. Her brother and sisters would do anything for me.

Following several efforts to find the rest of my family and friends in the Philippines, results have been mixed. The Tsuyas moved to Japan with PP several years ago, and I haven't tracked them, yet. I've been unable to locate either Mother Avita or Master David. Everyone else I grew up with is dead, as far as I know. Rumble is also dead, having refused to eat after I left.

Despite several trips to the Philippines, always under the radar, my attempts to locate my siblings have been futile, until recently. I've now found them all.

Isabel, following the flooding of Ormoc City in 1991, and consequent drowning of *four thousand* street kids, assumed that Chile and I were dead, and had indeed held a funeral for us. (We were in Davao by then).

She was definitely not expecting me.

She opened the door, "Yes?"

"I'm Mark."

"Mark who?"

"Just Mark, *your brother*," I got a kick out of saying.

"Wait," she cried, looking into my eyes. "Mark? It can't be!"

"It *is* me."

"I... can't believe it; we thought you drowned!"

"Nope."

She rushed into my outstretched arms, and held me for a long time, "You're *here!*"

She looked beautiful to me; I'd have known her anywhere—older, still with silky hair past her waist, thick and shiny as oil on a puddle, now streaked with gray.

Her mouth dropped open with astonishment. She stared, deliberately not blinking; perhaps afraid I'd disappear again. She tilted her head to the side, and finally called into the kitchen, "You won't believe who's here!"

José and 2Tall, even taller now, came from the kitchen, and upon realizing who I was, tackled me to the floor and we had an affectionate rumble. Isabel glowed watching us, but then suddenly burst into tears. We rose to comfort her.

"I'm so, *so* sorry," she cried, "I've felt guilty all my life for not wresting you away from Uncle Anton. I should have fought harder. I didn't know how terrible they were. Can you *ever* forgive me?"

"That one's *easy*," I said.

With that she embraced me, releasing years of pent-up tears.

"I'm grateful for you, and for all you've done for the family," I reassured her, "and feel so blessed to have found you."

"We all live here," José said, a moment later, "including our wives and children."

"All in this tiny apartment?"

"We're close," Isabel laughed.

They all laughed the same laugh and smiled in unison.

"Where's Francisco?"

"He passed away. I'll tell you about it later," 2Tall said. "And Chile?"

I shook my head. "He's also dead."

I met a few nieces and nephews, Isabel's husband, and two sister-in-laws, who couldn't do enough for me. Segundina was still single, and looked quite a lot like Isabel, with silky hair past her waist. When we compared our ages I realized I'd been mistaken in estimating my age. I'm two years younger than I thought!

*How cool is that?*

They'd heard about Chile and me, and had gone to our funerals. I caught them up to date with some of our adventures, and about Bonifacio. We stayed up all night visiting, and in the early morning hours, José, 2Tall, and I watched a recorded Manny Pacquiao fight. After the children went to school, and those with morning work shifts left, I asked about Francisco.

"How did he die?"

"Murdered," said José.

2Tall said, "He was in an auto accident. The man in the other car died, and his family blamed Francisco. It wasn't his fault, but they shot him for revenge."

"His wife and sons live about an hour away," José said, "and you still have three hours until your flight. We could go see them, but we won't have much time."

José, 2Tall, and I drove to visit Francisco's widow and sons. They lived in a tiny stucco house the size of our garage in America, but offered me the best food they had. I had very little time and didn't want to eat, but told Francisco's wife we'd take food for the car. Just one of the boys was home, and we had only a few minutes together. He was handsome, intelligent, and named after me. I was impressed that he wanted to go to college.

"What do you want to do?" I asked.

"Be a cop."

"Why?"

"So I can kill the guy who killed my father," he said. "I'm going to avenge my family."